The Baron's Betrothal

DANGEROUS LORDS BOOK ONE

BY
MAGGI ANDERSEN

BOOKS FROM DRAGONBLADE PUBLISHING

Dangerous Lords Series by Maggi Andersen
The Baron's Betrothal

Also from Maggi Andersen
The Marquess Meets His Match

Knights of Honor Series by Alexa Aston
Word of Honor
Marked by Honor
Code of Honor
Journey to Honor
Heart of Honor
Bold in Honor
Love and Honor

Legends of Love Series by Avril Borthiry
The Wishing Well
Isolated Hearts
Sentinel

The Lost Lords Series by Chasity Bowlin
The Lost Lord of Castle Black
The Vanishing of Lord Vale
The Missing Marquess of Althorn

By Elizabeth Ellen Carter
Captive of the Corsairs, *Heart of the Corsairs Series*
Revenge of the Corsairs, *Heart of the Corsairs Series*
Dark Heart

Knight Everlasting Series by Cassidy Cayman
Endearing
Enchanted
Evermore

Midnight Meetings Series by Gina Conkle
Meet a Rogue at Midnight, book 4

Second Chance Series by Jessica Jefferson
Second Chance Marquess

Imperial Season Series by Mary Lancaster
Vienna Waltz
Vienna Woods
Vienna Dawn

Blackhaven Brides Series by Mary Lancaster
The Wicked Baron
The Wicked Lady
The Wicked Rebel
The Wicked Husband
The Wicked Marquis
The Wicked Governess

Highland Loves Series by Melissa Limoges
My Reckless Love
My Steadfast Love

Clash of the Tartans Series by Anna Markland
Kilty Secrets
Kilted at the Altar
Kilty Pleasures

Queen of Thieves Series by Andy Peloquin
Child of the Night Guild
Thief of the Night Guild
Queen of the Night Guild

TABLE OF CONTENTS

Prologue

France, 1793

"BEAT YOU TO the river," Vincent called.

Guy Truesdale rode with his twelve-year-old twin brother over the grounds of their father's chateau. "If you ride that horse too hard, Papa will have your hide, Vincent."

Vincent kicked his horse's sides and forged ahead. "You're just afraid I'll win," he called back. "And the steward's daughter won't gaze at you with calf eyes anymore."

"Just to the giant oak, then." Guy had stolen his first kiss behind that oak tree and wouldn't mind repeating the experience. She was a pretty miss, older than him by two years. Said she might have married him one day if he hadn't been born a baron's son. Guy had laughed. Many years stretched ahead before he married, and he intended to live life to the full until then.

As Guy rode past him, Vincent swerved his horse into Guy's mount, almost unseating him. Guy drew on the reins and trotted after his brother as he raced hell-for-leather over the meadow. He reached the tree and threw his hat in the air with a shout. It was always the same, Vincent had to win, had to be best at everything. As if he resented being born second.

When they returned home, pandemonium had broken out. Some of the staff had abandoned them, including the steward and his daughter.

Papa called them into the library, his forehead etched with deep lines. He placed his arms around their shoulders. "I don't have to tell you that France faces troubling times," he said. "I have ordered our trunks packed and our most valuable possessions removed from the chateau. It appears we may have to leave at any moment. There are bread riots in Paris, and the Sans Culottes are trawling the countryside wreaking havoc. I believe I've been a fair master and many of my servants will remain loyal, but I shan't have them die for us, so best be prepared."

"But Papa, you are English," Guy said.

Papa shook his head. "But your mother is French, and my children are half French."

Guy stared at Vincent, whose blue eyes dark with fear reflected his own. Shock at facing the guillotine sent icy water flooding through his veins. He could find no words.

During the night, Guy woke and sat up with a start, as the lick of flames engulfed the chateau walls. Smoke poured into the room. He threw back the bedclothes, coughing and struggling to breathe in the thick smoky air. "Vincent!"

His brother's bed was empty.

"*Mon dieu!*" Guy fought his way to the window and stared out. The gardens flickered with flaming lights. Wild shouting reached his ears. Bands of peasants and those wearing the red liberty hats of the sans culottes, mostly workers and shopkeepers who despised the aristocracy, ran about the grounds with lighted torches. Paintings and furniture was dragged from the chateau onto the lawns and their horses led from the stables.

"Where is your brother?" His father appeared at the door with Maman, a handkerchief held to her face, her eyes enormous with panic as she held his sister's hand.

"I don't know, Papa," Guy said, his voice tight with fear.

"I shall find him," his father said grimly. "Look after your mother and sister."

From the carriage hidden in the wood, Guy, with his sobbing maman and his younger sister, Genevieve, watched the west wing of the chateau crumble to the ground in a haze of sparks.

"The kitchens!" Genevieve gasped.

Guy's father appeared, running through the trees. "Quickly, into the coach. We must leave now!"

"Vincent? Where's my son?" Maman cried.

"I'll find him, Papa!" Guy yelled about to spring forward.

His father grabbed his arm. "No, my boy, you will not. He is gone," he said bitterly as he herded them into the coach. "Vincent was with the chef in the kitchen. No one has seen either of them."

As the horses raced away along the country road, while his maman and sister wept, his father leaned across and placed a hand on Guy's knee.

"When you are a man, you must return to England, my son, and claim what will be rightly yours at my death."

Chapter One

London, 1816

H E HAD WAITED so long for this. Guy Truesdale, the sixth Baron
Fortescue, stood on the lawn verge of Golden Square and gazed
at number twelve across the road with the bitter taste of disappointment in his mouth. The impressive size of the three-story townhouse
was as he imagined, and the gardens in the square still well-ordered,
but Soho was not as elegant as in his father's time. It appeared to have
changed considerably from the last century. The aristocracy had
moved on to more salubrious areas. Back in those days, his father's
neighbor was a fashionable countess who held lavish balls. It was now
a warehouse for musical instruments. The swell of an Italian aria
emanated from an open window, sung by a tenor accompanied by the
harpsichord and violin.

The door of Guy's townhouse, now leased, opened to display
peeling wallpaper and scuffed tiles. Two modestly dressed men
emerged and walked across the square.

Glad the rain held off, Guy made his way back to his hotel. Tomorrow, he would leave London for Digswell. Perhaps what he found
in the country might please him more. Any hope that his father's
loving descriptions of England would make him feel less a stranger,
began to fade, as he continued through streets completely foreign to
him. He straightened his shoulders. He'd come to England to claim his
inheritance and claim it he would. There was no returning to France
now.

Dusk fell, too early for the gas lamps, and ominous shadows crept across the footpaths. On impulse, he took a shortcut, a shadowy laneway which by his calculations, would lead into a main thoroughfare.

He was halfway along it when the sound of running feet made him spin around. Two men appeared out of the gloom and advanced toward him.

Guy moved back until his shoulder brushed the wall. "What is it you want?"

When neither of the men answered, cold sweat gathered on his brow. His glance flicked ahead to where the laneway joined a busy road. "*Répondez-moi,*" he demanded. His throat tightened in fear. Was he to meet his maker before he even reached Rosecroft Hall?

"'E's the one all right," one of them murmured. They separated, and each took a menacing step closer, blocking off any avenues of escape.

The moon sailed above the narrow gap between the buildings and shone on the knife held by one of the footpads.

Guy drew the sword from his cane. "Back away."

At the sight of it, they stepped back, hesitated, and stood regarding him.

A feint might work. Once they were off guard, he'd run for it. He moved away from the wall and drew circles in the air with his sword. "Come on, you want to fight? I'm willing."

"He can't take both of us," the tallest of the two muttered.

"Yer, but he might run one of us through," the other replied. "And we weren't paid enough for that."

"Shut up, you fool."

Surprised, Guy stilled, his heart thudding in his ears. "Who paid you?"

"Say nothin'," the tall man warned. He then whispered something to his companion.

Guy watched them, his swordstick at the ready. Did they mean to kill him?

As the taller man raised his arm to throw the knife, Guy lunged to the left. A pistol shot blasted through the confined space, rattling the nearby windows as the knife hit the wall, and clattered to the ground.

The tall man shrieked. "I've been shot."

"You there!" Highlighted by the light from the street behind him, a caped figure strode toward them from the main thoroughfare, a pistol in each hand, one smoking. "Next time I'll aim to kill."

The pair turned and ran back the way they'd come.

Guy picked up the knife. He would have liked to get hold of them and find out who sent them. He turned to face the man who'd likely saved his life.

As their footsteps faded into the night, the gentleman tucked the pistols into the pockets of his multi-caped greatcoat and came over to Guy. "Saw them follow you. I'm sorry I didn't get here faster, but I turned the corner and wasn't sure which direction you took."

With a swell of gratitude, Guy sheathed his sword, shelved his suspicion that he'd been followed for later, and bowed. "I am indebted to you, monsieur, one obviously needs to be well armed in London."

"It is wise to be on your guard. Footpads will tackle an unarmed man."

Guy clutched his cane. He'd been armed, but it hadn't deterred them.

"We'd best get out of this dark place." The man led the way toward the lit street. "New to London? I don't advise you to walk alone around these parts at night."

"*Oui*. I arrived from France this morning."

"You can't think much of us then, an attempted robbery on your first day."

"It seemed more personal." Guy studied his rescuer. He was of a similar age to himself, somewhere in his early thirties with an air of solid confidence about him. Whatever reason brought him here, Guy could only be grateful for it.

The large, fair-haired man raised his eyebrows. "The war might be over, but not all the English can forgive and forget."

A grim smile tugged at Guy's mouth. "I'm sure that's so, *mon ami.*" He remembered the footpad's words, *he's the one.* It was him they were after. Who would want him dead here in England?

"Where are my manners?" His rescuer held out his hand. "John Haldane, Earl of Strathairn."

Guy shook his hand. "Guy Truesdale."

The earl's brows met in a perplexed frown. "I know that name. Truesdale? Why, that means you're a…"

Guy nodded. "Fortescue, *oui.*"

"A relative of the baron?"

"I am Baron Fortescue."

"Why this is grand news! Your father and mine were close friends." John frowned. "But it also means that your father is dead. I'm sorry. Not by the guillotine one would hope."

"No, not directly." They crossed the road. Beneath the halo cast by an oil lamp, Guy's gaze sought the earl's. "Thank you for what you did tonight. I hope to repay you should we meet again."

The earl slapped him on the back. "Nonsense, Fortescue. Where do you stay?"

When Guy told him, Strathairn said, "Not one of our best hostelries. You must come home with me."

"I couldn't presume…"

"Not another word. Father, if he still lived, would have been justifiably angry if I failed to offer you hospitality. We reside in Berkley Square and have plenty of room. I'll send a servant around for your luggage. Feel free to stay as long as you wish."

"*Bon*, but I'm riding into the country tomorrow."

"Your seat is to the north, Hertfordshire, I believe."

"My estate borders Sherradspark Wood in Digswell."

A hackney appeared around the corner, and Strathairn stepped into the road to hail it. As the jarvie pulled the horse to a stop, the earl gave directions and whipped open the door.

Guy settled on the squab beside him. "I am most grateful."

Strathairn dismissed the sentiment with a wave of his hand. "Nonsense, Baron. It's been my pleasure. But once my sisters get a look at you, I may change my mind."

"I'm not sure of your meaning." He'd been proud of his English heritage, but since he arrived in England, he'd felt terribly French.

"My dear fellow. If you aren't used to ladies fighting over you, you soon will be."

Guy shook his head with a grin.

Malforth Manor, Digswell
WITH THE THRILL of expectation, Hetty Cavendish removed the clothes she kept hidden in the back of her clothespress. The maids' work done, they'd gone downstairs, so she would not be disturbed. She'd discovered these men's clothes in a cupboard after they moved into the house. Although she'd intended to give them to the church, she'd tried them on instead.

The buckskin breeches slipped over her thighs and hugged her hips like a second skin. Men were fortunate. Breeches offered so much freedom of movement. But then, men had much more freedom than women to enjoy. She pulled the cotton shirt over her head and shrugged into the gray wool coat. The loose cut disguised her breasts without the need of binding. A black ribbon secured her chestnut hair in a queue while the knitted green scarf concealed her throat.

Hetty settled the shabby, square-cut, wide-brimmed black hat, rifled from the back of her father's armoire, over her hair and pulled the brim low to shadow her face. Glad for once that she'd inherited a tall boyish figure, she sat to pull on the boots.

She stood and considered her reflection in the mirror, narrowing her brown eyes and lowering her eyebrows as a man might.

Confident she could be taken for a man, an exhilarating sense of independence stole over her, a rebellious, guilty pleasure. No longer did Miss Horatia Cavendish, spinster daughter of Colonel Rupert Cavendish, appear before her in the glass. She'd been replaced by a young man, able to go anywhere unaccompanied. But she must still be careful, for they lived a mere few miles from the village, and a stranger in these parts stood out like a cuckoo in a dovecote.

Her father planned to spend the night with Aunt Emily in Mayfair. Since he'd retired from the army, he'd developed an intense interest in his finances and visited his solicitor every week. She hated to deceive him, but every time he was away from home, she felt compelled to ride his stallion, The General. It was after Papa refused her Aunt Emily's invitation to chaperone her for a London season, that it became necessary for Hetty to have a secret life of her own.

With the riding crop tucked under her arm, she left by the servant's door and passed through the door in the walled kitchen garden to cross the gravel drive to the stable mews. She held a finger to her lips and the groom, Simon, chuckled. "Looks like snow, Miss Hetty." The big, fair-haired man fetched The General from his box. Hetty trusted Simon with her secret. She would trust him with her life if it should come to that.

Simon led the chestnut out and put her father's saddle on him. The General whinnied and dug at the ground with a hoof, eager for a canter. Hetty patted his nose. "You don't mind a bit of snow, do you, fellow?"

"The General will be glad of some exercise, and knowing you ride like the very devil, I daresay you'll return before the weather turns."

She grinned. "I'll be back in time for tea, Simon. Rest assured."

If only her father had such confidence in her on horseback. Since a fall from a horse had caused her mother's death in India, he insisted she ride the small mare he'd purchased for her. She adjusted her seat on the saddle which was more comfortable than the sidesaddle. And safer.

Hetty rode past the cream-colored walls of the thatched manor house, its barren garden in winter slumber. The General sailed easily over the gate, and they continued down the lane. Simon was right. Ominous gray clouds edged with silver piled up on the horizon, and there was a hint of snow in the air.

Confident that the snow storm was hours away, Hetty took her usual route across country where she was less likely to be seen. The General knew the way, taking the right fork with little urging. They always enjoyed a gallop along the straight road to the first bend in the narrow country lane. The General obliged, his powerful legs lengthening his stride.

Hetty threw her head back and laughed out loud. How good it was to have the sleek and elegant thoroughbred, carrying her swiftly over the ground. To be free with the brisk breeze washing away the sluggish disposition that overtook her when she was too long in the house.

Her rides had been curtailed after her father began to attend to business by correspondence. But a matter with Lloyds needed to be dealt with in person and demanded his presence in London.

At the thought of Aunt Emily's intriguing poetry recitals and her neat townhouse, which was just a stroll from Hyde Park, Hetty huffed a regretful sigh. So close to museums, art galleries, and shops, indeed, all that London had to offer.

The General cantered over a meadow, drawing glances from cows chewing the cud, and splashed through a shallow stream.

Her father purchased the farm, Malforth Manor, set on twenty-five acres, for his retirement. He enjoyed the quiet country life, while Hetty, at seventeen years old, was ready to tackle the world. Five years had passed since they'd returned from India, each more uneventful than the last. The one bright spot in her life was when her godfather, Eustace Fennimore, came to dinner and regaled them with stories of London life. But that only made her more restless. A very popular man, revered in local society, Eustace was a close friend of her father's. For a time, they were in the same regiment in India.

Her mother's death affected her father very deeply. It seemed to Hetty inadvisable to depend on another human being so completely for your happiness that one was devastated when that person was no longer there.

To relieve the boredom of living in Digswell, she'd taken to writing poetry. She still clung to the hope she might one day live like Aunt Emily and become a renown poetess.

Above her, a sparrow hawk making lazy circles in the sky suddenly swooped on its prey. Hetty rode on, composing her latest poem. She quoted a few lines aloud. The General pricked up his ears. "What do you think, Gen? Needs work, doesn't it."

An hour passed before she turned the horse toward home. Distracted by her thoughts, she'd ridden farther than she intended. The storm bank began moving swiftly with a fierce wind behind it. Forced to take the village road, she urged The General into a gallop.

Malforth Manor was still some miles away. She would be lucky to reach home before the storm hit. She eased the horse into a trot as they approached a sharp bend in the road, the way ahead hidden by a stand of elms.

Once around the corner, Hetty gasped and reined in her horse.

A man lay sprawled on the road.

Highwaymen tried this ruse she'd heard. She edged her horse closer and made a quick search of the landscape. A horse disappeared over a hill with its reins trailing. An accident then. Hetty dismounted but still approached the man with caution.

A gentleman. Beneath the open folds of his multi-caped greatcoat the brown coat revealed the skill of the tailor and the cream, double-breasted waistcoat looked to be of fine silk. Tight-fitting, buff-colored, suede pantaloons encased his long legs. His mud-splattered top boots showed evidence of loving care.

Barely a leaf stirred. It was oddly still, and the air seemed hushed and quiet as death before the coming storm. It matched her mood as she stood wondering what to do about the problem before her.

He moaned.

Hetty squatted beside him. "Are you all right, sir?"

When he failed to answer, she seized one broad, hard shoulder and attempted to roll him onto his back. Blood tricked from a nasty gash over his forehead and into his dark hair.

"Can you hear me, sir?"

His eyelids fluttered.

She shouldn't stare at him while he remained unconscious, but she couldn't draw her eyes away. His dark looks reminded her of a painting she'd seen of Lord Byron. More rugged perhaps, but an undeniably handsome face, his olive skin more tanned than one usually saw in an English winter. A hint of shadow darkened his strong jaw. She gingerly picked up his wrist and peeled back the suede leather glove, relieved that his pulse was strong. An expensive gold watch swung from its chain having escaped his pocket. Not robbed then. It was likely that he'd hit his head on a tree branch and knocked himself unconscious. But how did he come to be on the road?

A gust of chill wind caused a shiver, forcing her to take note of the sky. Ash-gray snow clouds hovered overhead. "I have to move you, sir."

Hetty stood and looked around. The road ran along the boundary of the Fortescue estate. There was a small hut over the hill among the trees, used for storage and hunting. She used to peer inside when she roamed the woods, but she hadn't been there for years and had no idea what state it was in now. The first icy flurries of snow drifted down, sending a shaft of urgency through her. What to do? Her godfather, Eustace, spent part of the year in the Fortescue mansion, Rosecroft Manor, but that was miles away.

The hut was the only option. But trying to get the man at her feet onto a horse would be almost impossible.

He was a big man, tall and muscular. Could she move him? She glanced at the deserted road with the hope that someone might come along to help. Unlikely for anyone to out in the storm. Unless it was the vicar, and she'd rather not meet him.

She might manage to drag him under a tree then ride for help. As she considered this, the snow grew heavier. It settled over the ground, and the prone man and touched her face with icy fingers. She couldn't leave him out in the open, prey to the elements while she rode for help. She was halfway between home and Digswell village. By the time she rode in either direction, the man would be dead or certainly near to it. Somehow, she had to move him off the road and under shelter.

Hetty bent down, wrapped his limp arm around her shoulders, and caught a whiff of expensive bergamot. She took hold of his firm waist and tried to pull him toward the trees, but he was too heavy. She eased him down again. She removed her coat, and shivering, tucked it around him.

The wind gathered force. It howled through the trees and whipped the snowflakes into chaotic spirals of white.

Panicked, Hetty took hold of the man's arms and made another attempt. Fear made her strong. In small spurts, she backed closer to the scant shelter of the nearest tree. She broke into a sweat despite being without her coat in the frigid air.

Severely winded and gasping, Hetty reached the tree. It was a victory of sorts but afforded little protection.

As she was attempting to prop him up against the trunk, he opened eyes of a startling light blue. He stared uncomprehendingly at her.

Hetty grabbed her coat and turned her back to button it. "You've suffered an accident, sir." She lowered her voice. "We're in a snow storm. I need to get you under cover. Can you help?"

He nodded. With a grimace, put a hand to his head.

"If I help you onto the horse, do you think you could stay in the saddle?"

"You are kind, sir. But that is something I shall not know until I try, *n'est pas?*"

French! Was he a spy? It seemed unlikely for the war was over. She didn't fear him. His baritone voice sounded woolly, and she doubted he could manage much.

"What is a Frenchman doing in Digswell?" Hetty queried in a gruff tone, relieved because he hadn't seen through her disguise. She'd almost forgotten it herself because his blue eyes were so distracting.

"*Oui.* So, I have reached Digswell? Do not be afraid. I am not your enemy."

She ran over and grabbed his hat, dusted it off, and handed it to him. "I'm not afraid, monsieur."

"*Bon.*" He settled the brown beaver over his black hair.

She whistled to The General, and the stallion came to nudge her hand.

With the use of the tree, the trunk behind him, he slid to his feet. "I am as weak as a *bébé.*" He clamped his jaw, his eyes filled with pain, but succeeded to keep on his feet. He placed a heavy hand on her shoulder. "Have you seen my portmanteau?"

"No, monsieur." Aware of his big hand, Hetty moved toward the sixteen-hand horse. They shuffled forward. The General obligingly waited, although his big dark eyes showed a lot of white. She took hold of the reins. "If you put your foot in the stirrup, I shall help you, monsieur."

His black eyebrows rose. "I am no feather-weight!"

The wind howled around them while The General shuffled about. "We don't have much time. The weather is worsening. Please try."

The Frenchman seized the pommel. He placed his foot in the stirrup, leaning into her. She fought not to crumple under his weight. He staggered, and they almost fell. On the second attempt, he managed with a grunt to throw his leg over. He slumped in the saddle, his body sagging over the stallion's neck.

"If you can hang on, monsieur, I'll take you to a nearby shelter."

He closed his eyes, and she feared he would pass out again, but she wasn't about to wait for that to happen. Hetty grabbed the reins and led the stallion off the road, up through the bushes, and into the woods. How fortunate that The General was sweet tempered.

The frigid wind moaned high through the tall pines. She shivered.

"You're a good lad," the man muttered through clenched teeth.

"Not far now." Hetty worried about the furor her male garb would cause when she rode to the village for help. A terrible scandal would erupt. Her father would be furious and disappointed in her. But it couldn't be avoided. A man's life was at stake. She knew only too well how risky it was to ride around like this, one of the reasons she liked to do it. Hetty imagined she would have to leave the village forever. Perhaps enter a convent? No, that wouldn't do, for the nuns would find her very difficult to live with.

Her scattered thoughts served to keep her composed as she trudged through the sludge underfoot. Her feet were completely numb, but at least, the Frenchman managed to stay in the saddle, although his chin rested on his chest.

Hetty sighted a roof through the trees. "There's the hut ahead. I'm sorry, this must be hard. You can rest soon."

She hoped the hut still had a roof. The baron left England well before she was born after he'd shot and killed some lady's husband in a duel. It was said he'd escaped to France. Her godfather, a distant cousin of Fortescue's, remained in charge of the property ever since.

Their way was slowed by dense underbrush and fallen trees blocking the trail. Hetty pulled her coat free of brambles again, alert to shove the man upright if he slipped sideways. He managed so far to remain in the saddle, a hand resting on her shoulder. He uttered a string of what she assumed were French curse words. She was relieved that she didn't understand them, but to hear a man curse made her aware of just how difficult her situation was. She was alone in a forest with a stranger and a Frenchman. Well, there was no one to blame but herself, for his was not the light touch of a dance partner at a ball. It was the hard hand of a man whose countrymen had fought and slain many English. Perhaps he'd been a soldier in Napoleon's army. She was eager to ask him what brought him here. But that would have to wait.

Chapter Two

I N THE FAILING light, Hetty led the horse to the old hut which was wedged between two aged oak trees. She feared it was a ruin, but on closer inspection, the roof and walls seemed to be intact, although covered in creeper. The lean-to at the side, where wood was stored, would provide shelter for The General.

She brought the horse to a halt, and the man slid off and sank to his knees. "*Zut!*" He rubbed his eyes with an impatient hand. "Give me your arm. I think I can make it inside."

She braced herself and helped him stand. He leaned against her and staggered to the doorway.

"*Merci beaucoup.* I am most obliged to you."

He wavered, one hand against the wooden planks of the hut as she wrestled with the door. The wood was damp and swollen, and the door stuck fast. Frustrated and aware of the large man who struggled to remain on his feet beside her, she put all her weight behind a kick. It flew open with a bang.

He took two unassisted steps into the room, then collapsed onto a pile of horse blankets, sending dust into the air. As she was about to check on him, he groaned and turned to nod at her.

Hetty darted out to tie The General's reins to a branch and gave him a pat before returning inside.

The interior of the hut was sparsely furnished with a bench along one wall with shelving and a narrow cot against the other. Logs were stacked beside the fireplace, plus a box of tapers and a flint on the shelf above. The wherewithal to light a fire, heartened her. If the tapers weren't damp, she'd find kindling and get the fire started.

The man lay with an arm over his eyes.

"Sir?" She touched his arm, and he raised his head and looked at her. Once again, she was caught by the contrast between his tan skin and blue eyes, a foreign and exotic blue like the Mediterranean sky she'd seen in paintings. "I'll need two of those blankets for my horse. May I?" He rolled to one side with a soft moan.

"Sorry, your head must pain you."

"It's like my head is on a blacksmith's anvil and the blacksmith is pounding it," he murmured as Hetty eased the blankets out from under him.

She sneezed. A thick layer of dust covered every surface, and there was the lingering odor of game birds. A few odd feathers fluttered about in the draught and cobwebs swayed from the ceiling. Outside, the storm gathered pace, and the shutters began to bang against the two small window frames. Aware she must go outside, she seemed caught by the sight of him lying there and was unable to drag her gaze away. She turned briskly to the door. "We need kindling and I must tend to my horse. Would you like me to help you onto the bed?"

"*Non, merci.* See to your horse."

The General tore at a patch of grass while the trees whipped around him. Under the slope of the roof, she removed the saddle and threw the blankets over his back, then secured them around his neck. A trough nearby was almost full of rainwater but iced over. She found a sturdy branch and hammered at the ice until it broke, aware it would form again. She would have to check on it later.

She patted the horse's neck. "I hope you'll be all right here, Gen. If anything happened to you, I would never forgive myself and neither would Papa."

Already, the pines were dusted white like sugar on a confection, and a blanket of snow covered the ground. She tried not to dwell on how long she would have to stay here and continue the pretense. Alone with the Frenchman, she had no choice. Her disguise would protect her, she hoped.

Hetty shivered as she left the shelter of the lean-to, and a fierce icy wind numbed her face. She took the opportunity to answer a call of nature and darted behind one of the broad oaks. The wind slapped at her naked derriere like an unwelcome hand. She did up her breeches and gathered up an armful of small branches and pine cones, still reasonably dry. Hetty returned to the hut which was just as cold inside as out. She levered the door shut against the force of the wind with her foot.

He'd managed to move and sat on the cot with his head in his hands. He looked up as she entered. "Wood. *Bravo.*"

She'd struggled to get used to the cold after living in the Indian climate for years. Her father believed the cold to be healthy; it thickened the blood. He instructed servants not to light fires unless it was freezing. Hetty didn't enjoy a cold bedchamber, so she often lit a fire herself. There was a trick to it, she'd discovered, and she was good at it. But there was no coal here. Relieved that the taper lit, she knelt before the fireplace. The kindling caught with a small hopeful flame. It spread, a comfortable sight that would soon remove the chill from the small space.

Hetty sat back on her heels and turned to him. His long fingers prodded his scalp and raked through his coal-black hair. Which fell back into neat waves. "Any better?"

"*Oui.* My head aches a little."

"Can you tell me what happened?"

He moved his feet as if about to rise and then had thought better of it. "I forget myself." He bowed his head then winced. "I am Guy Truesdale."

Hetty recognized the name immediately. "You are a relative of the baron?"

"*Oui.* I am the sixth Baron Fortescue."

She stared at him, aghast. Should she bow? She wasn't entirely sure she could carry it off. "Lord Fortescue left England years ago. Your father."

"*Oui,* my papa. I was born in France, but now that the war with England is over, I am here to reclaim my ancestral home."

"You are but a few miles from it, my lord. Your relative, Mr. Fennimore, is in residence."

"You know him then?"

"I know *of* him." Startled, Hetty realized she'd forgotten her ruse. It was becoming tiring. "A groom don't hobnob with such as him," she said in a growl.

Fortunately, he appeared too distracted to notice her appalling effort to speak like a servant. And she'd forgotten to earlier. As a Frenchman new to England, he may not wonder at it, so she decided not to try it again.

He rubbed the back of his neck. "I was riding up from London. Bandits shot at me but missed. I outrode them, but as I congratulated myself at having lost them, I ran into a low branch. *Zut!* It almost knocked my head off. I must have fallen off my horse." He gave a rueful grin. "But I digress. What is the name of my savior?"

Hetty bit her lip. A name hadn't occurred to her. She plucked her groom's name from the air. "Simon Rawlings, my lord."

He nodded. "My most heartfelt thanks, Simon." As if the gesture hurt him, his dark lashes dropped.

It seemed he had accepted her. Hetty leaned back. She began to relax in his company. Masquerading as a man had unsuspected advantages as she could study this attractive male at close quarters. She changed her mind when he pulled off his cravat and loosened his shirt. The dark hair at the base of his strong brown throat held a certain fascination but made her nervous. The room suddenly seemed to close in.

She prodded at the fire, which was burning nicely, with a stick. She wrapped her arms around her knees. "Highwaymen ain't been round here for years."

"If that's what they were."

"Who else could they be?" Hetty asked, swinging around to look at him.

"I don't know, young Simon."

It worried him, that was obvious. Could it have been more than a chance attack?

He frowned and pointed to two dusty bottles on the shelf. "Would that be whiskey? It's usual to keep some for lost travelers such as we."

When Hetty shook one of the bottles, it was half full. She pulled out the cork and smelled it. "It is whiskey. We can use it to sterilize your wound and then we should cover it somehow to prevent infection."

"Does it smell brackish or reedy?" he asked.

She shook her head as spicy oak smells greeted her. It reminded her of her father's favorite Scottish malt. "No, it's still good."

"*Merci.*" He reached for the bottle. "Sit beside me, Simon."

Hetty's throat tightened at the thought of joining him on the cot. Desperate, she tried to think of the way Simon walked and his mannerisms. She strode over to the bed with a masculine swagger and handed the bottle to the baron. He took a long swallow and gave it back.

"Drink, Simon."

On the narrow cot, Hetty tried to keep a space between them. She spread her knees and rested a hand on her thigh as she'd seen Simon do. The position made her feel oddly exposed. Hot and flustered, she crossed her legs at the ankle. She held the bottle up to her nose. While she recognized whiskey, sherry and a glass of wine with dinner were the strongest drinks she'd had.

Hetty took a manly swig and wiped her mouth with the back of her hand. The fiery liquid burned its way down her throat into her stomach. It took her breath. She gasped and coughed. As she spluttered, his lordship moved closer and slapped her on the back. The shock of his touch made her rigid.

"I gather you're not used to it?"

His smile had an odd effect on her heart, which gave a little leap. It was quite the most attractive smile she'd seen, his teeth white against his olive skin. He took the bottle from her and put it to his lips. After another swallow, he offered it to her again.

"No, thank you, my lord," she rasped.

"Go on," he urged. "'Twill warm you."

When Hetty took the bottle from him, his fingers collided with hers. Acutely aware of his touch on her skin, she took a hasty gulp. The liquid slipped down the back of her throat and spread through her to warm her extremities, right down to her toes.

The baron took the bottle back. Hetty's muscles seemed to have loosened. Aware she'd slumped on the cot, she leapt up. Dust rose from the rug as she settled again by the fire, now warm both inside and out, she leaned back on her hands and straightened her legs in what she considered a mannish pose. Conscious of his every movement, she watched him stretch his long legs over the cot while the room filled with the fire's crackle and hiss.

Hetty didn't consider herself sheltered from men's company. She'd been kissed at a ball held at Rosecroft Hall after she and a young man strolled in the garden. She hadn't liked him much beyond his looks. He was the spoiled son of a wealthy man, and when he returned to London the following day, she hadn't missed him. But it was the memory of that kiss which had the power to thrill her rather than the man who delivered it. And he had not affected her equilibrium quite the way the baron managed to do with little effort. Perhaps it was the situation they were in, but he made her wish she wore her prettiest dress and he would gaze at her in quite a different way.

Chapter Three

T HE GROOM SAT on the floor beside the fire. "What is it about a fire that draws one's eye? It has a certain fascination."

"As long as it's contained," Guy answered, with a swift rush of memory.

Simon's shoulders drooped into a relaxed pose. He was quite graceful for a man, the shape of his hip and thigh rather feminine. Guy fought an absurd pull of attraction as he studied the slender column of his neck and the curve of his cheek. The lad had delicate skin like a woman. Guy pulled his gaze away. These feelings were very strange. *A la Greque* had never interested him. A woman's body offered enough delights for him.

To distract himself from this absurd and peculiar sensation, he began to speak of his childhood in France. "My mother was French," he said. "We were forced to flee France during *The Terror* and lived in Brussels for a time. While we were away, our properties were seized and our relatives, who remained, were murdered by guillotine. The shock and strain of it made my mother ill. After she died, my father quickly followed. Before he passed away, I vowed I would return to England and claim what was rightly ours. That I would marry and have sons. It was his dearest wish."

He climbed to his feet, relieved the dizziness had abated and made for the door. "I shall have to brave the cold to relieve myself. Will you join me?"

Simon ducked his head. "No, I'm right. I, um, went before."

A LOG TUMBLED onto the hearth, and Hetty jumped up to kick it back into the fire as the baron returned and slammed the door shut behind him. He sank onto the cot and scratched somewhere near his groin. Hetty peeped at the bulge there. She had tucked a rolled-up stocking into her breeches, but it was small by comparison.

"Did you join the army?" she asked to distract herself as well as him.

"I suspect we have bugs in this bed. I do hope not. What I would give for a hot bath, would not you, Simon?" He frowned and continued. "France was at war on many fronts when Napoleon seized power. Every able-bodied man was forced to join the army. I contracted a fever, which brought me low for some months, and by the time I recovered, the situation had changed, and they had forgotten me. I was glad. After what happened to my family, I had little sense of patriotic duty, I'm afraid. And my father had instilled in me a pride in all things English."

"Why didn't your father return to England when the other French émigrés began to desert France?" she asked.

He gazed down at his hands. "No doubt you know the story?"

"There has been some mention of a duel."

"The thought of being tried by his peers deterred him." He shook his head. "I suspect Father suffered great shame. He had not intended to kill the man and wasn't proud of what he'd done as a callow youth. He hesitated too long. He did not wish to subject my French mother to the cruelty the *ton* would inflict on them. And by the time we had to leave, Maman was not strong enough to endure the journey to England."

Filled with sympathy for his sad life, Hetty didn't trust herself to speak. She stared at the fire as the room became hushed.

SIMON HALF-TURNED TOWARD him. "Do you have any family still living?"

A woman would be glad of such a profile. Guy was almost sorry the silence had ended. It had become strangely companionable. "*Oui*, I have a sister, Genevieve, she is married and lives in Paris." He frowned. "I had a twin-brother, Vincent. He was lost after our chateau was ransacked by peasants and set on fire in the days of *The Terror*."

"That must have been devastating."

"We were twelve at the time. My father risked his life searching for Vincent. He continued to look for him when we returned to France but found no proof that he lived. It was very difficult for Papa to accept that Vincent had died in the fire. It broke his heart."

"How sad. You will remain in England?"

"*Oui*. It is a nobleman's duty to marry and secure his lineage." He shrugged. "Whether he loves the woman he chooses or not."

Simon jumped to his feet and snatched up a bowl from the table. "I'll fetch some snow. We can melt it for water. I have sandwiches and an apple in the saddlebag. I planned to stop for a bite but then forgot."

"Sandwiches?"

"Bread and cheese, meat and pickles."

"*Bon.*"

Guy watched Simon wrestle with the door as wind and a flurry of snow blew into the room. The temperature dropped, and the flames in the fireplace flattened, then roared.

The groom managed to slip through and close the door behind him. Guy was left with the thought of a female derriere, though where it had come from, he knew not. Bemused, he recollected that he hadn't enjoyed a woman for a while.

HETTY WAS PLEASED to find the sandwiches still edible, if a trifle squashed, in their brown paper wrapping. She fed the apple to The General.

Despite the strain of keeping her secret from his lordship, she enjoyed his company. His affection for his rakehell father, mother, and sister, shone through, and she liked him for it. She supposed he would seek a suitable bride in London. But her friend Fanny, the daughter of a baronet, would be perfect for him. She was sweet-natured and very pretty. Hetty wasn't sure why, but she didn't relish remaining in Digswell to witness it.

Hetty shivered as she checked the stormy, dark sky. What if they were snowed in? The thought terrified and enticed her in equal measures. *Bother!* She wished she understood these feelings, so new to her. She had accepted her independent nature would make it difficult to accept marriage, but now she wanted so much more, and there wasn't the remotest likelihood of her experiencing it in this small country village. After scooping snow into the bowl, she hurried to the hut.

"Ah, you are back." He lowered the bottle. For a moment, she suspected that he might be in his cups, a worrying circumstance she hadn't considered, but he looked far steadier than he had an hour ago and seemed to hold his liquor well.

She unwrapped the sandwiches and placed them on the table beside him. "I'm not sure if you have pickles in France," she said. "Would you prefer cheese?"

"I have not eaten them, but I am ready to try all English foods," he said with an uneasy smile.

"Half of each, then." She offered him the meat and pickle, curious to see how he fared with it. He took a bite of the meat along with a slice of pickle, and his dark brows rose as he chewed.

"A curious flavor." He washed it down with whiskey.

Hetty almost giggled and pulled herself up sharply. "Perhaps the cheese will be more to your liking."

"I am grateful for the food," he said. "It has been a long time since I ate. But your pickles might take a little getting used to."

"You were telling me about your family, my lord."

"Was I? How about you tell me more about yourself, Simon?"

"There's very little to tell. I work for Colonel Cavendish, a retired army man at Malforth Manor."

"Is the manor far away?"

"About six miles as the crow flies."

There was a pause while he studied her, making her glad the light was poor. He nodded toward the door. "That's a fine piece of horseflesh out there."

She bit into the sandwich and took her time chewing. "The General is progeny of a stallion the colonel rode in India. Let's me exercise the horse when he's away, he does."

"That is remarkably good of him. Will someone be worried when you fail to return?"

His scrutiny made her nervous. Tired of the effort required to continue with her fabrication, she struggled to come up with an answer. "I live over the stables, so I doubt that's likely," she said finally.

He chuckled. "You don't wish to tell me the truth of it?"

"There's nothing to tell, my lord. I was exercising the horse. With the colonel's permission, of course."

"Of course," he echoed with amusement in his voice. "As long as no one awaits your return."

Did he suspect she'd ridden the horse without permission? Might he suspect she was on her way to meet a lover? Hetty was quite comfortable with that. It was a virile thing for a groom to do, after all. She settled on the rug by the fire again, and they finished the sandwiches in silence.

The pleasure and ease she had begun to feel in his company was broken when he stood up. He looked very big and strong as he eased out of his greatcoat. She ducked her head when he joined her on the rug. He drew up his long legs and clasped his knees with his hands. The wind howled around the creaking hut, and the flames popped and spluttered in the fireplace as they ate into the wood.

When his arm brushed Hetty's, nervous prickles traveled up her spine. Alert to every movement, she resisted moving away. He made it worse when he patted her on the shoulder. "I cannot thank you enough, Simon." He smiled. "I would be lying dead out there, but for you."

"'Twas merely luck, my lord." She was glad that dusk had fallen because his features had begun to blur in the glow of the fire. "You should treat that wound."

"Would you do it for me?" He took a clean handkerchief from his pocket and handed it to her. "You can use my cravat to tie up my head, if you will be so good."

He closed his eyes. Hetty knelt at his side, and her pulse leapt at the prospect of touching him. She firmed her lips and edged closer, to dab at the wound with the handkerchief dampened with whiskey, wiping away where the blood had run down into a black eyebrow. The cut had stopped bleeding. His soft breath tinged with whiskey touched her cheek. She swallowed. "No need of a stitch." Her gruff voice sounded unsympathetic to her ears.

"Then it will not leave a scar and spoil my good looks."

"I doubt it." Indeed, it might serve to make him more attractive. As she moved, so did her unfettered breasts beneath her coat. Her sensitive nipples rubbed against the material and she leaned backward in fear he might discover them at any moment. Luckily, his eyes remained closed.

"You have a gentle touch for a man, Simon."

"My work with sick horses and foaling taught me to be gentle."

"Such good work you do. I would like to work with animals."

"You would?"

"*Oui*. Animals are noble. I cannot say as much of some people. I have had dogs and horses I could rely on for my life." He frowned. "I hope my poor horse has found shelter."

She drew away and bit down on a sigh. "You are very lucky, my lord. You could have been killed." She wound the cravat around his head.

"Well, there is no wife or child to mourn me," he said cheerfully. "Do you have any family?"

"Yes, my father," Hetty said, unable to lie about such a thing.

"No siblings?"

"No, but I wish I did." A sister or brother would be a distraction for her father.

"And your father. He works with horses, too? On the same estate?"

"No. He's retired. Lives in the village."

"You get on well together?"

"Most times. One doesn't always agree with a parent, does one?"

He chuckled. "*Non*. But most times?"

"Yes. My father is a fair man. He's kind and wishes the best for me." Hetty realized this was true. She had not behaved well, and a sense of shame washed over her. If she was discovered, she could destroy his life as well as hers. If she escaped censure this time, she would not ride The General again.

"There, all done." She tied the cravat ends and moved away.

He climbed to his feet, looking rakish and handsome in his white turban, like that sketch she'd seen of Lord Byron in Albanian dress.

"I'm much better already. It's so dark, there's nothing to do but sleep. If you were a woman, it would be another matter, *oui*?" He laughed and tossed her the pillow.

Unbalanced by his remark, she fumbled and almost dropped it. She held it against her chest, wondering what unnerving thing he would say or do next.

He sat on the edge of the cot. "Would you mind doing one more thing for me? Help me with my boots?"

"As you wish, my lord." A tingle climbed her spine, and she marveled at her calm voice. How dangerous this had become. What would he do if he discovered her sex? She shivered.

"You are cold?"

"A little. The room is warmer though."

He raised his leg and rested his boot on Hetty's thigh. She grabbed the boot and pulled. It didn't give an inch.

"Perhaps if you turn around?" he said. "My valet used to do it that way."

She turned her back and reached her shaky hands down as he threaded his riding boot between her legs. The boot rubbed against her most vulnerable spot, stirring something within her. She started as he rested his other boot against her derrière. Frantic to get it over with, she grasped the boot and tugged with growing alarm as heat radiated out from her nether regions. She let out a relieved sigh as the boot came away in her hands.

He repeated the procedure with his left boot. It was an exquisite torture.

"You're a slim young man, Simon," he said from behind her. "When you're a bit older, you will fill out and put on more muscle." Was he studying her derrière? She quickly sat.

By the time his lordship stood in his stocking feet, Hetty's face burned so hot it must have rivaled the logs in the fireplace. Adding more, she raised a cloud of sparks with the hope they would last the night. Then she pulled off her boots before he suggested he might help.

When he stood to loosen his trousers, she spun around and fussed over the arrangement of the horse blankets on the bed. She turned back as if compelled to watch him as he ran a hand over his chest beneath his shirt.

He winced in pain. "I might have bruised a rib. Have a look, will you?"

"I doubt I can be of much help, my lord," she said. "I doubt there's a bone broken. The pain would be more intense."

He unbuttoned his waistcoat and lifted his shirt. "I doubt that, too, but just look, will you?"

She had never seen a grown man's naked chest before. Sucking in a breath, she bent to examine him. Small brown nipples jutted from his sculpted chest, and his stomach was ridged with muscle. A soft mat of dark hair disappeared into his breeches. Her stomach clenched as his manly smell teased at her and her fingers curled into her palms with the need to touch him. What would happen if she did? Her tentative finger traced a rib. She'd never expected a man's skin to be so smooth.

The desire to sweep it over the planes of his chest caused her to pull away. "You're right. There is a bruise here."

"Thought as much." He yawned then yelped, cradling his forehead. "Devil plague it!" He patted the cot. "We can throw those blankets over us and sleep top to tail. Not ideal, but 'twill do, will it not?"

He looked so trusting he made her ashamed of her dishonesty. "I can sleep anywhere. Curled up on the mat by the fire will do, 'tis all the same to me," she said in a tight voice. That she found him so attractive surprised her when she wasn't sure she approved of him. But then, Byron's transgressions only served to make him more charismatic.

He patted the cot. "I won't hear of it. There's plenty of room here."

She nodded, her throat too tight to speak.

"You're a gentlemanly fellow for a groom, Simon," he said. "I haven't got you into trouble, have I? No doubt your colonel will think you've absconded with that horse."

Hetty knelt at the foot of the cot. "I'll set that to rights in the morning." She suffered a pang of guilt. Simon would be worried. But he would have to wait for the storm to pass before he could search for her.

She'd ride to Rosecroft Hall for help at daylight, even though it would risk revealing her identity to Williams, the head groom. Williams seemed a decent sort of fellow. If she pleaded for his silence and made a quick getaway before her godfather, Eustace, saw her. Her disguise wouldn't fool him for a minute. She must arrive home before her father came back from London. Heaven knew what the servants would tell Papa if he arrived before her. Simon would be forced to take the servants into his confidence. Some knew she rode The General, and would rally to protect her, but she hated to make them witnesses to her deceitful behavior.

"You look most uncomfortable." He spread his greatcoat over them, then lay down with his hands clasped behind his head. "Aren't you going to take off your hat?"

"Keeps my ears warm," she mumbled.

"No man wears a queue these days. You should get your hair cut short like mine. Short hair is *de rigueur*." He ran his hands through his hair, careful not to disturb the makeshift bandage.

Frenchmen were far too concerned with their appearance. Fops, many of them, she decided, warming to the idea. It was uncharitable of her and possibly unfair, but it helped her keep her distance.

"I haven't been accused of snoring. Do you?"

"I don't believe so." She wished her voice didn't sound so strained. The gruff voice made her throat hurt.

He raised his head to gaze at her with those blue eyes, his well-defined lips stretched into a grin. "You do not know?"

She shook her head.

"Even in this poor light I can see your cheeks are smooth as a *juene fille*. I take it you are not old enough to have enjoyed feminine company?"

Hetty shifted her gaze to the cobwebs on the ceiling as she tried to work out a way to extricate herself from this mess of her own making. "Old enough yes ... but no."

His deep laugh made her catch her breath. "We men are always old enough, are we not? You have much to enjoy when you do throw a leg over. Ah, *mademoiselles*." He gave an appreciative sigh. "What would we men do without them? I've known some great beauties in my time."

How boastful! She wished she wasn't so intrigued.

"You must become a good lover, my friend. It is a skill that requires much study to perfect."

"In what way?" Oh, why had she asked that? She'd just invited him to tell her. She bit her lip, half wanting to hear it and half fearful of what he would say.

"By listening," he said, surprising her. "What lies beneath her words can give you clues."

"And if you learn nothing?"

"You ensure the woman has her pleasure before you take yours, using all of your body, your hands, your tongue, and lips, as well as your cock. When she comes, you will hear it, see it, feel it, and delight in it."

Hetty dipped her head to hide her hot cheeks as he elaborated on what he liked a woman to do to him. He must notice her rapid breath. Women would need little encouragement she was sure. She slanted a glance at him under her lashes as he ran a careless hand across his broad chest. A desire to move closer, took her by surprise. Such an arbitrary thought horrified her. There was far more at risk here than her reputation.

"But don't fall in love with the first one you bed." His fingers rasped over the beginnings of a beard. Would it be prickly against her cheek? "I don't allow my cock to rule my head."

Startled, her wayward thoughts vanished. Aware she gaped at him, she shut her mouth.

"I'm aware of my obligations," he continued, "particularly since most of my family has been wiped out. The only male left, apart from me, is my English relative who has been caretaker of the estate these past years."

"Mr. Fennimore is well known hereabouts, my lord. A friend of the colonel of long standing, he often dines at the manor."

"I have not warmed to him in our correspondence, but the English are known to be reserved."

This surprised her. She was very fond of her godfather, who was a gregarious soul. "Were your father and Mr. Fennimore close at one time?"

He frowned. "No, but I owe him a great debt of gratitude for his care of the estate in our absence. I am keen to marry and make my home here."

"I expect you shall seek your bride from the debutante's during the season, my lord. I've heard Almack's is the perfect marriage mart."

He smiled. "I might find one prepared to live with my bad habits."

"You take after your father, my lord?" Was he bragging about his rakish ways? Annoyed, Hetty yearned to put him in his place.

His eyebrows rose at her impudence, but he laughed good-naturedly. "Papa was fond of the ladies, and it got him into trouble when he was young. But when he met my mother, he knew what he wanted."

"And was he faithful to her?" An even more impertinent question, but she was compelled to ask it.

His gaze roamed over her, and she bent to smooth the blanket. She must hold her tongue and be more careful. Had he become suspicious?

"I saw no reason to doubt it." His eyes remained on her, and she resisted tugging her hat lower. "But there are many fillies who will wish to snare you, so beware, Simon. A handsome *jeune homme* like you …" His voice drifted off, and his dark brows rose.

She held her breath.

He propped his head in his hand. "Do I embarrass you, young Simon? This knock on my head has addled my brains."

"Not at all, my lord." She dropped her gaze to her hands, to find herself arranging the blanket like a maid would do. "You must be tired. I shall allow you to sleep."

He turned on his side and closed his eyes.

With some small measure of relief, she settled ramrod stiff on the cot, determined not to touch any part of him, but it was so narrow it proved impossible. Her feet ended up settled against his back while his stocking-clad feet were somewhere behind her head. He smelled pleasantly of Bergamot soap, overlaid with male, leather, and horse.

He was soon asleep, his breath slow and even.

What would it be like to lie in his arms, safe and comfortable? Well, perhaps not so comfortable. Or so safe? She nestled her feet close to his warm back, she listened to the creak of the roof timbers and the snap of frail branches breaking under their burden of snow. The General shuffled in his makeshift stall. No doubt, the horse was hungry. She was, too, and a little light-headed from the whiskey. She must be gone at first light before the baron saw her in broad daylight.

Now that he had recovered his wits, it wouldn't take him long to realize she was a woman.

Hetty doubted she could sleep in such proximity to a man who made her pulse leap when he smiled. She tucked her cold hands between her legs. Such powerful emotions this man stirred in her. Tomorrow, she would leave. How could she ever view life in the same way again?

Chapter Four

HETTY WOKE TO find she was spooning the baron's lower back. She eased herself away and sat up. Gray morning light struggled through the small square of dirty windowpane. The blanket had fallen away. He slept deeply, his lips parted, and his strong chin darkened with a day's growth. A fringe of thick dark lashes lay on his cheek. Why did men have fuller eyelashes than women? She liked the shape of his nose and the way his nostrils flared above a generous mouth.

His bandage had unraveled during the night to reveal his wound, which had clotted nicely. She studied his big hands and the swell of his muscled arms beneath his shirt. Her gaze ran the length of him, studying his strong thighs and the contour of his trousers. His very maleness tempted her to consider what it would be like to lie on his broad chest and press her body against his... She jerked upright. She had slept overlong and must leave before he woke.

Her hat had fallen off, and her hair had escaped its bonds, spilling over her shoulders. Her chilled fingers tangled in the knots as she attempted to draw it back. She managed to braid it into what she was sure was a bird's nest at the back of her head then eased her feet to the floor. She located her flattened hat beneath her hip and jammed it on. The blanket stirred, and dust motes rose. She sneezed.

His eyes opened.

"Zut! It is cold." He sat up and blew on his hands, rubbing them together. "Did you sleep well?"

"Yes, thank you." Annoyed with herself, she bent to pull on her boots. "I hope you did also?"

"Quite soundly. Shared body heat was an excellent idea."

She flicked a glance at him. "You feel better, my lord?"

"I do. Hungry though." He grinned. "I could even consume a big English breakfast."

Sometime during the night, the fire had gone out. The room was so cold that steam floated out of their mouths when they spoke. Hetty stood and wound the green scarf around her neck and the lower part of her face. She stirred a log in the fireplace with a toe. "I'll light the fire before I leave."

"You do not intend to abandon me here?" He pushed up from the cot.

She raised her head to glance at him. How tall he was. Now that he'd recovered, his masculinity filled the room with an almost overpowering presence.

She turned toward the door. "I'll ride for help. The sooner I go, the quicker someone will come for you."

"No need for that." He snatched up a boot and sat to pull it on. "We can double up on that big horse of yours. Mr. Fennimore expects me. My letter will have reached him several days ago. Because of the storm, he might have sent a search party out for me."

She watched helplessly as he buttoned his waistcoat and shrugged into his coat. He reached for his cravat. "You can have something warming to eat and feed your horse before you return home."

Hetty's heart sank. Not only would her godfather recognize her in broad daylight, the baron would learn who she was. If she took him into her confidence now, could she trust him to keep silent about her escapade? She couldn't be sure. Neither could she dispute his suggestion, for it made sense. There was very little dry wood left, and in daylight, the hut had lost any pretensions to comfort. Not only was it a miserable place to be cold in, it was dirty and smelt of mold. She chafed, wishing to be gone. She would travel much faster alone, but as a lowly groom, she must obey him. With no option but to take him with her, she pulled her hat down over her eyes. "As you wish, my lord."

He dressed quickly, and they left the hut. The stallion snorted his impatience and shuffled, unhappy with his makeshift stable.

"I'm sorry, boy. It has been a long chilly night." Hetty patted his neck.

"He will be glad of a feed and a warm stable."

"Yes, indeed." Hetty pulled off the blankets and saddled The General, relieved that long practice made it appear easy.

She mounted the horse and removed her foot from the stirrup for the baron. He threw his leg over the rump of the horse and sat close behind her, his thighs rimming hers. As she returned her foot to the stirrup, his hand settled at her waist, driving the air from her lungs. "Do you know the way?" His voice sounded close to her left ear.

She threaded the reins through her hands and moved the horse on. "I do. I roamed these woods as a child."

"Did you?" He sounded surprised, and she realized she'd become so relaxed in his company that, for a moment, she'd forgotten she was a groom. She bit her lip. How could she remain on guard with him so close?

She forced a laugh. "I should not admit my trespass to the owner, perhaps."

"You have my permission to roam my woods for the rest of your days, Simon."

"Thank you, my lord."

She tried and failed to ignore his muscular thighs and the warmth of his hands at her waist as she turned the horse. The trees were heavily laden with snow. As they rode along the woodland trail they brushed against branches, scattering snow over them.

She was surprised by how overgrown the woods had become, thick with bracken, fallen trees and dead branches. Had her godfather lost his forester? Several seasons ago by the look of it. Might he be short of money? There'd been no sign of it, for he dressed well and still enjoyed the London season in his Mayfair townhouse. The arrange-

ment with the baron's father was not her business. For many years
during October, London society had come for the grouse shoot. The
village had come alive like a parched plant given water. Some very
important personages attended Eustace's dinner parties and balls. But
two years ago, they had ceased because of his health–or that was what
she had been given to understand. Since then, Eustace had not
entertained in even a small way.

"I know a shortcut. If it isn't too overgrown, we'll be there in an
hour or so." And the sooner the better, she thought, as his arm
reached around her to push away a pine branch and his warm breath
stirred the hair at her nape.

As they negotiated a rise, The General stumbled over a rock hidden beneath the slush. The baron's thighs gripped hers, and his tight
hold on her diaphragm sent a wave of heated anxiety through her.
Distracted, the reins slipped through her grasp. She steadied herself
and urged the horse on. They had to reach the house soon.

"What did you like to do when you roamed these woods as a
child?"

"Oh, I collected robin's eggs. Climbed trees and picked wild flowers." She went rigid with horror as her mind searched for an acceptable
explanation. "My aunt liked to press them into books."

He dropped a hand from her waist and shifted away from her.
Chilly air rushed into the space where his warm body had been.

There was a long pause as the horse crunched its way through the
snow. The icy wind stung her nose while she berated herself for her
stupidity. The more familiar with him she became, the more difficult it
was to pretend. At least he was no longer so close.

"Do you prefer the company of men, Simon?"

She almost missed his quietly spoken question. "I have several
friends," she said, deliberately misunderstanding. Might he now
suspect her to be one of those Romans Catullus spoke of in his poems?
She clamped her lips shut on a nervous giggle. In India, she'd found a
French translation in the library of their rented house. Her French was
good enough to make some sense of them. Those poems had shocked

her, but she couldn't help continuing to turn the pages. There had been a collection of Persian literature, too, some with pictures, and she'd smuggled them into her room and poured over them late at night by candlelight.

"We play cards and hunt when we get a day off," she said.

"But you are of an artistic persuasion, no?"

"There is artistry in many things, my lord," Hetty said with a shrug. "The skill in crafting a fine saddle, for instance." The comment would not stand up under scrutiny, she knew. But fortunately, it had the effect of silencing him. Were doubts now planted in his mind? When next he met her, as he was sure to do soon enough, would he recognize her and be angry enough to denounce her?

They continued with just the creak of saddle leather and the cry of the birds wheeling overhead in the frigid, gray sky.

"We seem to have reached the main thoroughfare," he said with obvious relief.

Hetty could only agree.

She guided The General out onto Rosecroft Hall's rutted gravel drive lined with knobby, aged oaks. The hall sat in queenly, if shabby, grandeur on a rise, its clusters of blackened chimneys highlighted against the sky.

"You know the history of the house?" he asked, pride warming his voice.

"A little, my lord." Of course, she did, but a groom wouldn't, and she wasn't about to disappoint him.

"Rosecroft Hall was built in fifteen-ninety by William, the first Fortescue. It consisted of little more than the great hall, solar, buttery, and bedchambers. Lord Robert, the third baron, extended it in the seventeenth century. He added the west wing and gatehouse. The fourth earl added the sash windows and water closets. All of the Fortescues are buried in the crypt in the parish churchyard in Digswell, except for my father."

Hetty made an encouraging sound in her throat. She had roamed the churchyard and studied the ornate crypt of which he spoke.

"Rosecroft Hall's great chamber boasts a carved minstrel's gallery, where many fine paintings hang. It is renowned for its Elizabethan panels and plasterwork ceiling. But more than this, *mon ami*, there's a secret door below the solar with a tunnel that leads to the woods. My father used it when he was a boy. I intend to find it."

She smiled at his boyish enthusiasm. "I wish you luck in finding it, my lord."

"The gardens are known to be *magnifique*. Created by England's famous gardener, Capability Brown, before my papa left England. He was very proud of them. The lime walk, the topiary…" His voice fell away as they rode farther on and the neglect became more obvious, with unclipped hedges and rangy gardens beneath a layer of snow.

Hetty remembered two years ago when she'd last visited. The house and grounds needed attention even then, with cracked plaster and faded draperies. She doubted much had been done since. Men were not always aware of such things. It needed a woman's touch, and Eustace was a widower. He never spoke of his wife. Perhaps her passing still weighed heavily upon him as her mother's did her father.

"The grounds need work," he said. "I wonder why it wasn't done before winter."

"I heard Mr. Fennimore's not been well," Hetty said, disliking any criticism of her godfather.

They approached the rambling Elizabethan stone house. The columned forecourt was covered in a flowering creeper, the walls thick with ivy. She reined The General in. The long, mullioned windows looked blankly down. A footman rushed out to greet them. Thankfully, there was no sign of Eustace.

"Please come in and partake of some breakfast," the baron said to Hetty. "I'm sure Mr. Fennimore would like to thank you."

He jumped down and stretched his back with a groan as Williams hurried around the corner from the direction of the stables.

"Most kind, my lord." Hetty eyed the approaching groom. "But I must ride straight home. I'm concerned about my master."

He bowed his head. "Thank you, Simon. I am indebted to you."

"No need to thank me, my lord. Anyone would have done the same." She sank her chin beneath her scarf and ignored Williams's penetrating stare. He would recognize The General. She turned the horse's head, directing him back the way they'd come with a sigh of relief. If Williams didn't question his lordship too closely, she might pull this off, but she had yet to face what lay in wait at home.

As The General cantered down the drive, she turned. The baron stood, legs apart, and hands on hips, staring after her. He raised a hand in farewell. She wondered where Eustace was, for he still hadn't appeared at the door. He would be relieved to find his relative had arrived safely.

She swung her arm in a casual mannish gesture of farewell and rode on. Instead of the expected relief, she found herself saddened, as if she was saying goodbye forever to a friend. How odd. Lord Fortescue wasn't a friend, and now would never be.

GUY WATCHED SIMON ride away down the drive. He'd felt off balance in the groom's company. He'd been unsettled the whole of last night and this morning, in fact, and he wasn't able to pinpoint the reason. The knock on the head he supposed. His temples still ached a little. Eager to meet his relative, he introduced himself to the butler who admitted him and strode into the paneled great hall. He released a long breath as he stood looking around. Dust faded the fine woodwork, and the ceilings were stained with smoke. The damask drapes at the long windows were threadbare, almost in tatters.

Guy tried to suppress his annoyance and disappointment as he pulled off his gloves and handed them, along with his coat and hat, to the butler. "*Merci...?*"

"Hammond, your lordship."

"Is Mr. Fennimore at home, Hammond?"

"Yes, my lord. He is in the library." Hammond snapped his fingers, and a footman led the way up the wide, carved oak staircase.

Guy could have found the library by himself. He had discussed the house so often with his father he knew his way around as if he had lived here.

The footman scratched at a set of double doors, and a man's faint voice requested they enter.

Guy walked in to find Fennimore leaning back against the green velvet cushion of his wing chair. His foot on a fringed footstool. Despite the fire glowering in the marble fireplace, the room smelled of damp. The green silk at the windows had holes which emitted the light. The bookshelves were dusty, and the cedar furniture dull with the lack of polish. Long windows looked down over the terraced Tudor rose garden. Through the murky glass panes, he glimpsed woody roses grown out of shape. Mildewed statues wearing a mantle of snow rose like ghosts from the tall grass.

"*Bonjour*, Eustace." Guy walked over to shake his relative's hand. Eustace's plentiful ginger hair was streaked with white. He had an attractive cast to his face and must have been good looking in his youth, despite a receding chin. His faint smile failed to banish the bleakness in his eyes.

"So, Guy, you have arrived at last." When he failed to rise, Guy leaned down and shook his limp hand.

"I expect you wondered what had happened to me."

"I did, my boy. I did." Eustace nodded toward the window where a watery sun broke through the clouds, turning the snow a luminous white. "I daresay the storm was fierce. You'll need a good breakfast."

"*Merci*. I'm as hungry as a bear." The man looked as if he suffered from some malaise. Simon might have been right. The logical reason for the estate to be in such a bad way.

As if reading Guy's mind, Eustace said, "I'm afraid I have a touch of the gout. Forgive me if I remain seated."

Guy nodded. "A painful disease. I heard the Prince of Wales suffers from it."

"He does. Prinny offered me a remedy, but I am yet to try it." Eustace waved a languid hand toward the damask chair opposite him.

Guy wondered what remedy Eustace employed. Then he turned to more pressing matters. "I require a bath and a change of clothes. I trust my trunk has arrived?"

"Yes. A strange horse turned up at the stables during the night. Would that be yours?"

"*Oui.* I'm glad the animal found shelter." Guy frowned. "Did they bring in my portmanteau?"

"No. There was nothing on the horse bar the saddle."

Guy groaned. "Then my portmanteau has fallen off somewhere."

"Indeed?" Eustace dabbed at his mouth with a monogrammed silk handkerchief. He was far better dressed than the house, wearing an elaborately patterned silk banyan over a fine linen shirt, and pantaloons. "I shall need evidence to prove you are Fortescue."

Guy gazed at him shocked. He had not expected such a poor welcome. "My papers were in my portmanteau. Lost somewhere out there where the horse and I parted company. I shall have to go and search for it when the weather improves."

Eustace eyed Guy's wounded forehead. "You fell from your horse?"

The man's yawn behind his hand outraged Guy. "I was set upon by bandits. As I outrode them, I collided with a low branch and was knocked out. A man from the village came to my aid."

Eustace leaned forward in his chair. "Lucky to find anyone on that road. Who was it?"

"Simon Rawlings, a groom in the employ of Colonel Cavendish of Malforth Manor."

"You were fortunate." Eustace picked up a bell from the table next to him and rang it. "A servant will show you to your chamber. We have much to talk about. I'll join you in the breakfast room after you've bathed."

Guy followed the footman to his bedchamber, noticing further evidence of neglect. He had been given one of the lesser suites in the east wing. Apparently, Eustace felt no need to vacate the famous blue suite where royalty had once slept. It had been Guy's father's bedchamber and his grandfather's before him. Perhaps he would now.

The chamber hadn't been prepared for him. Guy rang for a servant and gazed at the dull paneling and faded yellow brocade.

"Please have the maids clean this room and air the bed."

"Yes, my lord."

It appeared that Eustace resented him being there, despite the house remaining at his disposal should he wish to stay. Guy made that clear in his letter, and he was becoming angry at the man's attitude. Ill or not, it wouldn't be difficult for Eustace to offer him a hospitable welcome.

Over breakfast, Eustace didn't see fit to question where Guy had spent the night, so Guy didn't tell him.

"I plan to leave for London in spring, when the season begins." Eustace raised a tankard of ale to his lips.

"You are welcome to live here," Guy said, making sure Eustace understood.

Eustace's smile did not reach his eyes. "Thank you, but as soon as parliament sits I shall leave for London. As I have told you, the lease on your London townhouse does not expire until July. And when it does, it will take considerable time for the rooms to be made fit for your use. You'll reside with me in Mayfair, of course."

"Thank you for the offer. I expect I shall sell the townhouse and buy another in a better part of Town."

"You have chosen a bride?"

"No. But I intend to marry as soon as possible."

"You can select one from the next season of debutantes."

"I am grateful for your kind offer, but I don't plan to return to London immediately. There is much to see to here," Guy said with a careful glance at Eustace. "I should like to visit the tenants. There does not seem to be many servants, and the house needs repair." He ignored Eustace's frown. "Come spring, the gardens can be tackled."

"I did my best." Eustace's shoulders stiffened. "The war might have ended, but revolutionary talk fills the pamphlets and the newssheets. Workers prefer the city and bigger towns to the country now. It has been extremely hard to find suitable staff."

"London appears to be filled with homeless soldiers and sailors, and the half-starved unemployed," Guy said. "I wonder if I might find some suitable servants among them."

Eustace shook his head. "Untrained and unscrupulous men are worse than none."

"Then I shall write to a London employment service."

"The cost to keep an estate this size has become crippling in recent years."

It was Guy's turn to frown. "And the tenant farmers?"

"The long years of war have left England impoverished," Eustace reiterated. "There's little money to be made on the land. Once you've recovered, I'll instruct the office manager to show you the ledgers."

His nostrils pinched, Eustace rose and excused himself, leaving Guy to eat alone. He cut up a piece of bacon. Things must change, and fast. He beckoned to the lone footman standing against the wall in his threadbare livery.

"Moodie, isn't it? What is the estate manager's name?"

"Mr. Ellis, my lord."

"Find him and inform him I shall expect him in the library with his books at eleven o'clock."

The footman bowed and left Guy to plan his day, attempting to ignore a persistent headache. If the weather permitted, he would ride out and search for his portmanteau. Guy was eager to visit the tenant farmers and see for himself what the true situation was. He needed more information before he accepted Eustace's excuses. Throughout the years in exile, his father had found a way to send money, and his relative had been given a generous stipend for the upkeep of the estate.

Annoyed, Guy threw down his napkin and rose. What if the evidence Eustace demanded had been burned in the fire in France? Would he then be cast out as an imposter? It didn't bare thinking about. He couldn't sit around and do nothing. He'd hire workmen and gardeners who could begin preparing for spring. And he would call on his neighbors. Perhaps Digswell society would prove good company.

No time like the present to learn the English ways.

The butler assisted him into his coat and handed him his hat and gloves. Guy walked out into fragile sunshine along the graveled drive to the stables. Perhaps his future wife was to be found here. The extraordinary happenings of the past few days troubled him, but when he tried to replay them in his mind, instead of the attack on his life, his mind returned to Simon. He gritted his teeth, which made his temple throb.

"*Zut!*" he muttered, startling the groom who hurried to greet him.

WITH A SINKING heart, Hetty spied her father's carriage standing in front of the house. She rode straight into the stables. "We've been so worried, Miss Hetty." Simon hurried to assist her down. "The storm was so fierce we couldn't begin to search for you until this morning. Joseph and I went out at dawn. We've just got back."

Hetty felt a stab of remorse. "I'm so sorry, Simon. Please thank Joseph. As you see, The General and I have suffered no injuries. I had to spend the night in the old Fortescue hunting lodge when the weather turned nasty. How long has my father been home?"

"His carriage has just arrived. I'm so relieved you're here. I was wracking my brains for a way to tell him."

"Before you tend to the carriage horses, could you see to The General, please? He is very hungry."

"At once, Miss Hetty." He led the horse away.

At the relief on Simon's face, prickles of shame climbed Hetty's neck. She ran through the walled kitchen garden and entered the house by the servants' entrance. She met no one on the servants' stairs and arrived at her bedchamber just as her father called to her from the bottom of the stairs.

"Are you there, Horatia? Where is that girl? Doesn't she wish to greet her father?"

Hetty threw off the offending clothes, tucking them back into their hiding place in the clothespress. She glanced at her bed, which of course had not been slept in. Sally would say nothing to give her away. Hastily buttoning her morning gown, she left the room. She hurried down the corridor, hearing her father's purposeful tread on the stairs.

"Why does no one know where my daughter is? I have news. *Horatia?*"

She met him on the landing. "Here I am, Papa. What's amiss? Did you have a good trip?"

"My trip was satisfactory. I've been home for fifteen minutes. Why did you not come to greet me? Have you been in your chamber all morning?" He sat his pince-nez on his nose to study her. Through them, his magnified gray eyes looked suspicious. "I smell wood smoke! Have you had your fire lit again? I don't like that unhealthy bloom in your cheeks."

"I was reading and didn't hear you arrive."

"You've been reading? I hope it's not that fellow Byron's poetry again. I've heard distressing rumors… Oh well, never mind that. Why don't you read Pope? Now's there's a poet. But I digress. We have been invited to dinner this Saturday!"

"How agreeable, Papa, where?"

"Lady Kemble." He beamed and tucked his thumbs into the plaid waistcoat that strained over his stomach. "I'm sure you're as pleased as I am. She always puts on a splendid dinner."

"Yes, she does."

He held up a finger. "Wait until I tell you all. Lady Kemble plans to invite Lord Fortescue. The sixth baron that is. At long last, he's arriving from France to set his estates to rights."

Hetty chewed her bottom lip. "I see."

Her father rubbed his hands. "She is to kill the fatted calf in his honor."

She followed him down the stairs. "I'm not sure if I'll be well enough by then. I fear I am coming down with a cold. My head aches."

"What? But you always wish for more society! Of course, you have a headache, reading all morning in that overheated chamber of yours.

Don't try to pull the wool over my eyes! You've had the fire lit, when it's sunny out."

"Papa it's been snowing. We had a violent storm last night."

"I know about that, but it's passed over now, and the sun is shining. Come and have a cup of tea, that will fix your headache. If it doesn't, have Mrs. Bentwood make you a tisane."

Short of being on her deathbed, Hetty accepted that her father wouldn't take no for an answer. She sighed as they entered the breakfast room. But she was hungry, having missed dinner last night.

"Wear that gown the color of a new penny which suits your lovely hair, so very like your mother's," he added in a wistful tone. He eyed her askance. "I'm not sure I like the way you're wearing it today."

Hetty put her hand to her hair. Drat. She'd forgotten she'd dragged it back to wear under the hat. It must look like a fright. "It was an experiment, Papa, a new style in a fashion magazine."

"Hmm. Don't care for it. Well, there's naught that can take away from your looks, Horatia, but you should embellish them, my dear." He put his hand to the fringe of graying hair that clustered around his ears. "A few curls, you know, the way women do."

"Very well, Papa. I'll tell Sally to arrange it like that."

Hetty settled at the table and poured them both a cup of tea from the teapot. When the maid brought toast, she buttered a piece and added strawberry jam. She took a bite, but at the thought of meeting the baron again, she almost choked. She had to admit the prospect was exciting. He was the most fascinating man she'd ever met, although, by his own admission, he had been a rake, as was his father in his youth. It was his intention to marry and have his heir, but would that put an end to his rakish ways?

He would have left a trail of broken hearts in his wake. Even if she was a suitable choice of bride for him, which she was not, being gentry, he would not break hers. She had the advantage of being forewarned.

Chapter Five

DESPITE HETTY'S WISH that Saturday never come, it arrived to deepen her anguish. In the afternoon, Fanny Kemble came to visit in her carriage. She hurried into the house wearing a fur-trimmed blue pelisse and bonnet, a hand thrust into a matching fur muff.

"Fanny, how nice you look. Come into the parlor. I'll ring for tea."

"I had to promise to be home by four, otherwise, Mother would not have let me come. But I couldn't wait to tell you the news," Fanny said. "Lord Fortescue called on us yesterday, and Mama's invited him for dinner and there's to be dancing afterward."

Sarah brought the tea tray in.

Hetty poured the tea into cups. She wanted to share her secret with Fanny, but, dear practical Fanny would think her mad, and she couldn't always be relied on to keep a secret. Not that she would deliberately hurt a living soul, but her inherently honest nature made it impossible to keep things to herself.

She often wished she was more like Fanny who knew exactly what she wanted from the moment she left the schoolroom. A home and a family. Fanny was bound to marry soon as her Aunt Caroline was to chaperone Fanny for the London season.

"Oh, Hetty, the baron is so handsome." Fanny clasped her hands to her breast. "And so very charming. What is it about a French accent? It makes even the simplest sentence sound romantic. Everyone in the village talks of nothing but the prosperity the Baron's return will bring to Digswell. Lord Fortescue told us of his plans to improve the house and grounds. I was rather shocked that Rosecroft Hall had become so shabby when Mama and I were last there. It is most exciting." She trilled with laughter. "Mama is beside herself!"

"That will liven up Digswell society," Hetty said, dismayed at being forced to keep secrets.

Fanny widened her eyes. "Is that all you can say? Dear Hetty, if you won't take your nose out of a book, I declare you'll end up a spinster. And you are far too pretty to be one of those poor wretches."

"Not every woman who fails to marry is a poor wretch," Hetty said. "I prefer my independence. Husbands have complete power over their wives. As a single woman, I may inherit, buy, sell, and own my own property. If I marry, I must relinquish it to my husband."

"Oh, pooh." Fanny gestured with a currant bun. "No woman would pass up someone like the baron for spinsterhood. And why would you want to worry about all that when a husband takes care of it for you?"

"To become devoted to the idle graces? Married to a nobleman, my days would consist of visits to the dressmaker, carding, and formal visits. Unlike my grandmother who lived a useful life and managed my grandfather's estate after he died. Why, today, noblemen even have a means to prevent women bearing children once they have their heir and a spare."

Fanny's eyes widened. "My goodness, Hetty. You put me to the blush. Where do you learn of such things?"

"On a hot night in India, after a long-drawn-out dinner, and much wine, many topics were discussed by the guests, and I admit I eavesdropped." Hetty laughed. "I learned far more from listening to the women in the drawing room after they'd left the men to their port."

Fanny giggled. "How fascinating. You must tell me more. But your poetry won't warm you at night, Hetty. And I'm sure the baron would."

"He might be half-English, but not all the villagers will put out the welcome mat for him." She sounded like a meanspirited old spinster.

What was wrong with her?

"He's an English nobleman by birth. And Mama has learned on good authority that, although his father's French properties were seized during the Revolution, he continues to be wealthy."

"Then he will be of great benefit to the district," Hetty said grudgingly.

"Oh my, you are like a bear with a sore head today. What has happened?" Fanny didn't wait for a reply before rushing on. "What are you wearing tonight? I have the most exquisite new gown. It has been made especially for my come-out, but Mama told me to wear it."

"Father wants me to wear the bronze with the figured lace."

"What? That old thing? Buttoned up to your chin? Finish your tea and let's go up to your chamber. You must have something better."

"If I had something better, I would wear it." Hetty wished her father's economizing didn't extend to her wardrobe.

Fanny put down her napkin and rose, brushing her skirts. "We have hours to spare. Come, let's see."

In the bedchamber, Fanny pulled out all Hetty's dresses and threw them on the bed. None were particularly alluring. There hadn't been much call for glamour in this quiet place, but Hetty had a sudden urge for it.

"All right, it's the russet silk," Fanny said with a moue of distaste. "We might lower the neckline. Do you have any spare lace?"

"I do as it happens. It came from India. I'll fetch my sewing box."

Several hours later, Hetty tried the gown on again. Fanny had cut the neckline into a deep scoop and edged it with a border of fine old lace that Hetty had been keeping for a special occasion. What better occasion than now? There was enough lace left to embellish the hem, shortened to give a glimpse of the ankle. Fanny was an enthusiastic seamstress but had little chance to enjoy it, for her mother had all her gowns made.

Hetty gave her a hug. "You are the best of friends, Fanny." She gazed in the mirror, and her hand fluttered over her chest. "But it is barely decent. Perhaps I should add a fichu."

Fanny gasped. "You know they aren't worn any more, especially in the evening. Why, Mrs. Braithwaite at the lending library might wear one, but she's in her dotage and might have need of it. Someone young, like you, does not." She took the scissors and cut a thread. "The neckline is perfect. You have lovely skin, Hetty. And the gown is quite modest, really."

That evening, Hetty took an unconscionable amount of time with her appearance, and when she came downstairs, her father remarked on how well she looked.

"That gown complements your fine brown eyes, my dear. I don't remember it being so…" He waved a hand across his chest. "Perhaps a shawl? We wouldn't want you to catch a chill. Those curls frame your face so becomingly. I'm pleased you took my advice."

More ringlets clustered about Hetty's ears than she cared for, preferring smooth braids. Aware that Fanny would hate it, she had added a little black net to cover the crown of her head, like a dowager in mourning, in the faint hope it might disguise more of her appearance. The low neckline of the gown afforded her figure some womanly curves, and she trusted she now bore no resemblance whatsoever to the groom Lord Fortescue spent the night with. She bit her bottom lip in dismay. What a reckless fool she'd been! If their night together was discovered, the ramifications would spread far wider than she'd envisaged. But surely the baron would be too distracted by Fanny's loveliness to notice her.

The carriage passed through the gates at Kemble Court and approached the three-story, symmetrical building of stucco brick. It pulled up in front of the porch flanked by two pillars.

The property was situated farther from the town than Malforth Manor and enjoyed a much larger park. However, it paled into insignificance beside the magnificent Rosecroft Hall. Lady Kemble had mentioned on more than one occasion that, although smaller, her property was far better laid out, with very little wasted space. Hetty thought her a fearful snob and considered it fortunate that her attitude had failed to rub off on Fanny.

A footman assisted Hetty down from the carriage. She eased her tight shoulders, sure that an awkward and disconcerting evening awaited her.

She entered the hall on her father's arm where a maid took her evening mantle and her father's coat.

Lord Kemble now deceased, had gained his knighthood for his service in the navy. His widow stood waiting in the entry hall, eager to present her special guest.

"So rarely are we honored with a visitor of this stature to our community," she gushed. "And to think that he plans to remain among us."

Lord Fortescue stood beside her, handsome in beautifully tailored dark evening clothes, his linens white against his olive skin. "And such a prepossessing personage," Lady Kemble added with a flirtatious glance in his direction. She introduced Hetty's father to the baron. Then Lady Kemble's glance alighted on her, and her features took on a disgruntled expression. "Miss Horatia Cavendish."

Hetty forced her knees into a curtsy after taking note of the small bruise on his forehead and the cut which had almost healed.

"My pleasure, Miss Cavendish." He bowed. His gaze flickered over her from her hair to her chest and back to her eyes. She had not forgotten those blue eyes. She searched them for a sign he recognized her but saw nothing beyond politeness.

He moved on to greet Mr. and Mrs. Shelton, who had arrived after them. Hetty might have been an aged dowager for all the interest he showed in her. Perhaps it was that cursed bit of net. After the first studied glance, he'd looked right through her. And he a practiced rake! She fumed, ignoring the fact she should be relieved. Her breasts suddenly seemed pale and exposed, and she pulled her shawl closer.

Hetty entered the salon on her father's arm. Beside the fireplace, her godfather, Eustace, held court, and her father went to greet him.

Apparently, Lady Kemble had cast her net wide, bringing suitable personages from the surrounding towns. Some twenty guests milled about in the long room and several had brought their daughters. The three young ladies watched Lord Fortescue in frank admiration.

Eustace left her father and came to kiss her hand. She noticed his limp. "My dear, you are the belle of the ball this evening."

"You flatter me, Eustace. I hardly compare with some beautifully gowned ladies here tonight," Hetty countered with a brief smile. "Is your gout bothering you very much?"

"It has been troublesome, my dear. Thank you for noticing."

"I'm so sorry. Have you tried that remedy the apothecary suggested?"

"I try everything, but little seems to help, save laudanum."

"Are you pleased to have your relative returned?" Hetty was surprised he had not mentioned the possibility of an heir when he'd come to dinner last.

He smiled. "But of course. Handsome is he not?"

"Yes, I suppose so."

Curious as to what Eustace might make of him, she said, "Do you think him a good man?"

His brows rose. "Good? I pray it is so. He has been unable to supply me with proof that he is Baron Fortescue."

"But surely, he's the baron." Hetty had never doubted it herself. He knew the Fortescue history and could describe the estate as if he'd lived there.

"He might have been a servant of the baron's," Eustace said with a frown. "After all, this time, I require evidence as does the Committee of Privileges."

Hetty eyed Lord Fortescue doubtfully as he moved gracefully through the room. He looked every inch the aristocrat. "Could a servant be so at ease in society?"

"There are upstarts everywhere, my dear."

"But the family likeness…"

Eustace shrugged. "His father's hair was brown. Not coal-black."

"But his mother was French," Hetty said. "What about his eyes? Are they not unusual?"

"The family does produce blue-eyed children, but they are common enough."

Hetty didn't find the color of his eyes at all common. "He would most likely tell you more about his family should you ask him."

Eustace raised his ginger eyebrows. "I'm surprised that you defend him on such short acquaintance. I cannot afford to be so trusting."

Hetty gave a start. "I heard he has a sister who lives in Paris."

"Oh? And where did you hear that?"

"He told Fanny, or her mother." Hetty blushed at the lie.

"I have written to the Duchess Châteaudunn who will be able to confirm or deny he is who he says he is." Eustace gave a sad smile. "Poor girl, this whole business has concerned you more than it ought to. You are wasted stuck away here in the countryside. Your father must be persuaded to let you go to London."

"He refuses to consider it."

"He doesn't trust your aunt's ability to care for you, believes her to be a bit of a flibbertigibbet. Too wrapped up in her literary society. But I shall also be in London. Perhaps that might sway his opinion?"

Hetty doubted it. It would be wonderful to stay with her aunt, especially while Eustace was there, but her father had been adamant, and she saw no reason why he would change his mind. She snuffed out the faint hope before it burst into flames. Watching her godfather greet guests, she marveled at how he put others at ease. Even Sophie, the doctor's shy daughter, blossomed under his attention.

The guests laughed and chatted, more than was usual. Lady Kemble had been right, the village of Digswell had never seen Lord Fortescue's like, at least not since his father had lived here, and few could remember those scandalous times. At twenty-two, Hetty certainly didn't.

The baron moved among the guests, bowing gracefully, and, after a brief conversation, left spellbound expressions behind him. He approached the small group where her father stood chatting. She held her breath, fearful that he intended to mention Simon to her father. If she could speak to the baron, she might find a way to prevent it.

Fanny rushed up to her, dainty in a gown of jonquil satin with an overdress of spider-gauze, her blonde ringlets bouncing. "How lovely you look, Hetty." She peered and frowned. "But what's that thing on your head?"

"Net. You're like an angel, Fanny. That gown is perfect for you."

"Mama had it made by a dressmaker in London," Fanny said, hitching a glove up her arm.

Hetty smiled fondly at Fanny, then her gaze swept the room, searching for an opportunity to speak to the baron alone.

Lady Kemble sailed toward them like one of Nelson's frigates, on which her husband had once served. She gave her daughter some unspoken direction with a lift of her eyebrows and a jerk of her head.

"It appears your mother wants you to mingle," Hetty said. "We must compare notes later."

Fanny grinned and moved away.

The chatter around the room centered on Lord Fortescue's encounter with the highwaymen. Digswell in Hertfordshire was some twenty-two miles from London. It lacked a toll road, the closest being at Ayot Green, and nothing so dangerous had happened within the environs for some years. It was as though his lordship brought trouble with him, riding into their midst wreaking havoc, especially for her. She appeared to be of no special interest to him, but an appeal to his better nature might work. Apart from his rakish ways, he'd shown himself to be trustworthy.

"Have you summoned the magistrate?" Lady Kemble asked Lord Fortescue with an exaggerated shiver. "And given him a good description of the rascals?"

"But of course. I expect they will be miles away from here by now." He glanced at Hetty, and a tiny frown puckered his brow.

Hetty lowered her eyes and busied herself with smoothing her gloves. When she looked up again, his gaze still rested on her. Was that a speculative look in his eye? She could not allow the conversation she'd intended having to take place in her father's presence. As soon as a waiter approached with a tray of champagne flutes, she backed against the wall and dropped her fan into an urn.

"Oh dear," she said to her father. "I must have dropped my fan as we came in, and it is close in here with all the candles lit. Shall I go and see?"

"No, my dear," her father said. "I'll tell a servant to find it."

As he moved toward the door, someone claimed Lady Kemble's attention. Hetty seized her moment and stepped closer to the baron. "My lord, I'm sorry to see you have suffered an injury. As it occurred a few miles from our home, I am anxious to learn more of your dangerous encounter."

A dark brow peaked above his amused eyes. "*Enchanté*, Miss Cavendish, although it has been blown out of all proportion, I assure you."

He offered his arm, and they strolled away from the throng. Everyone watched them, and no doubt thought her extremely forward when they walked out of earshot to the far end of the long salon.

Hetty said, "I have a favor to ask of you, my lord."

"A favor?" He smiled. "When so charming a lady asks such a thing of me, how can I refuse?"

Hetty frowned. So, he switched the charm on and off when required? "Please do not mention your acquaintance with our groom, Simon, to my father. Papa was away from home that night, and I am the only one who knows Simon rode his horse." She searched his face for a sign he might have discovered her ruse. If he had, he hid it well.

"I see." A gleam brightened his eyes. "We shall share your secret, no?"

"If you wish to put it like that," she said, growing cross.

"You obviously have a close friendship with your groom, Miss Cavendish."

"No, I… He has been with us for some time and does confide in me, yes."

"You find him attractive, your groom?" He lifted that black eyebrow again. So imperious.

"I hadn't noticed." Annoyed, Hetty wished she had her fan to use as some kind of barrier to hide from his astute gaze.

He moved closer and dropped his voice. "You share this secret with your groom?" He made a *tsk* noise with his tongue and shook his head.

Caught by the shape of his mouth, she raised her head to find laughter in his eyes. She firmed her lips. He was toying with her. "I dislike the implication, my lord." Frustrated, and unsure where she stood, Hetty adopted her most effective stony expression.

"Why don't you order him to stop?" he asked, refusing to be deterred. "I'm sure Simon is eager to please his delightful mistress."

If he hadn't recognized her, he was flirting shamelessly, and no doubt would do the same with every woman in the room under forty. The French were known to be terrible flirts. She'd preferred his lordship when he believed her to be a man. "Simon is a very capable groom. Surely you would not wish him to be discharged for helping you?"

He held up his hands, palms toward her. "Trust that I will say nothing."

"Thank you, my lord." Relieved the matter was now well in hand, she turned and walked back with him to the guests clustered closer to the fire.

"My lord, ladies, and gentleman, dinner is served," Lady Kemble's long-faced butler announced in a grave voice. One might suspect a tribunal awaited them instead of a meal.

Lady Kemble tucked her hand through Lord Fortescue's arm while managing to send a scowl in Hetty's direction. "Mr. Oakley is to escort you, Miss Cavendish."

When Frederick Oakley, a rejected suitor of Hetty's, offered his arm, it caused an embarrassing moment to pass between them. He managed a faint smile that spoke of deep regret, and they proceeded at a stately pace through the doorway. Once seated at the long dining table, Hetty found herself between Mr. Oakley and the vicar, at some distance from the baron who sat at Lady Kemble's right. Eustace sat on her ladyship's left with her father across the table next to an attractive widow in a gown of deep violet silk. Mrs. Illingworth had just emerged from her period of mourning.

While Mr. Oakley paused to draw breath during his account of the abundance of vegetables produced by his new hot house, Hetty picked up her glass and sipped the light, fruity wine. Her conversation with Lord Fortescue had not turned out as she hoped. His flippant attitude failed to reassure her. She remained on tenterhooks. She drew her lower lip between her teeth. *Well, you wished for excitement and now you've got it.*

The footman served the soup, which was followed by halibut in cream sauce and a variety of vegetables. Hetty tucked in, finding her appetite unimpaired when the delicate, buttery aromas reminded her of how little she'd eaten all day.

The vicar talked of the weather, the babies christened in the last month, and last Sunday's sermon, where he'd discussed dealing with disappointments. Then, to Hetty's relief, having been in attendance last Sunday and suffered through it, he turned his attention to dissecting the fish. From the other end of the table, Lady Kemble begged Lord Fortescue to describe his ordeal once again in more detail.

That the baron didn't wish to discuss it was clear to Hetty despite everyone leaning forward eagerly to better hear him.

"There's very little to tell," he said almost apologetically. "I do not wish to scare the ladies. The worst thing to happen was that I rode into the branch of a tree and lost my seat." He laughed and put his hand to his forehead. "Then after almost losing my head, I lost my horse."

Hetty noted he withheld his suspicion that they were not highwaymen. His gaze sought hers, as if to conspire with her, and she almost choked on a mouthful of fish.

"And did you find your horse again?" asked the vicar who preferred all the threads of a story tied up.

"Fortunately, the animal had more sense than me. It turned up at Rosecroft Hall before I did."

At his words, a concerned murmur went around the table but faded as the third course—a dressed goose, roast beef, and a loin of pork—were brought in. The baron's gaze sought Hetty's again, and his eyes twinkled wickedly. *We have a secret*, he seemed to say. Did he know? She shivered, and her knife slipped from her nerveless fingers.

The conversation turned to other matters. Hetty motioned to the footman to pour her another glass of wine and earned a disapproving glance from the matron across the table. As she sipped her second glass, warmth spread through her limbs along with a much-needed boost of confidence. If he intended to torture her, he was succeeding. She clung to the hope that her imagination had got the better of her. He could not possibly have recognized her. She would emerge from this escapade unscathed.

After everyone rose from the table and returned to the salon, Lady Kemble made an announcement. "In honor of the Prince Regent, who some months ago introduced a new dance into society, the musicians are to play a Viennese waltz. All those who feel brave enough to attempt the dance are invited to participate. But I warn you, those in poor health should watch!"

With a murmur of delight, they filed into the ballroom where the local members of a string quartet tuned their instruments.

Hetty was immediately claimed by twenty-year-old, Henry Farr, whom she considered barely out of short trousers. Lord Fortescue escorted Miss Emma Broadhurst, the vicar's daughter onto the floor, and they formed part of the set for the country dance. The wine had banished Hetty's nerves. She met the baron's eyes over Emily's head as they moved toward the end of the line, and she flirted with Henry as the dance progressed. At first surprised by this unforeseen event, Henry needed little encouragement. By the time the dance was completed, he had become a clown, turning the wrong way on purpose, and making everyone laugh.

Henry returned Hetty to her chair and seemed inclined to remain by her side. Hetty batted her eyelashes at him as he hovered over her. "Could you see if they've found my fan, please, Henry?" She smiled sweetly at him. "It is so dreadfully hot."

Henry hurried from the room. Almost as soon as he disappeared out the door, a waltz was struck up. Lord Fortescue appeared at her side, beating Frederick Oakley, who approached her with the same intention, by a whisker.

Lord Fortescue bowed. "May I have the pleasure of this dance, Miss Cavendish?"

Hetty baulked at the thought. When news of the waltz had first reached them, lessons had been held at the assembly rooms in St Albans. Despite Henry partnering her and treading heavily on her toes, she'd enjoyed the dance but felt far from confident that she'd mastered it with any degree of grace. Manners dictated she must accept, although she feared it was the baron's intention to further torment her about Simon. She murmured a polite response and accompanied him onto the floor. There would be no doubt in his mind when he got this closer look at her. She almost welcomed it, for she wished to bring the whole charade to an end.

"This is a dance with which I'm familiar," he said, drawing her into his arms. "We danced it in Paris long before it came to England."

She supposed he considered England far behind Paris in most things fashionable. His arms tightened as he swung her into the dance. Her breath caught. "We do not dance this close in England, my lord."

He eased back in feigned surprise and left a space between them. "*Merci*. I did not know. You have saved me from making a *faux pas*."

She suspected he knew quite well, for the devilry in his eyes betrayed him. "You might learn by observing others, my lord," she admonished him.

At least now she could breathe. But this was so different to the night they'd spent together in the hut when her disguise had protected her. Did he find her attractive? She had no idea if his charm was merely part of his personality. It shouldn't matter, for he would choose a bride from the aristocracy, but somehow it did. His hand at her waist, guiding her, made her recall his indecent revelations of lovemaking. Her breath quickened at the thought of such an act perpetrated by him on a woman, or even possibly her. His proximity and the strength and pure maleness of him almost overwhelmed her. She breathed in the familiar woody Bergamot scent, intermingled with starched linens, and closed her eyes, but that made her dizzy. After examining his masterfully tied cravat adorned with a sapphire pin the color of his eyes, she raised her eyes to his. "I have not seen a cravat tied in that way before. Does it have a name?"

He smiled down at her. "The *Trone d'Armour*." The style hailed from France most likely. He was different to the English in other ways, too, which made him all the more intriguing.

He reversed her expertly, and as she gained confidence in his arms, she began to enjoy the dance.

She tried not to respond to his charm but when he smiled she had to smile back. She cautioned herself. Was he the real Baron Fortescue or an impostor? His familiarity with the Fortescue family seemed authentic. He'd talked so lovingly about them.

While she counted the steps, he spun her over the floor. Gasping, she fixed her gaze on the cleft in his chin. His full under lip might be a sign of a generous nature. A passionate one? Annoyed, she sought to silence her thoughts. "Is there a chance Napoleon might escape from St Helena?"

His mouth twitched up at one corner. Did he find her naïve? Amusing? He shook his head. "Bonaparte is a beaten man. The world will not see him, or indeed, his like, again."

Were they his true feelings for the French general? He must care deeply for the country of his birth. Despite his inheritance, could England ever mean as much to him?

"You dance divinely, Miss Cavendish." His hand at her waist tightened. "I am not making you breathless?"

It was not the exercise that made her gasp. "I'm hardly in my dotage, sir." She looked down to the swell of her bosom, pale in the candlelight. Her chest gave her feelings away, rising and falling as if she'd run a mile.

"I should never have known." He chuckled. "Why, you must be well past twenty. If I can be allowed to guess."

"You are not allowed, my lord. I'm shocked you would mention it." She wished she could whip the offending bit of net off her hair.

"I do apologize; I seem to have an aptitude for annoying you."

"Not at all."

It was his graceful moves that made her dance so well. They spun around and around. Her head, already a trifle woozy from the wine, spun a little. Their bodies were close again, too close for propriety's sake and her peace of mind. There was nothing she could do about it, so she gave herself up to the sensation. She lifted her gaze to his and found his expression had become earnest.

"If you permit, I shall call on you and your father." He paused as they reversed. "I desire to see Simon again. To thank him," he added, *sotto voce*. "I worry he may get into difficulty on my account."

Hetty's heart sank to her dancing slippers. At this precise moment, she had no idea how to deal with such a request. To refuse him would be considered bad mannered, and in his arms, the urge to fight him deserted her. Her wits lost, she scrambled for some excuse. "Simon is a modest fellow. I doubt he would wish you to pursue this further. You will embarrass him."

"*Tiens*! That is not my intention." He sought her gaze and held it. "I promise to take care. I shall call on Monday at two o'clock."

"Of course," Hetty said in a high voice, her mind blank with horror.

The dance ended, and he escorted her from the floor. "Would you care for a refreshment?" he asked. "Dancing does make one warm."

She settled herself into a chair aware her cheeks must be pink from the exercise. "Thank you, my lord."

"I see you do not have your fan."

Suspicious, she slanted a glance at him and caught his sympathetic smile. Somehow, she didn't trust it. Hot and extremely bothered, she determined to rescue her fan at the first opportunity.

He signaled to a waiter and returned with a glass of Madeira. "I see the musicians are threatening to play again." His eyes danced with amusement, and she wondered if he found them all terribly parochial. "If you'll excuse me, I must ask another lady to dance."

He bowed before Fanny. She curtsied and blushed prettily as he led her onto the floor as squares formed for the quadrille. What a handsome couple they made, but she wished Fanny would not giggle so.

With a quick glance around for rivals, Mr. Oakley hurried over. She suppressed a sigh as she rose to take his arm. His eyes, filled with hope, met hers as the dance commenced.

As soon as the dance ended, Hetty excused herself and slipped from the room. The salon was deserted. She plunged her hand into the urn and straightened with the fan in her hand.

A deep voice came from the doorway. "Ah, you have found it."

She spun around. "Why yes, it must have fallen into this vase."

"How extraordinary you thought to look there." The baron leaned against the doorframe.

"Yes, wasn't it?" She snapped it open and glared at him from over the top.

He gave a benign smile and offered her his arm. "Shall we join the others in the ballroom?"

With a stiff nod, Hetty accepted. He stepped beside her, and she rested her hand on his sleeve, aware of the sensual slide of fine cloth under her gloved fingers. Her skirts rustled against his leg as they walked down the long passage with the beeswax candles burning in their sconces scenting the air.

"Do you know, Miss Cavendish, I found your groom most remarkable."

Hetty swallowed and wished she could go home. "You did?"

"The way he cares for animals, particularly."

"Yes, he has a gift with them," she added, warming to her subject. Simon was a master with horses after all.

"I've heard it said that Englishmen love their horses more than their women."

"Indeed?" She removed her hand. "You should not believe all you hear, my lord. Why, I've heard it said, that the French are overdressed flirts? Most unfair I feel sure." She offered a regretful smile.

A grin turned up the corners of his mouth and sparked in his eyes.

"Most unfair. But as I require staff for the Hall, I must warn you, I may try to steal Simon from you."

So that was what this was about. She must stop them from meeting. "Simon will never agree. He is very loyal. I would advise you not to bother."

He smiled with an apologetic shrug. "At least I have been honest."

"Honesty does not necessarily guarantee good manners, my lord." They had reached the ballroom. Relieved, she saw her father approaching. "Ah, here is Father. It must be time to leave."

Her father thanked their hostess and excused himself to organize the carriage.

"I advise you to accept Mr. Oakley's offer, my dear." Lady Kemble pinched her lips. "He is more than acceptable, and your unfashionable height will bring few opportunities your way."

"Thank you for your advice, Lady Kemble." Hetty tried to ignore the sting of her words. "'Tis of no consequence, as I never intend to marry."

Lady Kemble's titter died away when the baron approached.

"How can you be sure of that, Miss Cavendish?" he asked. "You might meet your perfect match."

"It is my wish to pursue literary endeavors like my aunt." She now not only looked like a spinster, she sounded like one. It was his fault. His amused gaze unsettled her. It was unfair, one didn't insult a baron, and it would be all around Digswell tomorrow. "Aunt Emily has a remarkable circle of friends and acquaintances in London."

"A remarkable endeavor."

She curtsied. Did he find her foolish or worse, dull?

He bowed before returning to speak to his hostess.

Some hours later, when Hetty had settled in bed, her uneasy thoughts refused to allow her to sleep. She stared into the dark, recalling her conversation with the baron and their dance. It appeared he hadn't recognized her, and this unfortunate business would be at an end once she'd dealt with his wish to meet Simon, and a plan emerged. She would send Simon away on an errand. Then she would don the groom's attire and waylay Lord Fortescue before he arrived at the house. Her disguise would be safe in the shadowy stables. Once she'd assured him that he need not pursue the matter and refused any offer of employment he might make her, she could whip up the back stairs and slip into a morning gown. A lace cap would hide her hair. Convinced she could make it work she yawned, and closed her eyes, drifting off.

Chapter Six

THE FOLLOWING EVENING, after a day spent in fruitless search of his portmanteau, Guy wandered the Rosecroft gallery of portraits recognizing a feature or expression in some of his ancestors. His father had told him much of their history. He paused before a portrait of his father as a young man and his throat tightened. His father looked lighthearted, a lively humor shining in his blue eyes. Guy took a deep sip of the fine claret his butler had brought from the cellars, then continued on along the corridor which led to the west wing.

Art that his father had listed were missing from the walls, Meissen and Sévres china gone from the cabinets. Valuable items meant to be handed down from generation to generation, gone. There was a story here, and he wanted to hear it, but so far Eustace had managed to avoid his probing questions. He'd complained of the ague and retired to his rooms. Something was very wrong. Guy needed to delve deeper into the reasons behind the estate running at a loss. How was it possible for this to happen, with all the money his father had sent from France over the years? Could it be that Eustace had financial problems? Did he sell these pieces to pay his debts? Surely not, there must be another explanation. His father had written to Eustace, so he knew there was an heir who would one day come to England.

Guy sensed his father's presence more strongly here in England. He was saddened, not only because Eustace had so obviously mismanaged the finances—despite the comfortable living the estate had afforded him, but also, because his father had walked away from so much that had mattered to him. The portrait gallery displaying Fortescues over several hundred years had struck at the very core of who he was. It was the same for his father. Strathairn had told him what had taken place before Guy's father fled England's shores all those years ago.

When a brash young blade, his father had flirted with a married lady and stirred the ire of her jealous husband, Earl Spender, who had demanded satisfaction. Friends had tried to persuade the earl to walk away, for the sum of it had been a brief kiss in the moonlight, but the countess had a history of dalliance, and her husband intended to make an example of Guy's father.

The two men and their seconds met at dawn in Hyde Park. As the earl was known to be a poor shot, Guy's father intended to delope. Earl Spender's shot went wide. His father fired into the ground, trusting the seconds would then call a halt. But the earl insisted on a second shot and fired first. When Spender's bullet grazed his father's cheek, he fell back, and his pistol fired, ending the earl's life. Before daybreak, his father had left England, never to return.

What that made this tragic event easier to bear was the French-woman his father had married. Guy's mother's warmth and love for them all overcame everything. He swallowed the sorrow and loss that threatened to overtake him. Family meant everything to him. And apart from Genevieve, they were all gone. He must live his life in a way that honored them.

No doubt Eustace would be more approachable, if not more re-spectful, when Guy provided the proof of his birth. But as time passed, and he failed to find it, he wondered if it might have fallen into the wrong hands. The bag might have fallen off anywhere. Grateful the snow had melted, he would continue his search the next day.

Guy returned to the salon and poured himself a brandy. Eustace and the servants had gone to bed. The house was quiet except for the usual clunk of the mantel clock, the creaking of timbers, and mice scrambling behind the wainscoting. A candelabra throwing an eerie light before him, he made his way to the solar, below it was the secret passage his father told him about.

The steps took him down to a cellar, pitch black and airless. He moved along the walls but could detect no sign of a door. After a frustrated hour of searching, he gave up and returned upstairs.

He must deal with the matters at hand. Eustace certainly, but first... He paused and smiled. Simon.

WHEN MONDAY CAME, Hetty picked at her breakfast. She ate even less at luncheon, drawing a concerned comment from her father. Just to please him, she forced down several mouthfuls of ham and a slice of bread.

At half past one, she excused herself from the library where she'd knitted while her father smoked his pipe and read a book on fly fishing. She hurried upstairs and donned the groom's clothing, her fingers stumbling over the hidden button on the fall-front breeches.

Jim, the stable boy, chatted to Cook in the kitchen. Hetty slipped past without being seen. Jim had needed little urging when Hetty suggested he sample Cook's biscuits fresh from the oven.

Outside was blustery and cold, but snow hadn't fallen in days. The slush crunched underfoot while heavy gray clouds hung low. Hetty hesitated as the wind whipped around the corner of the house, a gelid touch on the bare skin at her nape. She'd forgotten her scarf. With an annoyed shake of her head, she hurried toward the cozy warmth of the stables. It would be flying in the face of fortune to return to the house for the scarf, and it wouldn't be needed if she kept to the shadows.

Pleased that the stables were gloomy, she hurried inside. The General whickered a greeting. Simon had gone to the village apothecary to fetch her father's medicine. That was the only reason she could think of, but as her father would soon be in need of it, the order caused no comment.

Hetty patted The General's nose and fed him an apple. By the time the last of it had disappeared, the clip of a horse's hooves sounded on the gravel drive. She peeped out of the barn door. The baron, tall in the saddle, rode toward the house.

Hetty stepped out and beckoned him. As he reined in and dismounted, she slipped back into the stables.

"Sorry, my lord," Hetty said, adopting Simon's gruff voice. "We have no footman here. No undergroom neither. I'll stable your horse."

"Simon, good fellow," he said warmly as he led his horse inside. "I came to thank you again."

"No need for that, my lord," she said. "Everything's right and tight here as it happens." She busied herself, settling his horse in a stall, then bent and swept the brush over the gelding's flanks.

He patted The General's nose, then came to rest an arm on the stall door. "I am relieved. If you should lose your job, you must come to work at Rosecroft Hall."

She straightened to brush the horse's back, confident of the poor light. "Mighty good of you, my lord. But not at all necessary."

"*Merci encore.* I must go to the house. They will wonder where I am." He turned toward the door.

Relieved it had gone so well, Hetty stepped out from behind the horse. She looked up to see if he had gone and walked purposefully toward the stable door planning to slip inside and change her clothes.

"I do hope you enjoyed our waltz."

Hetty froze where she stood and slowly turned to see Guy emerge from the shadows. The elation left her, and she took a deep, shaky breath. "How long have you known?"

"The red hair was a definite hint, even partly disguised beneath that hair adornment. I wondered how far you would carry this ruse."

She backed into an empty stall. "My hair's not red," she said incensed.

Guy followed her into the stall and reached over to whip off her hat. Her hair slipped from its perch and tumbled around her face. "Even in this light it looks red to me. Why deny it? Your hair is the color of an excellent burgundy wine. While I remain grateful to you for my life, I'm interested to hear what you have to say about your attempt to fool me with that disguise."

"I was a victim of circumstances, my lord." Hetty lifted her chin, her heart pounding loud in her ears. She would have to brazen this out.

"Oh? In what way?" Annoyed blue eyes stared into hers. "I do not like to be toyed with. I worried that the knock on the head had scrambled my brain."

"Have you had headaches?" she asked with an innocent expression.

"*Zut!* How you still toy with me! When you bent over in those breeches! From the first I felt a strong attraction that a man has to a woman. It confused me. And then, when I saw you dressed as one, I understood."

She scowled. "You deliberately teased me that night."

"A little of your own medicine, perhaps?" He placed his hands on her shoulders. "You sought to trick me. Was it because you didn't trust me?"

She shrugged off his hands. "No trickery, my lord. I was dressed this way when I found you if you recall. When we were forced to spend the night in the hut, I needed to keep up the pretense."

"So, it was a matter of trust. You thought I would ravage you if I knew you to be a woman? I can understand that. But not to continue the ruse fearing I would expose you. That has hurt my feelings."

"Then I apologize." Hetty was sure an arrogant man like him would get over it.

He widened his eyes. "But why dress like that?"

She couldn't explain her restlessness to him, how hard it was to be a woman and want the freedom of a man. She hung up the curry brush. "I prefer to ride astride."

He cocked a brow. "You like a strong beast moving beneath you?"

"As I prefer to ride alone, it's safer." He made it sound as if she'd gained some sort of indecent enjoyment from the exercise. Her face heated. She had known that riding astride was unfeminine, but it had never bothered her before this. It was an excellent way to compose her poems.

"Even so, it is risky. You like risk?"

"There is not much risk in Digswell, my lord." Hetty drew herself up. "I can handle myself well, perhaps not as well as a man, but Simon is an amateur boxer and taught me a few moves."

"I look forward to meeting this Simon." His gaze flicked over her. What was he thinking? She quivered under his scrutiny.

"I don't see why you should meet," Hetty said. "The matter is at an end."

"Is it? We spent the night in the same bed," he said bluntly.

The indecency of it made her want to block her ears. "I remember it quite well. You have no need to remind me," she murmured. "Although it sounds a good deal worse than it was."

His dark brows slammed together. "While I was half-conscious, I told you all my secrets, confound it!"

So, that was what worried him. Hetty's agitated breath eased a little. "You have nothing to fear from me. I am not about to mention it."

"I spoke to you as one man to another. *Zut!*" He raked his hands through his hair. "Now you've got me cursing!"

"I've heard far worse from your lips," she said with a wry smile.

"You deserved to," he said coolly. He appeared to rein in his temper and leaned against a post to shred a piece of straw.

"Really, your confessions were hardly scandalous," Hetty fibbed. She began to enjoy her new sense of power. "The French are so volatile compared to the English. You place too much importance on something of little consequence."

"You have a poor opinion of us it seems." His voice sounded dangerously honeyed as he shoved away from the post and stepped closer.

Hetty stifled a nervous giggle. She feared she had gone too far. She had provoked him. While she didn't fear he'd hurt her, she did fear he'd take liberties. She wasn't entirely sure she disliked the idea as he advanced on her. Her spine came up against the wall of the stall.

"We should go to the house," she said, unsteadily. "My father will be wondering where I've got to."

He towered over her. "And how he will enjoy your mode of dress." He offered her his arm. "Allow me to escort you."

He believed he had the upper hand, curse him. Hetty gulped down her alarm and tried to appeal to his better nature. She was reasonably confident he had one. It was just she, most probably, who brought out the worst in him. "Please... Lord Fortescue, allow me to go and change my clothes." She edged around him, but his hand on her arm stopped her.

He gestured at her breeches. "Is it right that you should do this behind your papa's back?"

"No. And I shall tell him. You will keep my riding The General a secret?"

His eyes caressed her. "What will you give me in exchange?"

Alarmed, with a gasp she pulled her arm free. "There is nothing I can give you."

His gaze settled on her mouth. "Oh yes, there is much you can give me. But I am not greedy."

Hetty drew in a long anxious breath. What was he suggesting? Surely not... A nervous thrill passed through her, coupled with a sense of shame. Did he consider her immoral? "I assure you, my lord, there is *nothing*."

He placed a finger under her chin and raised it, forcing her to meet his fiery blue gaze. She felt singed as warmth spiraled down to heat regions of her body she'd hardly been aware of. Her knees threatened to give way.

"You owe me a kiss, I think." He sounded entirely reasonable despite his outrageous request.

Hetty was quite sure she couldn't handle a kiss from this man with any degree of savoir-faire. He had the wrong idea about her entirely. "I owe you nothing of the sort." She decided to bluff it out and pushed past him.

She found herself on her back in the straw, with his lordship leaning over her. She struggled, but he held her down by her arms.

"*Roué!* Rake!" She fought her own desire as she attempted to evade him when he lowered his head to hers. It was useless, for he was too strong. He claimed her mouth, his lips cool and hard, and she stilled, shocked by the lick of excitement passing through her like a hot flame. He withdrew to look at her with surprise. "Horatia!"

She sucked in a breath. "I did not give you permission to call me by my name. How dare..."

His mouth claimed hers again. Hetty never knew a kiss could be like this. It was not an embarrassing collision of lips, quickly over. His lips softened as they moved over hers as she drew in his fresh male smell. Such raw intimacy stunned her. He stroked up her arms and clasped her hands, holding them above her head, a further shock of skin on skin, while crushed against his hard body. The body she knew well, having spent the night with him. How could he respect her now? And did it really matter? He would never be hers.

The fight went out of her. Had her hands been free, she would have pulled him closer still, driven by an insatiable curiosity.

Hetty was dimly aware that he taught her a lesson. Women could not live in a man's world. They would never get the better of a man physically. They should keep their place. Impotent fury rose along with the unwelcome passion.

Their heavy breathing filled the stable. The horses shuffled and whickered as he hovered over her, still holding her captive. She glared up at him, struggling against the desire he stirred in her. She fought to keep her anger close and nurture it to build a wall between them. "You have made your point," she hurled at him. "You are stronger than I am."

"You are such an innocent, Horatia," he said, suddenly serious. "I hope you now realize you can't go about teasing poor men in this manner. That is a dangerous world out there, even in this small corner of England. Promise me you mean what you say."

"I keep my word, my lord."

"My name is Guy. I believe we've moved beyond the formalities." His blue gaze roamed her face. "Has anyone told you your eyes aren't brown? They are closer to amber with touches of green and gold. Like some rare stone."

She turned her head away. "Let me go."

When he obeyed her, she shoved him back as hard as she could. She jumped up and left him lying in the hay, an infuriatingly smug expression on his face. "You are no gentleman, sir. It seems they teach very poor manners in France!"

"Ah, but we French know how to enjoy what life has to offer." He climbed to his feet and dusted the straw from his legs. He straightened, laughter in his eyes. "I've wanted to do that since I first saw you. The shape of your body in those breeches caused me some anguish, for which I may not forgive you!"

She put a finger to her swollen lips as another wave of helpless rage swept over her. "How ungrateful you are. I saved your life!"

"And I remain eternally grateful for it. Now go quickly and change before I decide to kiss you again. As fetching as you look right now..." His gaze roamed over her from head to toe, which made her suck in another frustrated breath. "I wish to see you dressed as a pretty woman should be. Your secret is safe with me."

What arrogance! Glaring at him, she searched for the right words to wound him. Fury tied her tongue into knots. He toyed with her because he was a man and could do whatever he pleased. Her restricted circumstances became so unbearable she was afraid she might explode.

She planted a smile on her face and swayed her hips as she came closer.

"*Mon dieu!*" He eyed her body in the formfitting breeches and shook his head with an approving grin.

She raised her arm and slapped him hard across the cheek, so hard her fingers tingled. She welcomed the smarting; it made her feel considerably better.

"*Coquine!*" Eyes open wide, he fell backward with a hand to his cheek.

"We Englishwomen are not to be toyed with, my lord!" She turned to make a grand exit but stumbled over a rake cast down in the hay. Extricating herself without injury, she hurried for the door. "I shall expect you for tea in ten minutes."

"Oh, I shall be there. Never fear. I wish to see your transformation," came the amused reply.

Chapter Seven

MORTIFIED, HETTY HURRIEDLY slipped on her best morning gown with a rose-pink pattern, hoping it would give her confidence. Confidence was needed to put the baron in his place. She discarded the lace cap and parted her hair to sweep it back in a smooth bun, secured with pearl-handled combs. If Guy had sought to show how weak she was when a man wished to take advantage, he'd succeeded. But in her heart, she knew he was concerned for her safety. The appearance of highwaymen had changed Digswell. It was no longer a quiet backwater. Did he fear he'd brought them here for some other purpose? To her shame, his kisses had made her feel passionately alive. She now accepted she needed passion in her life. How else could she write splendid poetry? But she wouldn't find passion stuck in Digswell for the rest of her days.

After a quick glance in the glass, she hurried downstairs. With a deep breath, she entered the drawing room, where Guy and her father were enjoying a slice of Cook's plum bread. Guy threw down his napkin and stood as she entered the room. "How good to see you again, Miss Cavendish."

Her father's brow puckered. "Where have you been, Horatia? I sent Molly to find you fifteen minutes ago."

"I was out in the garden, Papa, and had to tidy myself."

"You've changed your gown," her father said with a nod of approval.

So annoying to be fair and blush like a ruby rose in midsummer.

Henrietta curtsied. "So nice to see you again, Lord Fortescue." Unable to risk meeting his eyes, she stared at his left ear. "I expect you find the English weather deplorable."

He angled his head so that his eyes met hers. What she found there surprised her. Sympathy and compassion. Or was it pity? Her throat closed in horror. "Nothing about England is deplorable, Miss Cavendish," he said. "The beauty one finds in the countryside fair takes one's breath away."

"Well expressed, Lord Fortescue," her father said. "Horatia, that's more persuasive than that poet Lord Byron you're always quoting."

Hetty sat on the sofa beside Guy. "Oh, not so often, surely, Papa."

"Byron is a favorite, Miss Cavendish?" Guy seized on the information, and a delighted gleam entered his eyes. He was not about to let such a moment pass. "Surprising that a *roué* and a rake can produce such sensitive verse, don't you agree?"

Hetty scowled. "I agree that his poetry is very fine."

Knife poised, her father raised his head before buttering another slice of bread. "*Roué*? Rake? These are not words bandied about in English drawing rooms, my lord." He looked at her with a worried frown. "If Byron is one of these, I forbid you to read any more of his work."

Guy's eyes twinkled.

She leveled a glowing look at him. "I'm surprised you've read Byron, my lord."

His eyebrows peaked. "Do you mean that French poets are so sublime we tend not to read beyond our shores? We are a nation of romantics." He put down his cup. "I recently discovered a new poem of Byron's. Written this year, I believe." He began to recite it, his voice lending it just the right tone of regret.

> *"Fare thee well! and if for ever,*
> *Still for ever, fare thee well:*
> *Even though unforgiving, never*
> *'Gains thee shall my heart rebel."*

Hetty released the breath she'd been holding. She'd hung on every word. He quoted Lord Byron as if he truly understood the meaning behind Byron's words. With the memory of his kiss, she feared she was gaping like a foolish, smitten girl and bent her head over the teapot.

"Written to his wife, when his marriage ended after one year, I believe," Guy added, helpfully bringing her back to earth.

Her father replaced his cup in its saucer with a rattle. "Modern verse!" He shook his head and climbed to his feet. "I declare, I can't follow what young people talk about nowadays." He bowed. "If you'll excuse me, my lord, I'll go to the library, there's some business needs my attention. It has been a pleasure to have your company. I had no idea you were so interested in fly fishing. You must call on us again."

Guy stood and bowed. "*Merci*, Colonel Cavendish. I should be delighted to learn more from you before I embark on the sport."

With both doors left ajar for propriety's sake, her father settled by the library fireside.

After a glance at her father rustling his periodical, Guy turned to her. "Horatia," he said in a quiet voice, edging closer to her on the sofa. "Might we be friends?"

She needed time to build some sort of resistance to his charm. "Friends don't treat each other the way you did," she said in a small voice.

"I am sorry." He gave a Gallic shrug. "I could not resist. You were very beguiling."

She was? Hetty tried to ignore that. "You're not sorry at all."

"You did trick me, Horatia."

"I explained why." She glanced at her father who was intent on lighting his pipe. "I was right not to trust you."

Guy grimaced. "But you can trust me, I promise you." He tilted his head and smiled. "No one has been badly wounded by this escapade, have they?"

His words sounded so convincing, and she had to admit that the last few days had been quite extraordinary and certainly not dull. She would consent to a friendship for it put the relationship on a safer plane. "You'll tell no one…?" she whispered.

He chuckled. "Kiss and tell? That is not my code."

She allowed him to take her hand. He was quite convincing, despite his behavior in the stables.

When he turned her hand over and pressed a kiss on her palm, endless quivers of sensation raced along her nerve endings. She snatched her hand back. "That is not within the bounds of friendship!" An English gentleman would never behave so…

He held a finger to his lips, his dark lashes hiding his expression. She was sure his eyes were dancing. He was so outrageous she tamped down an urge to laugh. She must not give him an inch, he was likely to take a lot more.

"Forgive me," he said, a smile in his voice. "It won't happen again. Unless you wish it."

"Rest assured, I shall not. Let us talk of something else."

Mary came in and bobbed. "Shall you require more hot water, Miss Hetty?"

"No thank you, Mary."

"So, you're called Hetty?"

"Yes. Although my father prefers Horatia."

"Mm. I shall you call you Hetty."

She sighed and shook her head. It wouldn't do the slightest bit of good to argue with him.

"I have discovered an excellent library at the hall. I imagine you have availed yourself of it? You're welcome to continue. There are some excellent volumes of poetry."

"That won't be possible now. As you must know."

"Come dressed as Simon. I shall enjoy it to no end."

She glanced across at her father. It was lucky he was slightly hard of hearing. "You are impossible!"

His gaze roamed over her. "But I must confess, I do prefer you in that rouge-colored gown."

She gathered the folds in her fingers. "This hue is called rose-pink."

He laughed and shrugged in that Gallic way he had, which was so charming. "Rouge, rose-pink, chestnut?"

"They are all different." Her tone censorious, she resisted the urge to pat her hair.

"Well, the color suits you."

"You are a compulsive flirt, my lord." She shook her head but couldn't prevent a small smile hovering on her lips. "Weren't we to speak of other things? How is my godfather today?"

Guy shrugged. "He has taken to his bed."

"Poor Eustace. He suffers terribly from gout."

"So I believe." He fell silent.

"I'm sure he will rally soon and become better company."

"I do hope so. There is much for us to discuss."

"I daresay. Years to catch up on."

"I have tried, but he shows little interest in the family."

"Oh? Because he is unwell, I suppose." This surprised her, for wasn't it Eustace's wish to confirm Guy's right to claim the barony?

He looked doubtful. "Perhaps."

"Is Eustace returning to London?" Would he be cast out of his home after all these years? Surely Guy would not do such a thing.

"In truth, he has enjoyed my father's hospitality unencumbered for many years. It might be difficult to relinquish it."

"He enjoys living in Digswell," Hetty said. "He has made many friends here."

"I wrote to advise him. Did he mention it?"

"Not to me."

"Until he heard from me, he might not have expected an heir to appear after the bloody Revolution."

"Nevertheless, he would wish you to take your rightful place."

He shrugged. "Not if I had met my end on the way here."

What was Guy suggesting? She cringed. "Surely, you don't suspect Eustace to be behind the attack."

Guy looked down at his hands. "I've yet to find that out. As well as what lies behind the poor state of the hall. Until then, it makes no sense to discuss it."

Outraged at even the faintest suggestion of impropriety on her godfather's part, Hetty rose. "I've known Eustace for many years. He's a good man. He would want to do the right thing."

"It is hard to know the workings of a person's mind. We are strangers after all. He holds no affection for me in his heart."

"That's very different from…" She couldn't say the words.

He stood. "I must go. I hope we shall meet again soon." A grin tweaked the corner of his mouth. "On horseback perhaps?"

She sighed. "This episode has put an end to my riding alone. And Papa seems to have lost his love for it."

"That's regrettable. But it has become dangerous, as I've taken pains to explain to you."

He was just like her father beneath his bravado. His wife would have to obey him in all things. It hardly mattered, for it would not be her. Fanny, perhaps, with her biddable nature, would make him an agreeable partner in life. Hetty walked with him to the door. "You have much to do to put your estate to rights. I wish you well with it."

He pulled on his gloves. "A difficult but necessary enterprise."

At the parlor window, she watched him ride away through the trees. Guy must have met the real Simon at the stables who would have returned from the village.

She shivered and returned to the fireside. Did he really believe her godfather could be capable of such evil? Although to be fair, Guy hadn't come right out and accused him of it.

She wound the tassel on a cushion through her fingers. What had occurred for the hall to fall into neglect? Perhaps Eustace's condition was more serious than they knew.

Simon's voice came up the kitchen stairs. Hetty was tempted to go and ask him what he thought of Guy. The groom was a levelheaded fellow, and she trusted his judgment. No need for the matter was at an end. She sighed and patted the cushion back into place. Guy had expressed the intention to marry and safeguard his heritage with an heir. And, rightfully, his wife would come from the upper ten thousand. She must put him out of her mind. A season in London had become imperative. She must find a way to persuade her father.

Chapter Eight

S EVERAL WEEKS PASSED, each day was very much like the last. The only visitors her father received were the widow, Mrs. Thompson, and her sister, Alice, and self-appointed organizers of all matters relating to the church. They took great delight in discussing the fascinating new member of the parish. Hetty suffered through their fulsome praise of Lord Fortescue, how charming he was, and how he'd granted a substantial endowment for improvements to the rectory.

To fill the long days, Hetty wrote letters, played the piano, and read, but even Byron's poetry failed to captivate her for long. Her own attempts at verse were uninspired. She organized the maids in their duties and began to embroider a new sampler, but, after pricking her finger for the third time, threw it down in disgust.

It was hardly gardening weather. Undaunted, she forked the frost-hardened soil in the vegetable patch to prepare it for spring. It was a pastime she usually enjoyed, but she found herself furiously attacking the dirt with the garden fork as if a highwayman hid there.

Hetty made daily requests for her father to accompany her on a ride and tried to quell her temper when he usually refused. She hated to see The General shuffling in his stall, but it was too cold to put him in the paddock.

Her father, perhaps tired of her low spirits, suggested an outing to the village for afternoon tea. He would invite Lady Kemble to join them. Hetty seized on the offering even though it meant coming under the scrutiny of Fanny's mother. She wore her smart moss-green wool beneath her pelisse. Although the weather remained chilly, there seemed little chance of snow.

The carriage rattled along through hills of oak and thorn, following the curve of the valley which led to the River Mimram. They passed the gray-stone church with the two cedars of Lebanon planted by Capability Brown last century, and then the rectory, with the Monks Walk and grove of sweet chestnuts. "Is this not God's country?" Papa asked.

She glanced out to where sheep dotted the rolling green hillocks and sheltered beneath spreading oaks. "Digswell is very pleasing to the eye."

"Would you really want to leave it for the teaming metropolis?"

"The city would offer a very different life," she said cautiously.

Her father cleared his throat. "I've been meaning to speak to you about Mr. Oakley."

Her heart sank to her half-boots. She'd begun to hope that her father had given up on Frederick Oakley. He hadn't called since Lady Kemble's dinner party.

"Oakley's a decent man, Horatia."

"Yes, he is."

Her father drew the rug up farther over his knees. "With a fine property and a decent income."

"That's true."

He studied her. "You might sound more enthusiastic."

"I don't love him, Papa," she said, distracted by the image of a pair of blue eyes.

"Marriage to a good man counts for a lot."

"You loved Mama."

His eyes turned sad, and she wished she hadn't mentioned it. "Our mutual regard grew into love after we married."

As the vehicle swayed over the road, Hetty smoothed the fur trim on her sleeve. "Father, I could never love Mr. Oakley. We are too different in our sensibilities."

He sighed heavily. "He dislikes poetry?"

She gave a small laugh. "He has no sense of humor."

"Oh, very well, then. I shall not insist, although some fathers might do so." He gave a sorrowful shake of his head. "You are two-and-twenty, most women of your age are long wed."

"Don't you like me living with you?"

He sighed. "That is the trouble, I'm growing to like it too much."

"Oh Papa!" Filled with compassion and a sense of helplessness, she kissed his cheek.

"And I suffer some guilt that you cannot go to London."

"Aunt Emily is more than willing to sponsor me."

"I tremble at the thought of what sort of life you would live there. Much as I love my sister, she is not in the ordinary way. When a fox got into the hen house, she was so distracted with her poems he ate several of our chickens before she shooed him out."

Did Papa liken Hetty to a chicken and fear that Aunt Emily would let the foxes in? Hetty sighed. She would never go to London.

The carriage pulled up outside the Duck and Cockerel, a wattle and daub building in the high street.

"Well, here we are," her father said with relief in his voice.

Hetty alighted with the hope that their afternoon would rise above tedious subjects such as an effective treatment for chilblains, recipes for the vegetables in season, when best to prune the roses and of course, when the wintry weather would finally abate. She yearned to learn what was happening in the world beyond Digswell, but she seemed the only person interested.

Frederick Oakley waited for them on the footpath. He bustled forward in his lanky gait to bow over Hetty's hand.

"How good to see you, Mr. Oakley," her father said, looking pleased. He hadn't quite given up on Frederick as a son-in-law it seemed. Had he encouraged this meeting? "We are about to take tea. Will you join us?"

Frederick kept hold of her hand rather too long. "Delighted." He smiled at her. Out of the corner of Hetty's eye, a tall, dark-haired man emerged from the general store. Guy crossed the road toward them. She pulled her hand from Frederick's, her gaze resting on Guy's face. He raised an inquiring eyebrow as he removed his hat.

After their greetings, her father issued an invitation to Guy, which caused an unattractive scowl on Frederick's face.

While they waited for two tables to be joined and the seating arrangements to be organized, Guy bent his head to her and spoke in an undertone. "Eustace has told the shopkeeper that he plans to remain here."

"Do you mind?"

"No. The house is big enough, I just wish things were better between us."

"Have you discussed your misgivings about his running of the estate?"

"I've not been able to talk to him. He's returned to his sickbed."

Hetty inhaled. "Is he very ill?"

Guy looked frustrated, his lips thinning. "I suspect it's a means to avoid me."

"You cannot be sure of that." She thought Guy unsympathetic. "I shall call on him when he rises from his bed."

"Have you two forgotten your manners?" Her father tapped her shoulder. "Look who's arrived."

Fanny, Lady Kemble, and Mrs. Illingworth entered the room. Mrs. Crimpton, who ran the establishment with her husband, promised them currant cake and gingerbread before rushing off to the kitchen.

Frederick held out a chair for Hetty and took the one beside her. "I have been hoping for a chance to talk to you, Miss Cavendish," he said with an earnest expression. "I have had remarkable success developing a new variety of squash. It is far bigger and a finer green than any I have seen. I intend to enter it in the village fair. The flesh is whiter..." Hetty caught Guy's eye over Frederick's shoulder. An enigmatic smile played on his lips before he turned his attention to Fanny.

Hetty set her teeth in frustration. She wanted to discuss Guy's problem with Eustace further, to try to help matters between them. It might be quite a while before she could visit Eustace, and the rift might widen and became impossible to mend. Especially, after Guy left for London.

It was an entirely unsatisfactory afternoon. Frederick discussed his successes in his garden in detail while Fanny giggled at Guy's droll remarks. Her father talked to the widow, Mrs. Illingworth. He spoke warmly of the lady's sound, good sense in the carriage on their way home. She'd invited him to visit the following afternoon to advise her on her investments.

If she hadn't been so distracted, Hetty would have shown more interest in this latest development. Was it possible this new friendship could lead to marriage? She had taken immediately to Mrs. Illingworth, a calm, fair-haired lady of some forty-five years, who always seemed to measure her words before speaking.

Hetty arrived home with a throbbing head.

The next afternoon, her father dressed in his best coat. He was quite effusive as he said goodbye. A fledgling hope sparked in Hetty's breast. She would write to Aunt Emily at once. If an invitation arrived, her father might agree to allow her to go to London while his attention was caught by Mrs. Illingworth.

In the library, Hetty sat at her father's desk. She drew a sheet of vellum from the drawer and trimmed a pen. Then, dipping the pen in the inkwell, she began, *Dear Aunt Emily*, then paused, thinking of her conversation with Guy about Eustace. She would not wait to hear if Eustace had risen from his sickbed. The letter forgotten, she went down to the kitchen to ask Cook for some treats to tempt Eustace's appetite. She would visit him tomorrow.

GUY WALKED BACK to the house from the stables. He'd spent the morning making himself known to his tenants, ensuring they had a plentiful supply of coal. He was disturbed by their primitive living conditions and promised to effect immediate improvements. Their children were thin and undernourished, their livestock in poor condition, and some of their roofs needed rethatching. The peasants were starving in France, but he had expected more from Rosecroft Hall. The estate manager had painted a grim picture, blaming the high price of bread on the Corn Laws last year. He'd complained about the decline of English trade owing to the war and Napoleon's Continental System, high unemployment, and high taxes. Despite the overwhelming obstacles, Guy remained determined to put all to rights here at Rosecroft. He would employ more staff as soon as possible, even if it meant traveling to London to find them.

He stood admiring the architecture of the old house when a vehicle rattled its way up the carriage drive. As it grew closer, he saw it was Simon driving a gig with Hetty seated beside him.

Guy helped her down. Hetty wore a green pelisse with a fur collar the color of her hair, and a pretty bonnet lined with amber silk. The breeze toyed with the hem of her skirts, revealing a slim ankle, as he considered what delights might lie beneath.

"Good day, Simon," Guy said with a smile. "I'm sure Williams will be glad of a chinwag."

"As will I. Thank you, my lord." With a bow, Simon slapped the reins and drove toward the stables.

"How ravishing you look today." Pleased to see her in a pretty dress, Guy took her basket and carried it. "What have you here?"

She nodded her thanks. "Cook has made some afternoon tea for Eustace. Is he still in bed?"

It wasn't the warmest of greetings. "No, he seeks the sun in the conservatory."

"That is good news."

"I hope you find him more talkative than I." Guy followed Hetty indoors, waiting while Hammond took her coat and bonnet.

She patted her hair into place, her big expressive eyes filled with doubt. "Perhaps he's not happy here."

"Not happy?" His shoulders tightened with a prickle of annoyance. He escorted her along the passage. "Eustace has been happy here for the best part of thirty-five years."

"Perhaps he feels you want him to leave."

Guy tightened his jaw. "I've made it perfectly plain he is welcome. The hall is large enough for several families to live in and seldom meet."

"That's not the point."

He took her arm and turned her to face him. "Do you think I'm being unreasonable to want the man to explain a few things to me?"

She gave him a quizzical glance. "I should think it would depend on your manner. Are you too forceful?"

Her lack of faith in him affected him far more than he would have thought possible. Perhaps because it was so unfair. "Forceful? I've held off on asking any direct questions that might upset him. I've assured him he may remain for the rest of his days. What more do you suggest? Shall I offer to rub his back?"

She narrowed her eyes and took the basket from him. "You are talking nonsense. Perhaps all he wants is your friendship."

Rather difficult when the man is as frosty as the weather, Guy thought. And then there were those unexplained attacks of which he was reluctant to accuse the man, not without proof at least. And perhaps because he doubted Eustace lay behind them. He exuded lassitude rather than menace. "I'm willing to be on good terms, but he must also make the effort. I shall learn what has occurred here even at the risk of upsetting him."

Having escorted her to the door of the conservatory, he bowed. "And I shall have it straightened out before one of us leaves for London." He left her and strode away.

If she couldn't understand his point of view, so be it. But when his outrage drained away, he felt decidedly flat. He made his way to the library and returned to his study of the estate books and articles on modern methods of farming. He had much to learn.

Chapter Nine

DISMAYED, HETTY CROSSED the tiled floor to her godfather. He sat with a shawl around his shoulders, a book opened on his lap. Guy's stern manner had surprised her, but Eustace did appear miserable.

He smiled and closed his book. "Horatia. How lovely that you should call on a dull, old fellow like me. What is that you have brought with you?"

She put her basket down on a table. "Some of Cook's shortbread biscuits, plum jam, and an apple cake."

"My, you do spoil me."

She bent to kiss him. Cloves. She was familiar with the smell of laudanum. He patted her hand. "You are the closest thing I've ever had to a daughter, Horatia. The kind of daughter to make a man proud."

Horatia was touched but couldn't help a rush of unease. Eustace's eyes looked glazed and his movements sluggish as he summoned a footman.

"Take these to the kitchen," he instructed the servant. "We'll have the cake with our tea, shall we?"

She looked around the conservatory as she sat down. The sun highlighted the dirt on the panes of glass and the cobwebs in corners. Once a lush display, the area was almost bare of plants. The orchids crowded their pots, in need of being divided and repotted, and the violets appeared to have rot. She'd noticed the lack of servants. It was not surprising everything was neglected.

"Where is Thomas?"

"The footman? He decided he was better off in London."

She thought it odd. Thomas had been there for some years. "You know Guy is happy for you to stay here, should you wish to."

"Yes, he's said as much to me, but I shall leave for London soon. The season is almost upon us."

"Will you be well enough?"

"I may as well suffer there as here. I hold out hope that I shall see you in London. Any luck with your father?"

Hetty shook her head. "Papa is taking tea with Mrs. Illingworth again this afternoon. Perhaps he is developing tender feelings for her."

Eustace's eyebrows rose. Warmth sparked in his faded gray eyes. "Really? There's life in the old dog yet." His face reddened. "I do apologize, Horatia. Not fit talk for a young lady's ears. This laudanum has me saying the darndest things."

"Father needs someone to care for him. And someone for him to care for."

"But he won't bother while he has you there to do it. Ah, here is the tea." A footman placed the tea tray on the table.

"Go and find his lordship, Moody. Ask him to join us," Eustace instructed him.

Hetty leaned forward and poured out two cups. She cut him a piece of cake and placed it on the plate.

Eustace stirred his tea. "So very nice to have company."

Hetty didn't like the way he looked. As if he would prefer to doze in his chair than talk to her.

Moments later, Guy walked into the room. He sat in a wing chair. "I've been to visit the tenant farmers, Eustace," he said, taking a cup and saucer from Hetty with a nod of thanks. "They all suffer great difficulty with leaking roofs and not enough to eat."

"As is the case for the rest of England." Eustace stirred his tea. "The Prince of Wales is a charming fellow, but a spendthrift, and there's no help from his father, for he is mad. Lord Melbourne's Tory government is coming under enormous criticism, but they're doing their best." He took a sip of tea. "I don't consider it polite to discuss these matters in front of Horatia."

Guy folded his arms and frowned.

"This cake is first rate. Please pass my compliments to your cook when you return, my dear," Eustace said.

Rather disappointed not to be part of the discussion, Hetty passed Guy a plate. He looked annoyed. If she'd hoped to lighten the atmosphere between them and make things better, she'd failed.

When the tea things were taken away, Eustace leaned back and yawned behind a hand. "Horatia, take Guy for a walk to the lake. I feel in need of a nap."

Eustace had clasped his hands over his stomach and closed his eyes before they left the room.

The gardens greeted them with the smell of damp earth, the rustle of wind through the leaves, the call of birds, and the hum of insects. Guy opened the gate at the bottom of the parterre garden and stood aside for her to pass through.

"Where did you learn to ride astride?" Guy asked her as they strolled together.

Hetty picked a bay leaf from the tree and held it to her nose, breathing in its aromatic fragrance. "In India. A servant taught me to ride when my parents traveled into the higher country for the rainy season. Life was more relaxed there."

"How long were you in India?"

"I spent my nursery years with Aunt Emily in England. Then I was sent to join my parents in Calcutta. It was different to England, but the English created a society as close to England's as they could make it. We enjoyed our tea, and they drank gin to keep malaria at bay. Cricket and polo matches were enormously popular. Not a heathenish existence by any means. It was every bit as strict as English society." A small community rife with scandal and rumor as she remembered it. *Much like the ton must be.*

The fountain was empty except for rotting leaves at the bottom.

They skirted around the lime walk which was so overgrown as to be impassable, walking over the lawns toward the glimmer of water. The breeze had lost its sharpness, and the grass no longer crunched underfoot. It was unlike Guy to be so quiet. "Winter is losing its grip," she said to fill in a long pause.

"It should be pleasant here in the spring."

"It's glorious. The trees with new leaves and every bush blooms with flowers."

"I look forward to it."

"Have I done something to annoy you?"

He turned to face her, placing his hands gently on her shoulders. She startled at his touch. He was so physical. Englishmen weren't so, at least not the ones she knew. His eyes implored hers. "Do you trust me?"

"Yes, I do," she said without hesitation.

His eyes searched hers. "You believe that I am who I say I am?"

"That you are Lord Fortescue? Of course, I do."

The deep timber of his voice sounded sincere, but more than that, she'd never detected any sign of deceptiveness in his manner.

"*Merci.*" He dropped his hands to his sides. "I hate living under a cloud like this. I feel... helpless. Something I'm not used to."

"You must be patient. Eustace has written to your sister—"

"It's not that, for this will be settled in time. It's a matter of trust."

"If you could just see it from Eustace's point of view, Guy—"

"Why should I?" he interjected. "Look around you at the state of this place."

"I'm sure there's a good reason for it."

"You're so loyal, Hetty." He took her arm and turned back to the path.

They reached the grassy bank and gazed out over the lentic calm of gray water dotted with waterfowl. "Let's not talk about it," he said. "When I'm with you, I want to think of other things."

"Like what?" She laughed. "The cost of bread?"

A wicked twinkle entered his eyes. "What lies ahead. And how much I like your laugh."

Pleased, she shook her head at him. "I do declare you would flirt on your deathbed." She recalled how close he'd come to it and put a hand to her mouth.

He took one step toward her and reached for her hand, rubbing his thumb along the underside of her wrist. "I don't wish to dwell on death. I want to think of life and how much I enjoyed kissing you."

"I think we should go back."

"Why? You're safe with me."

Safe, he was the last thing from safe. His gaze rested on her mouth, and she took a gasp of air. "I thought we'd decided to put that in the past. You would not dare to kiss me again."

His wicked smile warned her that he would. She seemed rooted to the spot as he traced the shell of her ear with a finger, moving down to outline her jaw. "I never turn down a dare."

"Such rakish behavior is unforgivable, my lord." She batted his hand away while fighting her own need. It was so hard to resist him.

"You have labeled me a rake, so I'm inclined to live up to your vision of me," he mocked. She saw hurt in his eyes as he lowered his head toward her.

She stilled. "It's a matter of trust. Didn't you just say so yourself?"

Guy straightened and shook his head with a slow grin. "Oh, that is utterly unfair of you, clever, Hetty."

He offered her his arm, and she took it. As they strolled back to the house, Hetty didn't feel clever at all, just regretful that he hadn't kissed her. But the closer they became, the more difficult it would be for her to face the fact he would never be hers. A baron must marry a titled lady, that was an undeniable truth.

Three weeks dragged by while it rained every day, Lady Kemble's card party the only bright light on the social agenda. If one could call it that. Both Guy and Eustace sent their regrets, but Mrs. Illingworth attended, and her father's courtship with the widow continued at a leisurely pace.

Bored and frustrated at not knowing what went on at Rosecroft

Hall, Hetty turned her attention to the plight of The General. She found her father in his favorite chair in the library, sorting through his salmon fly hooks, his new copy of Thomas Best's *A Concise Treatise on the Art of Angling* open on the desk.

"Father, we finally have a fine day. Would you like to accompany me on a ride this afternoon?" A ray of sunlight from the window fell on her father's face, revealing the deep lines and puckers. She almost gasped. He was getting old. When had his brown hair turned sparse and white around his ears?

"Oh, I don't think so, my dear." He pushed his pince-nez up his nose and examined a fly more closely. "I'm most comfortable here."

"Then may Simon accompany me riding your horse?"

"Must you? It looks like it might rain again."

"Father, can you not find someone interested in purchasing The General? It is cruel to keep him."

His eyebrows shot up. "My goodness, that's a spirited request, my dear."

"Forgive me, I don't mean to be disrespectful, but it worries me."

"I suspect you are right. But it will take time. I promise to ride him this Sunday."

"Why not this afternoon?"

He looked pained. "I heard talk yesterday in the village that a stranger has been seen lurking about."

A warning bell sounded in Hetty's mind. "A stranger? Where?"

"Mr. Thurston passed a shabbily dressed fellow on horseback riding along the road toward the village. The vicar saw him, too. He's not putting up at the inn. And after that episode with the highwaymen, one can't be too careful. Best we remain in our homes."

Hetty climbed the stairs, her mind in a whirl. She walked around her bedchamber with prickles of unease on her nape. Could Guy's life be in danger again?

She stripped off her gown and took her forest green wool habit from the clothespress. She must warn Guy. Although she detested defying her father when she'd promised never to do it again, desperate times required desperate measures. Her mare was too slow; she would have to ride The General.

Once on the road, The General lengthened his stride, and she was caught again by his grace and strength. He was far too good for her father's Sunday rides. The sidesaddle was her one concession to propriety although she disliked it. The rain held off, and the horse covered the miles rapidly.

It was a revelation when The General trotted up the carriage drive at Rosecroft Hall. Workmen labored everywhere. They had begun the immense task of restoring the Hall to its former glory. Carpenters replaced rotting timber and stone masons worked to repair the stone walls while other workmen filled in potholes in the carriage drive. Gardeners moved over the landscape as they pruned, clipped hedges, and weeded, preparing the beds for spring. Hetty dismounted and handed the reins to a footman. She picked up the skirt of her habit and walked to the door where the huge entryway dwarfed the waiting butler.

"His lordship's not here, Miss Cavendish," Hammond said, in answer to her query. "He left a short time ago to ride to the village."

"Is my godfather here?"

"He departed for London several days ago."

"Thank you, Hammond. Please tell his lordship I called."

She rode past the abandoned gatehouse, and once through the ornate wrought-iron gates, she reined in The General. It might have been one of the workers from a neighboring village that Mr. Thurston and the vicar had seen, for some employed up at the hall were new to the area. It would be sensible to go home before her father discovered her missing. She nudged The General's flanks and headed in that direction. But as she approached the turnoff to Malforth Manor, some unexplainable instinct drew her on toward the village.

Hetty heard the rattle and jingle of a horse-drawn vehicle. Not wishing to meet with disapproval and fuel gossip, she rode into the shelter of the trees. She watched from her leafy hideaway as Mr. Gantry drove by in his curricle. She suspected he was on his way to visit her father. She hoped it would distract him for some time as the two liked to visit the farm and discuss livestock feed.

When she'd come within a few miles of the village, she pulled The General to a stop. A mere presentiment brought her here before she had time to consider her actions. Going off half-cocked, her father would say. And he would rightly be angry with her. A brisk, cool breeze had sprung up and rain clouds hovered overhead. She would turn back as soon as she came to the end of Sherradspark Wood. The fields and farmlands would offer few hiding places for highwaymen. By now, Guy would be in the village. Most likely enjoying a tankard of ale in the oak-beamed coachman's parlor of the King's Arms. He would laugh at her and accuse her of being fanciful. Well, she wouldn't tell him.

When the road straightened out, she caught sight of a rider ahead. Guy, trotting his horse, safe and sound. Relief and embarrassment heated her face. He rode out of sight around another bend. She eased The General up, then turned his head for home before Guy saw her.

A pistol shot ricocheted through the quiet air.

Chapter Ten

THE GENERAL REARED as panic tightened Hetty's throat. Settling the horse, she urged him into a gallop. "Go boy!"

The General obliged. They rounded the bend in minutes. Hetty gasped. Guy had dismounted. A man shoved a pistol into Guy's back and pushed him into the trees.

For a moment, she debated whether to ride for help or follow them into the forest. There was no time. When she'd reached the spot where Guy and the highwayman had disappeared, she dismounted and looped the reins over a bush. She fought her way through the bushes and trees, the brambles snagging her habit. Broken twigs and trampled undergrowth marked the path the men had taken. The trail crunched under her boots. Their voices reached her, and she crept forward.

"Who sent you?" Guy demanded.

"None of yer business. 'Ere will do fine."

Hetty crouched and parted the leaves of a rhododendron. Her blood chilled. In a clearing, the assailant raised a pistol and took aim at Guy.

Hetty screamed.

The gunman swiveled to stare in her direction.

Guy charged him, toppling him to the ground. The man's shot went wild, spraying bark from a tree, as they rolled down a slope, locked together.

Hetty emerged from her hiding place, her chest tight with fear. She hesitated, unsure what to do next. Her clammy hands clenched into fists as she danced around them. They gained their feet. Guy saw her, and his eyes widened. Distracted, he failed to block the man's fist. It connected with his chin with a resounding thwack. He reeled back with a curse. "Get out of here, Hetty!" he yelled.

The gun lay close to Hetty's feet, but she had no means of reloading it. She snatched up a rock, ready to use it.

Guy returned the favor with a punch to the man's solar plexus.

"Oomph!" The rogue staggered but managed to keep his feet. They cursed and gasped for breath as they circled each other, trading blows.

The rogue pulled a knife from his boot and swiped at Guy, missing him by a whisker. The momentum carried him forward, and he stumbled and fell over a log. Guy followed and kicked him in the knee. He fell with a yelp of pain. Hetty had to bite her lip not to cheer.

The man scrambled to his feet and darted forward again, slashing the knife across Guy's chest. Guy dodged, but the blade caught him, slicing through his waistcoat. Guy managed to grab the assailant's wrist and twisted.

With a groan, the rogue dropped the knife.

Hetty's heart galloped. She was gasping as she edged closer. The attacker took note of her, and his eyes narrowed. He broke loose from Guy's grip and snatched up the knife again.

"For God's sake, run, Hetty!" Guy yelled as he darted away from the lethal blade. The rogue followed, slashing wildly at the air.

The attacker's back was to her. She could stand no more, one false move and Guy would be dead. She rushed up behind the assailant and swung the rock at his head. It connected with an alarming thud. For a moment he stood still, then fell forward onto Guy, and they both went down.

Guy rolled the unconscious man off him as blood spilled onto the ground from a gash on the man's pate. He climbed to his feet. "What if he'd killed me? He would have killed you, too," he said with a growl.

She put her hands on her hips. "How ungrateful!"

Guy's jaw clenched. "I would have bested him. You should not have intervened. Go home before you are missed!"

Hetty peered at the ruffian who lay on his back with his eyes closed, his narrow face pale as death. Her chest heaved in anguish. "Have I killed him?"

"No."

"W-who is he?"

Guy picked up the pistol, then knelt and searched the man's pockets. "He didn't seem obliged to tell me." He looked up. "How did you come to be here? Not following me, were you?"

"Well, how arrogant! As if I would. I was on an errand."

He stood and examined a piece of paper he had taken from the pocket of the man's grubby coat. He flicked her a quick glance. "Alone? And riding your father's horse, I suppose."

She raised her chin. "Yes."

"And your father remains ignorant of the fact."

"This is hardly the time..."

"I'll bet when you were a child, you never refused a dare."

"Well I..."

A muscle ticked in Guy's clenched jaw. "Do you now see how dangerous it is to ride alone, Hetty? This could have ended quite differently." He glanced at the fellow. "Once he had you in his power, he may not have killed you immediately." His eyes pinned her in place, his meaning clear.

She shuddered. "Well, I don't believe he was after me."

He scowled at her. "A woman should not go about on her own when there are dangerous *canailles* about."

"*Canailles?*"

Guy scrubbed his face with his hand. "You call them highwaymen." His eyes narrowed. "But you are well aware of my meaning."

Hetty put her hands on her hips. "I was the one who knocked him out, my lord."

"That's true, but I had it well in hand."

"It didn't look as if you did."

"You distracted me."

"Such ingratitude!"

"I didn't want to kill him until I learned who hired him. I must get him into custody, preferably before he comes to. I am *most* grateful. And should be pleased to show you if I had time."

Unsure what he meant by that, the possibilities made her heart leap. "Shall I go for help?"

He shook his head. "You cannot. There would be gossip for a month of Sundays."

Anger robbed her of breath. "Surely you don't care for such things."

"I care for your sake."

Hetty opened her mouth, then shut it again. "I do believe you are a man after my father's heart," she said finally.

His eyes widened. "How so?"

"You would keep a woman under your thumb safe from the world, because she is so helpless."

"There is nothing helpless about you, Hetty. You are reckless! If that was your father's intention, he has certainly made a poor job of it. But I don't blame him. It must be exhausting."

She clamped her lips down on a sharp retort and pointed to the prone man. He had not moved. She stepped closer.

"Are you sure he's not dead?"

"Quite sure."

"Can you reload his pistol? You can guard him while I fetch the parish constable."

He gave a mirthless laugh as he stripped off the man's belt. "You most certainly will not." He fastened the belt around the man's wrists. "That should hold him." He dropped the man's hands and straightened. "I'll get him up onto his horse. And you must go home."

As Guy dragged the man through the undergrowth, she grabbed the man's feet in an effort to help. He was heftier than a sack of grain and reeked of rancid sweat, tobacco, and onions. She wanted to hold her nose.

With Guy doing most of the lifting, they hoisted him sideways over the saddle, his arms and legs dangling.

Guy gave her a leg up onto The General. The stallion danced around, unsettled by the other horses. Hetty spoke to him soothingly and patted his neck.

When The General quieted, Guy mounted his horse and, with a pull on the reins of the highwayman's horse, he turned the animals toward the village.

"Did he try to rob you?" she called after him.

He turned back to her. "He didn't get a chance, although I doubt that was his intention."

She met his restless gaze. "Then what was? Have you no inkling why these people keep attacking you?"

"I will learn more when he wakes. Say nothing about this, Hetty."

"You can trust me."

He nodded. "I know."

"Will you come and tell me more, tonight? Come late, after dinner."

"Very well."

She glanced again at the limp form, fearing she'd dealt him a deadly blow. "I hope he won't die."

"He's in no danger of it." Guy's eyes flashed with anger. "It wouldn't concern me too much if he did, as he did intend to murder me."

"That's all very well for you. You wouldn't have been the one to have killed him."

Guy gathered up the reins. "I promise you, I shan't let him die. And I'll resist killing him, myself." He huffed out a heavy sigh. "It seems I am in your debt again. Thank you, Hetty. Now please, go home."

She watched Guy ride away toward the village, the other horse and its comatose occupant trailing at the end of the rein. She didn't wish him to be in her debt, but she was so happy he was alive that her heart soared. But her spirits soon plummeted when it occurred to her that the rogue had been hired to kill Guy. And whoever was behind it would no doubt try again.

Hetty rode The General home. Had Guy killed a man? He was not the consummate liar Eustace suspected him to be, but she sensed there was much more to Guy's past than he was prepared to tell her. Had he fought with Bonaparte? Eustace was right to demand documented proof. And she hoped Guy would be able to provide it.

One thing she did know. Should Guy need her help again, she would give it, whether he liked it or not. Even if she saved him for Fanny or some other lady, she thought, as a lump formed in her throat.

Simon led The General away with a raise of his eyebrows, but he didn't question her. The house was quiet when she entered. Hetty hurried up to her bedchamber. She washed and changed into a house gown, praying she hadn't been missed.

Her father was at his desk in the library. He gave her a sharp look. "Ah, my dear. I had a visitor, Mr. Gantry. We've been visiting the farm. I sent word for you to join us for tea, but the maids couldn't find you. Where have you been?"

"I went out for some fresh air."

He frowned. "On foot?"

"No, I rode, Father."

"Alone?"

"Yes."

He rose from his chair and came around the desk to take her hands. "I am surprised and shocked, Horatia. Without my knowledge and with highwaymen about? You are far too reckless."

Accused of recklessness twice in one day cut deep. Her chest squeezed at the disappointment in his eyes. "I'm sorry, Papa. I am...stifled here sometimes."

He studied her. "Stifled, eh?"

She had reached a stage where she couldn't dissemble, not even to spare him. "Yes."

"That's not good, Horatia. Not good at all."

Relieved that he didn't ask her which horse she'd ridden, she placed a hand on his arm. "I should not have gone out alone, Papa. I am sorry. I won't do it again."

He straightened his back, appearing more like the figure of authority he'd once been commanding his troops. "Raising a daughter is not easy for a man to do alone. But I've done my best. I'm hurt that you've kept your concerns from me."

"I'm sorry I've disappointed you," she whispered, as her eyes filled with tears.

He chucked her under the chin. "There now, don't cry." He smiled. "We all make mistakes, my dear. We shall speak no more about it." He returned to his desk. "Oh, by the way, Mr. Oakley called. He left some vegetables with Cook."

"How good of him. I'm sure they're splendid."

"I had planned to play faro at Mr. Broadbent's this evening, but I've half a mind not to go. I should stay and keep you company. The skies threaten rain."

"I am perfectly content to spend the evening with a book."

"Are you? Then I suppose I'd best not let Mr. Broadbent down. Are you sure you won't be bored here on your own?"

"No of course not, Papa." A deep sense of shame lowered her spirits. She was neither a dutiful daughter, nor was she honest.

Her father left after dinner in the curricle. When he'd turned down the lane, Hetty lit a lantern and slipped out to the stables. A light rain was falling. Familiar stable smells, warm hay, manure, and the sounds of horses snuffling in their boxes greeted her as she slipped inside. She pulled her cloak close, her nerves on edge. It had been a frightful day and she'd never hurt a living soul before. Her anguish faded to be replaced by a heady sense of expectation. The memory of Guy lying in the hay smiling up at her in that rakish way he had, his mouth on hers, made her want to throw all caution to the winds. Hooves rang on the gravel drive. With a deep breath, she hurried to the doorway.

Guy appeared through the misty rain and dismounted. He led his horse inside, his shoulders slumped with weariness.

She was immediately contrite. "Papa has gone out. Come into the house and sit by the fire."

"What about the servants? I don't wish to compromise you."

"Don't be so stuffy. Come to the front door. I want to hear what happened."

He glared at her, his eyes bloodshot, but didn't resist.

An unmarried lady receiving a gentleman alone at night showed a sad lack of propriety to heap on top of her recent misdemeanors. She was glad of her loyal servants, but she couldn't make herself care about etiquette. Not when it was a matter of life and death.

The maid answered the door and showed him into the library where Hetty waited. It was cozy with the walls lined with bookshelves and the fire lit. A reassuring smell of pipe smoke mingled with that of old tomes. Guy poured their drinks and settled with her on the leather chesterfield.

Hetty allowed her fears to ease as she sipped a glass of sherry and watched Guy nurse a brandy. Guy wore a drab green coat, but his linen was fresh and white against his olive skin. He looked worried. He seemed more vulnerable tonight, which made him even more attractive.

He turned the glass in his hands, watching the crystal catch the candlelight. "I found a map in the man's pocket. It detailed the roads surrounding Rosecroft Hall, in relation to Sherrardspark Wood. The spot was marked where he held me up. The ruffian recovered his senses but has refused thus far to say who hired him. I'm at a loss. The one person who benefits by my death is Eustace. No one else. But I'm not about to accuse him of it. Yet."

Hetty gasped. "I simply can't believe it of him. He doubts you are the real Baron Fortescue."

"He takes so much laudanum he's incoherent."

"He's in pain."

"He's become dependent upon it."

"Oh!" She had feared it herself.

"When the highwaymen attacked me on my way down from London, I lost my portmanteau. It contained all my important papers plus a letter from my father with his seal."

"Have you looked for it?"

"*Bien sûr!* I search every day."

"Perhaps I can…"

"No, you cannot!"

"There's no need to snap my head off." She caught her bottom lip between her teeth. "I can't anyway, I promised Papa I wouldn't go out riding alone again."

Guy's eyes widened. "He knows?"

"Yes."

"That you ride his horse while dressed in a man's clothes?"

She flushed. "No. But I won't do that again." She wasn't sure it would be good for her father's health to hear it. "What will you do?"

"Continue to search for my bag for a few days. Then I'll go to my solicitor in London. Once that's done, I'll pay Eustace a visit."

"Why?"

"To inform him of my new will, which disinherits him from all unentailed properties. I shall also tell him of my plan to marry." He frowned. "But I must find those papers."

"I'm sure you will have no trouble selecting a suitable bride. You are, for the most part, perfectly acceptable."

"For the most part?" He cocked a dark eyebrow.

"You are attractive, undoubtedly. And a nobleman…"

He gave a cautious laugh. "I seem to detect a 'but' in there somewhere. Unless my English…"

"Don't fudge," she scoffed, looking at her hands. "Your understanding of English is excellent."

He took her chin in his big hand and forced her to meet his gaze. "Then what?"

She shivered at his touch and tried to ignore the way her breath quickened. Annoyed, she pulled away from him. "Your wife must be prepared to obey her master in all matters. Entertain and embroider and keep the hearth fires burning while you hunt and shoot and visit your club in London or a mistress…"

His blue gaze heated, and he gripped her shoulders hard, making her wince, more from his closeness than discomfort. *"Mon dieu*, but you are a tease, Hetty!"

She wriggled out of his grasp. "Fanny Kemble is an excellent choice. She is very sweet-natured. Could it be Fanny?"

"Fanny? Where did that harebrained idea come from?"

"You flirt with Fanny every time you're in her company."

"Flirt? I? What about you and that beanpole Oakley!"

"You are not exactly short yourself, my lord." Beanpole described tall thin Frederick, perfectly, and she stifled a giggle. "Frederick called today while I was out," she said coolly. "He has asked me to marry him."

"He has? Impudent man." His eyes narrowed.

"Papa approves of him."

He gave a derisive laugh. "Since when do you rush to obey your father?"

She firmed her lips. "I have refused Mr. Oakley."

"That was kind. You would exhaust the fellow within the first year."

"I don't believe I would. In fact, I might reconsider. You are behaving like a boor, my lord."

"It is Oakley who would bore you to death."

She could say nothing to that, for she feared it was true.

He took her hands. "Let's not quarrel, Hetty." His eyes softened. "You might do more to help me."

"How?"

"As you know, I'm not yet able to marry. I have need of a fiancée, however. It will give Eustace something to think about. He is very fond of you. Would you agree? It would be only for a period until all this is settled."

She stared at him. "A faux betrothal? What would my father say?"

"I shan't ask you to lie to him. Again," he added, making her frown. "But he needn't be told the precise truth just now. You want to go to London, no? This offers you a good reason to visit your aunt.

You won't remain bound to me, and should something happen, well…
you are free."

"Nothing must happen. Guy you will be careful? London is a dangerous place."

He grinned. "The countryside isn't so safe."

"Digswell is usually." A faux engagement was deceitful, but he was right. For Eustace to learn her happiness depended on Guy would give him pause, should he be behind this. She pushed the thought away, ashamed at her disloyalty. Her father would at last agree to a season with her aunt. As Guy's fiancée, she would have the freedom to discover all those things in London that called to her. Her eyes met his and she nodded. This must be kept on a business footing. She must guard her heart.

"No kissing," she said, determined to make it clear before she weakened. "A business arrangement."

"If that is your wish," Guy said, and his smile widened.

"I must have your word, Guy," she demanded.

"You have my word." He cast her a hurt glance she didn't trust. "No lovemaking unless you desire it."

She wasn't sure she liked the way he phrased it. It sounded like a challenge. She shrugged it off as excitement gripped her. *London.* "Very well."

"You agree?"

"Yes."

"*Bon.*" He kissed her hand and jumped up. "I thank you with all of my heart. Now I must go. I will return to ask your father tomorrow."

"Ask my father?" She clearly hadn't thought it through. It all became very real.

Oh dear.

Chapter Eleven

A FTER HER FATHER enthusiastically embraced the engagement, Hetty was left to struggle with guilt. Not so for Guy. Closeted in the library with her father, the two discussed her dowry and the marriage settlement. That done, he and her father shared a joke while discussing salmon fishing and farm practices. A good deal of bonhomie and laughter floated out the door along with the smoke.

Guy emerged at last and told her of his intention to continue his daily search for his portmanteau. Whether he found it or not, he would leave for London two days hence. This time he would travel by coach with a footman riding shotgun. Hetty would see him again when she arrived at her aunt's the following week. He smiled down at her as they said their goodbyes at the front door.

"You needn't be quite so pleased." She wanted him to suffer at least a twinge of guilt.

His lips curled up at the corners. She took a steadying breath. He was not her true beau, and she must never forget it.

"Goodbye, fair Hetty." He bent his head and dropped a feather-light kiss close to the corner of her mouth as she turned her head away. "I'll count the days until we meet in London."

Hetty glowered at him. He'd come close to breaking the rules of their agreement already. "You will stay with Eustace in Mayfair?"

"I am invited to put up with a friend, Lord Strathairn, as my town-house is to be sold."

"You might improve things between you, should you stay with

him."

His eyes clouded. "I don't believe Eustace and I shall ever be friends. Even if he is innocent, he has doubted me from the first."

"But, Guy…"

His dark eyebrows slammed together. "I expected to be given the benefit of the doubt. You gave it, the people of Digswell have given it. Why not he?" She opened her mouth to argue in Eustace's defense, but he placed a finger to her lips. "Hetty, I suspect as a wife you will give a man little peace."

"Well, it's a good thing we aren't to marry, do you not agree?" she fired back incensed. She'd been trying to repair the rift, but maybe Guy was right. He and Eustace would never be friends.

"Mmm?" He gave her that annoyingly inscrutable look he adopted at times.

She considered it prudent to change the topic of conversation. "I wish you luck in your search. It will put paid to this uncertainty."

When he took her hand and stroked the inside of her wrist, she could feel the fast beat of her pulse.

"I'll have to see about a ring."

She withdrew her hand. "There's no need for that," she said breathlessly. "I mean, I understood it was to be just a matter of days and made known only to Papa and Eustace. Then we can end it discreetly."

"And leave you living with your aunt?"

"Yes."

He frowned. "It must appear real. And remain in place until everything has been set to rights."

Disconcerted, she tried to discern his thoughts. "But how long might that take?"

"Until my sister arrives. Unless I find my portmanteau before I leave for London." He tilted his head. "Doesn't a season in London appeal to you?"

"Oh, it does," she said, excitement creeping into her voice. "London offers so much. My aunt's poetry readings most particularly."

He firmed his lips. "Poetry is well and good, but it pales beside life experience, Hetty."

"And real life sometimes pales beside poetry," she said coolly. He could be so annoying at times.

He arched an eyebrow. "That would depend on what one experienced. And with whom."

Her cheeks heated. "Miss Fanny is in London. You might call on her. I shall give you her address."

"I would be pleased to," he said. "I like Miss Fanny."

Hetty watched him ride away. London and its charms awaited her, with the promise of a visit to the museum and the Tower, art galleries and literary soirees, plays and the opera. The prospect should thrill her. Instead, she turned away troubled. She doubted they could extricate themselves from this fine mess without someone being hurt. She prayed it wouldn't be Guy's reputation, for a broken engagement was frowned upon, but it was more likely to be her heart.

Two weeks later, in Aunt Emily's townhouse parlor, her aunt expressed her enthusiasm to at last have Hetty stay for a whole season. And how utterly thrilled she was at the news of the engagement. "A baron no less," she said for the fifth time. "The aristocracy don't generally marry gentry unless there's money involved. It's always a matter of finance. And surely the baron doesn't need to fill his coffers?"

"I don't believe so, aunt."

"Well. Then. Fancy." Her aunt fell silent.

Unable to continue weaving a web of lies, Hetty fell silent.

Aunt Emily wandered over to her desk. She picked up a pen and prodded her topknot with the end while studying the papers on the desktop. "This morning in anticipation of your visit, I penned a short verse in iambic pentameter. An *Ode to Spring*. Would you care to read it?" She held it out to her.

Hetty put down her teacup. Having just arrived, stiff and weary, and consumed with exhilaration at the sight of the big, bustling city, she'd never felt so little enthusiasm for rhyme. But she took the proffered page and read it.

"It's wonderful, Aunt Emily. I love the way you've rhymed 'tree', with 'free' and linked 'spring' with 'wing'. There is a deep sense of freedom when spring first sends up those green shoots after a long winter," she said warmly, when she'd finished, although she found it too flowery for her taste. Somehow, the idea of spending her days penning verse had lost its attraction, although she was sure it would return, after the excitement of being here had died down. She wondered again why Aunt Emily had never married. Might the loss of a lover be the cause of filling her life with poetry, literature, and art? She must find a tactful way to ask her. Eustace had hinted at a mysterious man in her aunt's past, but he'd been hazy on the details and her father had never mentioned it.

Her aunt tucked the poem into a book. "Stand up, Hetty, and turn around. Let me have a look at you."

Hetty obligingly stood and completed a slow turn, drawing a frown from Aunt Emily. "Your dress is woefully outmoded. That shade of green was seasons ago. And sleeves are fuller this year."

Her aunt's interest in fashion was surprising because it seemed so out of character. "Papa has been economizing. And there's not much of a choice of fabrics in Digswell. And if I order a gown from a catalogue, it's not always a good fit."

"My brother, dear as he is to me, is entirely too parsimonious." She tsked. "For goodness' sake, you are about to marry into the aristocracy." She crossed the room to sort through a stack of magazines. "The sooner we do something about your wardrobe, the better."

Her aunt selected a copy of the *La Belle Assemblee* magazine. She handed it Hetty. "This has just arrived. See what appeals. We shall require a French modiste. Paris fashion has taken London by storm this year."

Hetty guiltily admired the elegant gowns featured on every page. Might she have an outfit like one of these? Perhaps two would be more practical. She would get years of wear out of them in Digswell. She was struck by a ball gown with a stiff, ruffled collar. Extremely tall ostrich feathers decorated the lady's headdress. "I do like this."

Her aunt looked at the page. "Mm? One must not go overboard, perhaps."

"What about this sea green turban?"

"We shall discuss it with the dressmaker. She will know what is suitable for every occasion. Fortunately, you have an excellent figure." Aunt Emily pulled the bell to summon a servant. "You must tell me everything. I cannot wait to hear how this engagement came about."

Hetty bent her head to hide her hot cheeks. "It happened quite fast, Aunt. Lord Fortescue finds himself in need of a fiancée."

Her aunt sighed. "It's not a love match?"

"More of a business arrangement."

"But, you said he wasn't in need of money." Aunt Emily's eyes widened. "If that were the case, Lord Fortescue would choose a lord's daughter."

"Yes, but it's a matter of urgency."

Her aunt's eyes became owlish. "Urgency? I don't understand, dear. Then what? Is he seriously ill?" Her face took on a tragic cast. "Surely you aren't to be a young widow?"

Hetty twisted her handkerchief. She couldn't produce a convincing lie to save her life, and her aunt's understanding seemed a good deal sharper than her father's. Or were men just easier to fool?

"Hetty?" Aunt Emily's voice lowered accusingly. "There is a story here. I wish to learn it." She sat down and folded her arms. "Tell all, if you please."

Hetty sipped a glass of water. Her throat was horribly dry. She'd been pleading her case for over an hour. A study of her aunt's face revealed there was still more to be said. "You have made a very bad mistake, indulging him in this, my dear. Your father has been remiss, but men... well, they have little commonsense."

"But, Aunt..."

Her aunt held up a hand. "What will occur when the engagement ends? Tell me that."

"I'll return home." *To live with my dreams.* She would become an oddity in Digswell she supposed. A whiff of scandal would follow her about, which might help make her poetry more popular.

"It must be something from the baron's past," her aunt said with conviction. "I don't know him well, but I can't believe Mr. Fennimore capable of such a thing." She shook her head. "I understand your need to protect this man, but I can't see that it should be you. It's not wise." Her brows drew together. "If your father knew the truth—"

"Oh, please don't tell him, Aunt. I promise to when it's at an end. I doubt it will be for very long, and I don't want Papa upset unnecessarily. I have gained a good deal from this. After all, I'm here with you in London."

"I've a good mind to speak to this Lord Fortescue. He has placed you in an invidious position."

The maid appeared at the door and held out a calling card. "You have a visitor, Miss Emily."

"Now who might this be?" Aunt Emily said crossly. "I want to talk you out of this silly..." She read the card and looked up. "Just the man I wish to see. Send him in, Sarah."

Guy entered the room, tall and imposing, a silver-topped cane tucked beneath his arm as he removed gray gloves. He was dressed immaculately in fitted buff trousers, a dark blue superfine coat and spotless linen, a gold fob looped over his embroidered silk waistcoat.

Hetty's heart fluttered. He looked elegant, poised, and heart-wrenchingly handsome. Aunt Emily thought so, too. She curtsied and bid him welcome in a breathy voice.

"Delighted, Miss Cavendish." Guy bowed. "Your niece has told me of your celebrated literary *soirees*. I have looked forward to meeting you and hope to be invited to attend when next you have one."

Hetty stood, clenched her hands, and waited for her aunt to inform him that the engagement must be at an end.

Guy's gaze swept Hetty with unveiled appreciation. "You appear to be in excellent health, Miss Cavendish. I trust you had a pleasant and uneventful trip?"

"I did, thank you." Hetty was struck by how different he seemed. Back in Digswell he was undoubtedly handsome, but here he appeared so much more commanding and like the lord of the realm he was. Her aunt obviously thought so, too. Hetty fell silent, tamping down her impatience to ask him the latest news.

Aunt Emily smiled. "Please do sit, my lord. Would you care for a libation?".

"Nothing to drink, thank you." He removed a small box from his pocket. "I wonder if I might be permitted a moment alone with Miss Cavendish?"

Hetty's gaze flew to her aunt, who was eyeing the jeweler's box. "Certainly, my lord." Amazed and relieved, she watched as her aunt gathered up her shawl and glasses and hurried from the room.

She turned to Guy. "Did you find your portmanteau?"

He shook his head.

"Oh. I'm sorry. You've been to your solicitor?"

"I just came from Lincoln's Inn. A codicil is to be added to the will. I plan to see Eustace this afternoon."

"But without your papers, it has no relevance."

"It may force his hand."

"Does that mean you might be in more danger?"

"We shall see. I'm prepared for it, in any case."

She gazed doubtfully at him as Guy flipped open the satin-lined box.

Hetty dropped her gaze to the diamond ring. A veritable sunburst of light. She gasped. "It's beautiful."

Guy reached for her hand.

"I don't suppose I could accompany you to see Eustace?"

"No, you may not." Hetty's hand trembled in his. A frisson of excitement bubbled up inside her when he slipped the ring on her finger. Her attempts to remind herself their engagement was not real didn't seem to help. "It's beautiful. It fits so perfectly."

He nodded, pleased. "Good, then I guessed the size correctly."

"How clever of you." She turned her hand to admire the rose cut diamond set in a cluster of smaller emeralds which was only on loan to her.

"A kiss to seal the arrangement." Leaning close, Guy framed her face in his big hands. Before she could object, his mouth covered hers and her senses swam.

When he drew away, she was about to rebuke him, but remembered her aunt, lurking, no doubt, somewhere outside the door. He ran a finger over her bottom lip, and she shook her head at him.

He smiled. "Do you like what you've seen of London?"

"You hadn't told me how busy, smoky, noisy, and smelly it is. Someone is always rapping on the door to offer to fix one's chairs or sharpen one's knives. And night is only a little better with the town crier tolling the hour and carts and night carriages passing the door." She smiled. "But I still can't wait to see more of it."

He laughed. "You shall."

With a discreet cough, Aunt Emily entered the room.

"Would you like to see the ring, Aunt?" Hetty held out her hand.

Aunt Emily nodded her approval. "How tasteful."

"Can I persuade you both to accompany me to the Theatre Royal tomorrow evening?"

Hetty's heart leapt. The theatre! How thrilling, she glanced uncertainly at her aunt.

She needn't have worried; her aunt's eyes held an excited gleam. "We shall be delighted, my lord. Mr. Edmund Keane performs King Lear. Everyone talks of it. How fortunate that you have obtained seats."

"Most fortunate," Guy said. "A friend, Lord Strathairn, has invited us to join him in his box."

"Indeed." A pink flush crept over Aunt Emily's cheeks, and she put her hand to the locket at her throat.

Guy bowed. "Until tomorrow, then."

Aunt Emily looked pensive when the door closed behind Guy. Then she came to life, clapping her hands. "We must prepare, my dear. Such an evening awaits us!"

Hetty held up her hand to admire her ring as she followed her aunt upstairs. She was surprised and relieved that her aunt seemed to have changed her mind. Why she had was a mystery, but Hetty hoped it would continue for the length of the engagement. However long that would be. She'd given her word to Guy and would not break it.

On Friday evening, Hetty entered Guy's carriage wearing her sprigged muslin beneath her aunt's Spitalfield's velvet evening cloak of rose pink shot through with gold. Her aunt wore purple. Gas lamps lighted their way through the streets. Covent Garden was ablaze, the crowd a fascinating mix, from strolling prostitutes to flower sellers to the most admired members of the *ton*. In the theatre foyer, Guy introduced her aunt and Hetty to the Earl of Strathairn, a handsome, fair-haired man, and his two sisters, the married Lady Eleanor Fitzherbert, and the younger Lady Georgina Haldane, a vivacious brunette not long out of the schoolroom. Hetty envied the young woman's blush pink gown embroidered with rosebuds, so delicate a fabric it seemed to float around her. "So, you're the one who has snatched Lord Fortescue from under our very noses," Lady Georgina said.

"Georgina!" Lady Eleanor chided with an embarrassed laugh. Lady Eleanor, more subdued in saffron silk, was older than her sister by some years and looked more like her brother in appearance. "Welcome to London, Miss Cavendish. You must forgive my sister. Georgina has yet to learn to curb her tongue."

"Yes, Georgina, do apologize." Lord Strathairn frowned. "You have offended Miss Cavendish."

"Oh no, she hasn't at all." Hetty smiled warmly at the elegant brother and his two sisters. "I can but hope you'll forgive *me*, Lady Georgina."

Guy laughed. "Do not be harsh with Lady Georgina, John. She has become my stalwart friend, assisting me in all manner of English ways, of which I confess to ignorance."

They ascended the crimson velvet-covered stairs to the row of gilt-embossed doors and entered the box. Settled on gilt-legged chairs upholstered in the same crimson velvet, coffee was brought. A din rose up from the seats below. In the boxes opposite, people gossiped and waved.

Hetty leaned forward in her chair as the curtain rose on King Lear's palace. The audience didn't cease in their chatter, and many still roamed about when Edmund Kean appeared. Applause broke out. She turned to Guy and found his eyes on her. "Isn't this exciting?" she whispered.

"Life is exciting, Hetty. If you give yourself up to it."

Hetty frowned. Sometimes, Guy was like a picture puzzle. She couldn't fit all the pieces together. There was so much about him she didn't know. She'd entered this engagement foolishly, the prospect of a season in London tantalizing her so much she'd snatched at it, without thought. What did he really want with her? He was entirely too good at playing the lover. And there was the question of who wished him dead. Poor Eustace seemed incapable of it.

Had evil followed Guy to Digswell from abroad? She turned back to the stage to follow the play. But when the actor's monologue was drowned out by the audience, her thoughts returned to the man beside her. She must try to think clearly, but he was so annoyingly distracting it was like trying to rise out of deep water.

The box emptied at intermission when everyone other than Guy abandoned it to speak to friends. After Hetty's aunt excused herself to go to the withdrawing room, Guy leaned close, seemingly oblivious to the curious gazes around them. "I called on Eustace yesterday."

She studied his face. "How was he?"

"Well enough. When I explained the change to the will to him, he accepted it without rancor. In fact, he seemed disinterested."

She widened her eyes. "He offered no comment?"

"Merely expressed delight at our engagement. He said he understood that I was concerned for you. But as my wife, should I die before you, without proof of my birth, any legal document would be worthless."

"Oh," she said in a small voice. "How frustrating."

"I am a patient man, Hetty," he said. A muscle ticked in his cheek, belying his words. "I expect a reply from my sister any day."

"You will be careful, won't you, Guy?"

He smiled. "May I take you out for a drive on Sunday? I'm keen to show you more of London."

Pleased with the idea of seeing him again so soon, she glanced uneasily toward the door of the box, unsure of her aunt's reaction. "If my aunt agrees."

"As an engaged couple, I should think a carriage ride to Hyde Park would be acceptable. It's hardly clandestine. At three o'clock? We will be too early for most of the *ton*, but there are always riders exercising their horses and ladies promenading in the park."

Lord Strathairn entered with his sisters. He took the seat beside Hetty. "Do you enjoy the play, Miss Cavendish?"

"It's excellent, my lord. Mr. Keane is spellbinding."

"I've always found him rather overrated."

"Oh, surely not. He's slight in stature, but he portrays the character with such force."

He nodded before turning back to answer a question Lady Eleanor had put to him.

Hetty clutched her fan. She could find no fault with his manners, but Lord Strathairn's eyes were a steely gray. And she sensed that his thorough scrutiny of her was almost a habit and came from considerable experience.

Chapter Twelve

GUY ACCOMPANIED JOHN in his quest for a high stakes card game on Saturday evening. They entered a private house which was a gaming hell run by Lord Bromehurst. Guy did not share John's interest, but as the earl's houseguest, he was happy to keep him company. He drew the line at courtesans and opera dancers, however. John accepted it good-naturedly but expressed surprise. After all, Guy wasn't married yet.

Guy was somewhat surprised himself. There was a time when he would have enjoyed such women's company. His life was in such a state of flux, he had no intention of complicating it with courtesans. And the image of Hetty's sweet face seemed to get in the way. He had no idea what was in store for him, but he needed her in his life. And that meant dealing as honestly with her as he could while withholding anything that might encourage her to leap to his defense. While he admired her loyalty and bravery, he wasn't going to allow her to become his comrade-in-arms.

He followed John through the elegantly furnished rooms where a myriad of candles clustered on polished tables and a pair of fine Italian crystal chandeliers shone down. As they observed the play at the hazard, loo, and faro tables, ladies roamed the rooms in their evening gowns sipping champagne.

Strains of Handel swirled above the hubbub from a small orchestra as couples strolled to and from the adjoining supper room.

A dark-haired lady approached. "You are Baron Fortescue, no?"

Guy bowed. "Forgive me, I haven't had the pleasure."

The Frenchwoman gave him a flirtatious look and fluttered her fan beneath dancing dark eyes. She spoke to him in French. "Countess Forney, Lord Fortescue. My husband, Count Forney, wishes a word with you." She took a card from her gold beaded reticule and held it out to him. "Would next Monday at twelve o'clock be suitable?"

"I don't believe I know your husband, Countess."

"That is true, but he knows of you, my lord."

Guy bowed. "*Merci.*" He ran his thumb over the engraved lettering, considering whether to call on the Frenchman. Then he tucked the card into his pocket as she moved away.

John placed his hand on Guy's arm. "It would be wise not to further the friendship with either Forney or his wife."

"Can you tell me why I shouldn't?"

John cocked a brow. "The count is mixed up in bad company."

"I'm sure you offer good advice, John," Guy said, but his curiosity was piqued. "Forney most likely seeks the company of another Frenchman."

John looked back at the lovely woman who strolled about the tables dressed in a revealing gown. A pink garter at her knee showed through the embroidered cloth. "Perhaps it's his wife who is interested to see more of you."

Guy followed John's gaze. Countess Forney countered with a knowing smile and placed a gloved hand to her throat, drawing attention to her shockingly low décolletage. Her bodice skimmed her nipples and the rounded globes of her breasts shimmered pearly white in the candlelight.

Guy nodded to her. "Shall we move on, John?"

They entered the inner chamber, the air stuffy with beeswax, the rancid sweat of excitement and possibly fear. In this room, the players spoke little, and the atmosphere fairly crackled with expectation.

"Fortunes can be won and lost in one night," John said in an undertone. "Large estates signed away."

"What is this game they play?" Guy asked.

"*Twenty-One.* Each player tries to beat the dealer by having two or more cards equaling twenty-one or better than the dealer's hand without exceeding twenty-one."

"*Vingt-et-un.* Played in France."

"Care to join in?" John's voice was soft, but his eyes glowed with interest.

"Not I." Guy had no need for such excitement. "I prefer to control how I spend my money."

"You're a conservative fellow," John said, with a grin. "Might we see you in the House?"

"When my life has settled down." Guy was keen to involve himself in the state of the country and the people who relied upon him. At the green baize table, his attention was caught by a man leaning forward to place his bet. The candlelight brightened his rusty hair. Misgivings stirred Guy's gut.

He walked over to the table. "Good evening, Eustace."

Eustace slumped back in his chair, his eyes dull. A glass of whiskey at his elbow, he held the cards in a loose grasp. "Guy?" Losing the hand, he threw the cards down and pushed back his chair.

"Eustace, I don't believe you know Lord Strathairn. My lord, this is my relative, Mr. Fennimore."

Leaning on his cane, Eustace swayed into a bow, in danger of toppling. "How d'you do?" His gaze returned to Guy. "You've saved me the task of sending you an invitation. I'm holding a dinner party in a sennight. I should like you and Horatia to come."

"We shall be pleased to."

Eustace left the table and tottered toward the front door.

"You seem a trifle under the weather," Guy said. "May I accompany you home?"

"Thank you, Guy. I'm done here." Eustace shrugged. "Pockets to let, old fellow."

Guy raised his eyebrows at John. "Forgive me, but I must leave you."

Strathairn nodded. "Watch your back then, my friend. I shall take

Mr. Fennimore's place at the table."

It had rained, and mist curled around the buildings. The narrow lane was lit only from the lights shining down from a few buildings, and no sign of a hackney.

"Best we walk to the corner. Footpads wait for those with plump pockets in this dark place," Eustace murmured.

Guy offered his arm after Eustace stumbled over the slick cobbles.

They reached the lamp-lit main thoroughfare. Moments later, a hackney swung around the corner. Guy hailed it and helped Eustace inside. He leapt in to join him.

"I am pleased about the marriage." Eustace lay back against the squabs and closed his eyes. "I am very fond of my goddaughter. She has a good deal of resolve, and it's been a bone of contention between her father and me that he's kept her in the country."

Eustace eased himself into a corner, folded his arms and began to snore.

The hackney rocked through Pall Mall. Guy stroked his tight jaw as suspicion took root.

HETTY STOOD ON a stool while the voluble French modiste, Madame Bernard, draped and pinned materials around her while all the time arguing with Aunt Emily.

"While my niece is past the age of a debutante and may wear color, it must be subtle. Peach, primrose, pale pink, and apple green will suit," her aunt said testily after the modiste suggested eau-de-nil and tangerine.

"This bolt of silver net is pretty," Hetty remarked with a wistful smile, when she was able to get a word in.

"*Non!* Frost will not suit your complexion!" Madame Bernard cried, taking down a bolt of primrose sprigged muslin from the shelf.

Aunt Emily shook her head vigorously. "Madame is quite correct! You have golden tones to your skin, Hetty."

Hetty sighed, at least they agreed about something. "Ouch!" She flinched as one of Madame's pins found her derriere. It was going to be a very long morning.

Several hours later, Hetty followed her aunt into the house. While Aunt Emily spoke to the cook about luncheon, Hetty wandered into the bookroom. On a shelf was a likeness in a small silver frame of a young man with a pleasant open countenance and light-colored hair. Her aunt came to the door. "What do you have there?"

Afraid she was intruding, Hetty swung around, the likeness in her hand. "Who is this?"

Aunt Emily took it from her and gazed at the likeness fondly. "That was my betrothed, Robert Falkner. He was a naval officer. He died at sea."

So, what she'd heard was true. "Oh, I'm so sorry, Aunt."

"I was eighteen." Aunt Emily smiled mistily. "A long time ago now. I did wish…"

"What, Aunt?"

"That I'd defied convention and been with him before he went to sea. I would like to have more precious memories of him than the few I have." Her aunt replaced the image.

She kissed Aunt's cheek fondly, rendered silent by the sadness and regret in her eyes.

When Guy arrived, Hetty was happy to see him as always, but today his big, unruffled presence so soothed her soul she wanted to throw herself into his arms.

Dressed in a multi-caped greatcoat, a black hat at a jaunty angle on his dark hair, he assisted her into Lord Strathairn's phaeton. The magnificent matched pair of chestnuts stamped their hooves, impatient to be gone.

"Has something happened?" Guy asked, when he'd told the horses to walk on. "You're unusually quiet today."

Hetty opened her new frilly parasol. Her aunt's romance was too personal to discuss with him. "Between the modiste and my aunt, I've been pummeled to death," she said. "They could not agree on anything, and I shan't have the gowns I wished for."

Guy laughed as he skillfully executed a three-point-turn in King Street. "Never mind, Hetty. You shall have your pick of fine dresses one day."

"I don't know about that, but I would like to wear them while I'm still young enough to enjoy them."

"I trust an evening gown was ordered?"

"Yes. Why?"

"We have received some invitations."

"Oh?" Her heart thudded.

"Lord Strathairn's married sister is holding a soiree this Friday. And Eustace plans a dinner party the following week."

After dealing with feelings of inadequacy brought on by the thought of an elegant soiree, she turned to study him. "And you accepted his invitation?"

"I did."

"Why the change of heart?"

"I consider it to be judicious. I need to learn more about Eustace."

"You may even get to like him." She gripped the handle of the lemon-colored parasol as excitement threaded through her. "That's less than a week. I don't expect my gown to be ready by then." She frowned. "I shall have to wear my old one."

"Perhaps if the dressmaker is offered an inducement?"

"I can't ask that of Papa. I doubt he can afford it, and he's already been most generous." *Unusually so*, she thought.

Guy's brows met in a puzzled frown. "I understood your father to be comfortably off. Your dowry is most generous."

Hetty had not queried the amount, afraid she would embarrass her father. "Is it?"

"He didn't advise you of it?"

She shook her head.

"I don't see that it should be kept secret. It's twenty thousand pounds."

Hetty's mouth dropped open. Poor father! It must be every penny he had in the world. A good thing perhaps that he'd never have to pay it.

"I'd be happy to pay for your gown."

"No, Guy, I won't let you."

"And why not? As your fiancé…"

"But you aren't. I mean, not really."

"To all intents and purposes, I am."

"I shall never be able to repay you."

He gave her a quick look, his expression warm, before returning to watch the road. "How am I ever to repay you for saving my life?"

There he goes again! Hetty wasn't sure why she found his gratitude so disconcerting. Was that all he felt for her? "It was nothing, *really*."

"Well, that's all very well for you," he said with a grin. "But I happen to value my life."

They joined a line of carriages and traveled down the South Carriage Drive. Hetty became engrossed in viewing the fashionable set, the ladies in their spring bonnets and apparel. They craned their necks to view her, making her cringe and wish she wore something better than her old muslin. At least her aunt had lent her a stylish Italian straw bonnet adorned with cherries and red ribbons to match her red velvet spencer.

Several couples ambled through the park, enjoying the unusually warm day, and a rider cantered down Rotten Row.

Hetty sighed. "I should love to ride. My aunt is to take me to a tailor for a new habit."

"And when you have it, we shall ride. I can't leave the horses today or we could walk. Shall we come back next week?"

"Yes, I should like that." Her mind was already on the soiree, apart from the theatre where she'd been safely ensconced within a small party, this was her first experience of the *ton*. What would they make of her?

Chapter Thirteen

THE MODISTE HAD triumphed, delivering the gown by Thursday afternoon. Hetty adored the cream silk evening gown, lavishly decorated with silk gauze and floral work. On Friday evening, Aunt Emily's maid, Sarah, did wonders with Hetty's hair, confining her curls with a stylish bandeau. Hetty wore white satin slippers, white French kid gloves, and the pearl necklace and earrings which had been her mother's. She carried her aunt's ivory fan and a white silk reticule decorated with silver spangles and tassels. Never having been dressed in the first stare of fashion, she quite looked forward to Guy's reaction.

She stood when his carriage stopped in the street, patted her hair, and smoothed her skirts. He walked into the parlor and stopped, his gaze was like a physical touch, and her heart jolted. "You look beautiful, Hetty." He kissed her trembling fingers and turned to compliment her aunt before whisking her away.

Hetty studied him in the dim glow of the carriage lamps. How handsome he looked in his dark evening clothes, his crisp cravat white against his throat. "We've hardly seen you this week. Did you find a house?"

"No. I've been hiring staff for the hall. I now have a decent steward who will take some of the weight off my shoulders."

"Oh, that is good. Who will be there tonight?" she asked, willing herself to relax. She felt as if she was about to be thrown to the wolves.

"Apart from the earl and his sisters, I have no idea." He patted her hand. "Everyone will approve of you. You have no need to worry."

Hetty opened her mouth, then closed it. Why would they approve of her? She was a country girl, she didn't know much about society or the rules they lived by. Etiquette came as naturally to them as breathing.

Berkley Square consisted of huge mansions built around a private park. When a liveried footman came to take the reins from Guy, she stepped down with trepidation.

Guy took her arm and led her into the long drawing room, filled with exquisitely dressed guests who all turned to look at her.

Lady Eleanor came to greet them. "How nice to see you again, Miss Cavendish."

Hetty curtsied. "It was good of you to invite me."

"I should like you to meet some of my guests. Lord Fortescue is not known to some."

They were then taken around the room and introduced. The guests were coolly polite, for as a guest of the earl's sister, they would never risk offense. But Hetty saw through the veneer to the condescension beneath.

She was presented to an elderly dowager duchess who blinked at her, then peered at her through her lorgnette. "A Cavendish, eh? A descendent of William Cavendish?"

Hetty swallowed. "William? ah, that is, I am not sure."

The lady touched her old-fashioned wig with a hand. "I refer to the Duke of Devonshire who lived in Berkley Square at one time."

"Then no, I don't believe so," Hetty said, yearning to move on.

The dowager duchess nodded. "Then it must be Henry Cavendish, 2nd Duke of Newcastle-upon-Tyne's side of the family."

"No, I'm afraid not." Hetty cast an anguished glance around for Guy.

The lady frowned. "Lady Margaret Cavendish, who married John Holles Earl of Clare?"

Hetty lifted her chin. "The Digswell Cavendishes, actually."

"The *Digswell* Cavendishes?" Lady Wotherspoon lowered her lorgnette and raised her thin brows.

Lady Eleanor placed a hand on Hetty's arm. "You must excuse us, Lady Wotherspoon. Miss Cavendish has many guests yet to meet."

Hetty's nape felt moist as she was led around the room and finally left with Lady Georgina. "You look all in," she said, and gestured to a satin sofa by the window.

Hetty gratefully sat after Lady Georgina told Guy to go away, quite rudely Hetty thought. The earl's younger sister sat beside her, smoothing her dainty muslin skirts. She was a beautiful and elegant young lady, very much at home in her surroundings. And this setting took one's breath away. Huge oil paintings dressed the burgundy papered walls, and glorious painted landscapes edged with gilt molding on the ceiling.

"You must tell me all about yourself," Lady Georgina said.

As she tried to order her thoughts, Lady Eleanor joined them. "What have you enjoyed most in London, Miss Cavendish?"

"I have yet to see it," Hetty confessed. "I have been busy having a new wardrobe made."

"That is very pretty," Georgina said, eyeing Hetty's gown. "I should be happy to introduce you to Madame Celeste if you wish to have more gowns and hats made. Eleanor and I won't step out of the door without something fashioned by the Frenchwoman."

"Thank you," Hetty said weakly, acknowledging the criticism. It seemed her gown was pretty but not quite up to the mark.

Eleanor frowned at her younger sister. "Have you known Lord Fortescue long?"

"No. Only since he came to Digswell."

"It has been a fast courtship, then," Georgina said. Her eyes filled with light. "Love at first sight?"

"You are such a romantic Georgina," Lady Eleanor said. "And it is really none of your business."

Georgina pouted. "Then I shall take myself off."

Hetty drew in a deep breath, relieved when she flounced away.

Lady Eleanor put a hand on Hetty's arm. "She means well. She's young and impulsive. Were you not the same at seventeen?"

Hetty smiled and nodded, but she doubted she had ever been like Lady Georgina. Left alone with Lady Eleanor, their conversation turned to poetry and the hour passed more pleasurably.

Then Guy returned to her side and stayed for the rest of the evening.

"Well, how was it?" he asked as they drove home.

"I was utterly terrified."

He laughed. "You had no need to be. Lady Eleanor sang your praises before we left."

"I like her very much. Where is her husband?"

"He is an invalid. We don't see much of him."

"Oh. I'm sorry."

The coach drew up outside her aunt's in King Street.

Guy took her chin in his hand and pressed his lips to hers as Lord Strathairn's footman opened the door.

At her door, Guy bowed. "Sleep well, Hetty."

The maid opened the door, and Hetty walked into the front hall where her aunt lurked. "Well, how was it?"

"Very pleasant," Hetty said, following her up the stairs. "The mansion was beautiful, and Lady Eleanor and I enjoyed a lively conversation about Keats' poems."

"Oh. You must tell me all about it at breakfast."

In bed, Hetty put her arm under her head. She didn't fit into that world, but it was an exciting one. She feared returning to the farm would be very hard indeed.

WHEN THE HACKNEY stopped outside Count Forney's palatial home, Guy paid the jarvie and stepped up to the door. He presented his card to the butler.

"You are expected, my lord."

Guy followed the butler to an impressive salon decorated in the extravagant Napoleonic style the Regent had adopted at Carlton

House, the furniture a combination of oak, ebony, gilt, painted bronze, and marble. The walls were papered in a chinoiserie pattern of birds. It was a showcase for a beautiful woman like the countess, perhaps, but too ornate for Guy's taste.

The count was not one of those French émigrés who had arrived with barely the shirt on their backs and found it hard to survive. They flocked together at Grillon's Hotel in Albemarle Street where the Constitutional Monarch of France, Louis XVIII, had stayed in '14.

Count Forney was wealthy and openly displayed his penchant for Bonaparte, which, while unpalatable to the English, wasn't a crime. The Regent himself was known to have a deep respect for Bonaparte although he'd refused the general's invitation to meet with him when aboard the *Bellerophon* in Plymouth Sound. Guy suspected it was because Prinny had never stepped onto a battlefield and believed he would not present well beside the famous general.

A gilt-paneled door opened, and Count Forney, a narrow-faced, swarthy Corsican entered. He bowed with an exaggerated flourish. "Lord Fortescue. I must apologize for keeping you waiting."

He spoke in French with a slight accent Guy couldn't place. "Not at all, Count," Guy said in English. "You wished to see me?"

"*Oui*, please be seated, Baron." Forney waved Guy to a Louis Quinze chair. The count was dressed more elaborately than Englishmen favored these days, with lace at his cuffs and a waistcoat embroidered in a pattern of golden bees.

The count's eyes were yellowish-brown which lent him a wolfish air. "You wish to speak in the English?"

"We live in England now."

"*Oui!* England. I prefer it in the autumn when the shadows in the wood grow long." He paused for a long moment and studied Guy. "May I offer you a fine French brandy?"

"Yes, thank you."

"A rumor has reached my ears that you were a confidant of Bonaparte's, Lord Fortescue."

Guy stared at him. "You are mistaken. I've never met him."

The count poured liberal portions of brandy into two balloon glasses and placed them on the marble and gilt table. He sat opposite Guy, crossed his legs, and gave a tight-lipped smile. "How odd."

Guy shifted in his chair. "Rumors are often false, is that not so?"

The count swilled the golden liquid in his glass and put it to his lips while Guy, with growing uneasiness, left his untouched on the table. "I have it on good authority you were part of a group of men instrumental in Bonaparte's escape from Elba."

Guy leaped up. "Absurd!"

"You wish to deny it?"

"I do."

The count banged his glass down on the table, spilling its contents. He threw back his chair and strode to a pier table. He returned with a document he held out to Guy.

Guy took it from him and read the French words, which included his name and an accurate description of him, along with a detailed list of activities in which he never took part. What the French government accused him of would be considered treason by the British. His gut roiled in anger as he stared into Forney's strange eyes. "This is all a tissue of lies!"

Forney's thin lips stretched into a contemptuous smile. "It is not I who wrote it. As you see, it comes from a very reliable source."

Guy flicked the paper. "How did this document fall into your hands?"

"I have not the least intention of telling you how I got it. I had hoped you'd be honest with me. After all, we are on the same side."

Guy swallowed, the bile rising in his throat. Like his father, he believed in the sacredness of the hereditary monarchial government and wished to see the monarchy restored in France. The Revolution, which began with the good intentions of idealists, ended with the death of hundreds of thousands of innocent people. It had robbed him of his brother, and he'd witnessed firsthand the awful consequences of Bonaparte's ambition. The past still gave him nightmares. He read *The French Foreign Office* heading once more. "This can't be genuine. It is a forgery."

"It describes you perfectly. See..." He pointed. "Guy Truesdale, Baron Fortescue of Rosecroft Hall, born in Paris on..."

"There's no need to continue, I can read." Guy thrust the document back at him. "But it's a mistake, I tell you. Who is behind this? Name the person who gave you this."

"That I cannot do."

"You hand me that abomination of a document and won't tell me who accuses me?"

Count Forney adjusted his cuffs. "*Très bien.* I see that we have nothing more to discuss." He reached for the bell and summoned a servant. He and Guy eyed each other without attempting further conversation until the liveried footman entered.

"Show the baron out."

The countess hovered, a splash of vivid emerald in the gray marble entrance hall. It appeared she was adept at listening at keyholes. "I had hoped we might see more of you, Lord Fortescue. It seems you have chosen to put your past behind you, which may prove to be the wrong decision."

"I am not ashamed of my past, Countess Forney. You might examine your own more closely, as well as your loyalty to the country you've made your home." Guy bowed and put on his hat, noting the angry downturn of her mouth as the butler opened the door for him.

Was he to be accused of sedition? His name besmirched before he could begin his life here? It was outlandish. Rage and frustration twisted inside him as he stepped out onto the road in search of a passing hackney.

When one stopped, he climbed in with a grimace of distaste. The straw on the floor was soiled, and the carriage smelled of stale sweat. He leaned back, crossed his arms trying to deal with his anger and frustration over what had just happened. Could he confide in Strathairn? The English government must be aware of this. Guy no longer considered it a coincidence when John came across him in that alleyway and rescued him from footpads. He needed time to think, to find out more before he could act upon it.

At Berkley Square the next day, Guy received a note from the constabulary at Bow Street. It advised him the man who attacked him was to appear before the magistrate on the morrow. Odd that he had been brought to London and not dealt with in the assizes. Guy read the brief missive again, in case he'd missed something, then crumpled it in his fist. Now that Forney had shown him the French document, it was even more imperative that he learn who was behind the attacks on his life. Were they connected? Perhaps, the man might be persuaded to say who put him up to it when placed before the magistrate. Then Guy could begin to make sense of all that had happened to him since he came to England.

Guy decided to confide in Strathairn. The next morning, he awaited John to return from his morning ride. The library was as well stocked as any he had seen. John's father had been a keen reader of the classics.

Strathairn was a different beast to his scholarly father. He was a strong vigorous man of action who preferred to drink, gamble, and enjoy women rather than read. He strode into the library in riding clothes smelling of horse and threw himself down in one of a pair of oxblood leather chairs flanking the fireplace.

Guy wasted no time recalling his conversation with the count.

John's eyes lit up with interest. He tapped his boot with his riding crop. "Did he reveal any more information? Any names?"

"Nothing. He clammed up."

"A slippery figure, Forney is a known Bonapartist. He has been suspected of spying for the general during the war, but nothing was ever proven. Whitehall will be interested to learn of this."

"Naturally, I'm anxious to get this matter sorted out. These attacks may be connected."

John nodded. "You will visit Bow Street today?"

"*Oui.*"

"You've heard from your sister?"

Guy nodded. "She has decided to come to England."

"Go to Bow Street," John said. "I will visit Horse Guards. My old regiment, the Seventh Hussars may have heard a whisper or two."

Despite his anguish, Guy had to laugh. A whisper was a slight understatement. The Horse Guards housed the Grenadier Guards who guarded the Royal family. Frederick, the Duke of York, was their Commander-in-Chief. The most powerful men in England would seek information from them when they wished to learn of sub rosa activities. "I often wonder what you did during the war, John. Might you have been one of Wellington's spies?"

"Spies are not well-regarded by society." John crossed his legs and grasped a polished riding boot with his broad hand. "You have your secrets, too, Guy."

"Not so many, *mon ami*. I hope to have few secrets between Hetty and me when we wed."

"A noble plan, although somewhat difficult to achieve. But why wait? Why not marry the lady now?"

"I need first to satisfy the Committee of Privileges that I am the baron." Guy balled his hand into a fist and banged the arm of the chair. "And it now appears that I must clear my name with Home Office if I wish to remain in England."

"A challenging task, but not an impossible one."

"Time is of the essence. I'll see what can be learnt at Bow Street. This brigand may be persuaded to speak the truth."

"I'll accompany you."

"You might ask this question of your colleagues. If I am considered a French spy, working to free Bonaparte, why haven't I been arrested?"

John gave him an enigmatic look. "Perhaps you have an influential friend."

Guy bowed his head. "If that is the case, then I am indebted to him." He studied his friend's face, but John's expression was shuttered. Guy leapt to his feet in frustration. "Can't you tell me more?"

Guy turned as the door opened and Lady Georgina entered in a swirl of white muslin. "I need you both to escort me to a ball on the twentieth at the home of Lord and Lady Taylor."

Her brother frowned. "Guy is betrothed to Miss Cavendish, as you well know."

Georgina's gaze settled on Guy, considering him to be the softer option. "You will escort me won't you, Guy? Eleanor is my sponsor, but she'll tell me to ask Lady Mary because Gordon is ill again." She grinned. "What better introduction than with a handsome man on each arm?"

"Eleanor is right. Aunt Mary must be asked to chaperone you."

Georgina giggled. "Don't glower at me, John. Aunt Mary is so dreadfully old fashioned. You don't care for her company any more than I do."

John stood. "We must leave, Guy. I'll drop you off at Bow Street on my way to Whitehall."

"Bow Street? Why must you go there?" Georgina asked.

"Nothing to trouble your head over, my sweet." John patted her cheek.

Georgina pouted in disgust. "You treat women like idiots, John."

Her elder brother folded his arms. "Not if they have proved themselves to be otherwise."

"But will you escort me? I won't have to ask Aunt Mary?"

"Although I might prefer to have a tooth pulled, I see that I shall have to." John turned to Guy. "I'd appreciate your company. But I must warn you, there'll be a dearth of decent entertainment."

"Delighted." Guy bowed. "It will be my pleasure to escort you, Lady Georgina."

"It is settled, then." John attempted a frown, but a smile pulled at his lips. "And we have no need of Aunt Mary."

She squealed and rushed to hug him. John gave in to the embrace with a laugh.

"I shall hug you, too, Guy," Georgina said with a speculative look at her brother.

"You most certainly will not," John said. "And it's Lord Fortescue to you."

"I consider myself hugged," Guy said, backing off with a laugh.

An evening away from the gambling tables at White's was always an attractive prospect, although he suspected John wished him to come so that he could keep an eye on him.

Guy wasn't keen to go, because Hetty was not an invited guest, but he relished any opportunity to repay John for his generosity. He sighed inwardly. He had more than enough worries to plague him for this business with Forney must be kept from Hetty.

Chapter Fourteen

A S HE FEARED, Guy learned a frustratingly small amount at Bow Street. His attacker, whose name was Leonard Stack, appeared before the sitting magistrate, along with the usual sad array of prostitutes, thieves, and pickpockets. He'd given evidence that he was a victim. A Frenchman had threatened to murder him if he did not carry out his request. But he knew not his name and had not seen him well enough to describe him, for the man had pulled his hat low over his forehead and hidden most of his lower face with a scarf. The magistrate, unmoved by the man's pleas, bound him over for trial at the Old Bailey.

Was this something to do with Forney? Relying on the sparse details Stack had provided, Guy employed a Bow Street Runner to trace the Frenchman. It was possible that his portmanteau had fallen into the wrong hands. He'd spent hours searching the ground between where he and the horse had parted company and Rosecroft Hall. If he found out who this Frenchman was, he might be able to retrieve the evidence of his birthright. When Genevieve arrived from Paris, she would identify him, but he wasn't sure when that would be. Familiar with his sister's love for her children, plus her inability to travel anywhere without a huge retinue in train, he doubted she'd appear in London any time soon.

Guy left Bow Street and walked to the corner of Russell Street, searching for the carriage. The sunny day brought all manner of people out into the streets from nearby Covent Garden. Vendors, errand boys making deliveries, and ladies intent on perusing the shops. A street girl sidled up to him. "Lookin' for luv, sweeting?"

Guy smelled gin on her breath. She looked painfully thin and very young. He reached into his waistcoat pocket. "Have a drink on me." He tipped a handful of coins into her waiting palms. "Better still, have something to eat."

"A real pity, sweeting, I'd be happy to oblige you."

Guy raised his hat and smiled. When the carriage pulled up near-by, he ran for it.

The carriage stopped in Whitehall, outside Horse Guards where John was kicking his heels in the street. Guy noted his solemn expression as he climbed inside.

Guy told him the little he'd learned. "And you, John?"

"Not much more than I've already been told."

So, it was true. John had known of this all along. Guy wrestled with his anger. "And what is that precisely?" he asked through clenched teeth.

John stared at him fixedly. "That you're to be watched as you are suspected of being a French spy."

"Ridiculous!" Guy grabbed the door handle as the carriage swung around a corner. He fought the temptation to leap out and run away. He pulled his hand from the door and leaned back, casting John a cool glance.

"I don't distrust you, Guy. I found this hard to believe from the first," John said with a shrug of apology. "But I was instructed to follow you. I saved you from your attackers in that alley because I was ordered to keep you alive and away from harm until you led us to a nest of saboteurs known to be in England." He leaned over and placed his hand on Guy's sleeve. "But the more I got to know you, the more convinced I became that you were innocent of such a charge. It's a puzzling business. But I would bet my life on it."

Guy pulled off his hat and ran his fingers through his hair. "What the bloody hell's going on, John? I've never met Bonaparte, let alone arranged his escape from Elba. And yet, Count Forney has shown me a document from the French foreign office which confirms it." A moment passed as he searched his friend's smoky, gray-blue eyes, which revealed little. "You are under orders." Guy shrugged. "I wonder what you plan to do with me."

John released a sigh. "You might say I'm keeping you under observation. But that also means I'm watching your back, my friend."

Guy bowed his head. "Thank you."

"Until I'm instructed otherwise," John added, looking grim.

Guy nodded. "I understand."

Tomorrow he would take Hetty to the park and lose himself for a while in her charming company.

"SHALL WE WALK to the lake?" Guy pulled the phaeton over to the side. He tossed the reins to the tiger who had accompanied them today, and after instructing him to walk the horses, helped her down.

With her hand tucked in his arm, they strolled along a path through the trees. Early spring wild flowers added color to the scene while birds fluttered above building nests among the leafy branches.

They entered a copse of silver birch trees where dappled sun sparkled through a filigree of leaves. "Aunt Emily has a visitor this afternoon. The poet, Mr. Wordsworth."

"William Wordsworth? I met him in Paris."

"You met the poet?" Another new thing to learn about him.

"He was there to visit his daughter, Caroline. We discussed his interest in exploring the relationship between the human mind and nature and he allowed me to read some of his poetry. *Tintern Abbey* is quite remarkable. A deeply thoughtful poem."

Delighted, Hetty was eager to discuss it. "The lyrical ballad is remarkable. The lines *"The still, sad music of humanity..."* She gasped. "What are you doing?"

After a quick glance around, Guy had drawn her off the path and deeper into the shadowy copse. He removed her parasol from her hand and put it down, then tugged at her bonnets strings. "I'm going to kiss you," he murmured, and pulled off her bonnet. The look in his eyes was so intense that her pulse fluttered, and she caught her breath.

Guy lowered his head and covered her mouth with his. The intense pleasure of his closeness wrapped around her, and abandoning her demand for propriety, she looped her arms around his neck and kissed him back. His tongue teased at the seam of her lips, and she opened to him. When he dove inside, she melted and clutched onto his coat. Their breaths quickened as he pressed her against him. Taking in deep breaths of him, his fresh manly smell, she suffered a strong urge to lie down on the grass and pull him with her. She moaned against his mouth.

"*Mon dieu!*" Guy groaned and thrust away from her.

Suddenly aware that she'd forgotten her intention to keep him at arm's length, Hetty pushed at him. "Guy! What is this about?"

He removed his curly-brimmed beaver and ran a hand through his dark locks with a distracted look. "I didn't intend it to go that far." He smiled, charmingly apologetic. "I desire you, Hetty."

She took a deep breath. He was so utterly disarming. "You do?"

"Why do you think I've arranged this engagement?"

"Because of Eustace. Because you were in danger."

"I should have left you safely in Digswell." Guy shook his head. "But I wanted to get you away from that bean pole."

"Mr. Oakley?" Hetty was stunned. "But I told you I refused him."

"We'd best walk." Guy offered her his arm.

Thrilled as she was to learn how he felt, she told herself sternly that Guy could never marry her. The newspapers would have a field day. She must not forget that she was not one of the Cavendishes that mattered, she was the daughter of a retired army man of modest means. Even her aunt had been astonished at their engagement although Hetty found her abrupt change in attitude difficult to fathom. Aunt Emily did appear quite shrewd when she allowed herself to focus on something other than poetry.

Ahead, sunlight danced on the Serpentine. "Shall we walk to the water?" Guy asked.

"Yes, lets."

He seemed intent on his own thoughts, and she returned to hers. Had either of them considered what effect a broken engagement would have on her life when the news reached Digswell? They'd hardly been discreet, openly revealing their relationship before the *ton*. Perhaps these things were done differently in France. The French were so much more relaxed about matters of the heart. It was second nature to them, while the English... Hetty gazed into Guy's troubled face, a face she'd grown to love. She wanted more of his kisses. Desperately, because soon she would lose him.

If a scandal was to follow her home, why not have a good reason for it? Guy would know how to protect her, and they could both gain much from it. After all, once back in Digswell, she would never marry.

They paused at the riverbank to watch a man propelling a rowboat over the water with strong strokes of the oars. "I quite like the idea of an affair," Hetty said, testing him.

"*Quoi!*" Guy swiveled to stare at her.

If she hoped he would fall at her feet with delight, she was mistaken. Although this was hardly the place. As excitement built within her like a fire fanned into a roaring blaze, Hetty continued to stroll along the bank. "I prefer never to marry," she said bravely. "You must agree I will write far better poetry with some experience of life."

Guy's hand on her arm swung her around to face him. His eyes flashed. "So, if not me, then Mr. Beanpole will provide your life experience?"

"Good heavens, no." Hetty laughed at his description. "You're not jealous of Mr. Oakley?"

He pressed a kiss on her gloved palm, which produced a cry of encouragement from an elderly gentleman sitting on a seat nearby. "I will be the only one to make love to you."

"You?" Hetty's eyes widened. She took a deep breath. "Oh, Guy, I want that, too." She stared over at the man, thankful he was out of earshot. "But where?"

Guy pulled her by the hand. "Come on."

Thrilled, she gasped. "Where are you taking me?"

"Back to your aunt."

"What? Why?" Guy's stride was so much longer than hers. He dragged her along. Her bonnet fell back onto her shoulders, suspended by its cherry ribbons, and she almost dropped her parasol.

"Because if I ever climb out of this mess I'm in, I intend to do the thing properly."

Hetty wasn't quite sure what he meant by "the thing", but she was more than keen to find out, as her intention to keep her heart safe from hurt evaporated.

She was not to learn of it today, however. Guy, tight-lipped, escorted her to the phaeton and drove her directly home. He answered her questions in monosyllables, and she eventually gave up trying. Then he left her with her aunt with a bow and his apologies, murmuring that something had called him away.

Her aunt frowned. "Did you have an argument?"

"No. At least I don't think so," Hetty said, bemused.

"A business concern, perhaps?" Aunt Emily suggested with a hopeful lift of her brows. "Never mind, Mr. Wordsworth is to arrive soon. You'll enjoy meeting him, I'm sure."

In normal circumstances, Hetty would have enjoyed it immensely, but her own concerns intruded. When Guy had thought her to be Simon, he had confessed to all sorts of amorous adventures. Had she shocked him? Was it possible to shock a rake? Her mind whirled, and when introduced to the slim, brown-haired man of some forty-five years who would once have thrilled her to the core, she offered him an abstracted smile.

All through Mr. Wordsworth's scholarly conversation and her aunt's animated replies, Hetty pondered Guy's behavior. He waged a war within himself. The passionate rake was a conventional man at heart. She wondered which would win where she was concerned.

The week proved busy with trips to the mantua maker and the modiste for further fittings, in between sojourns with her aunt to the museum and the Tower. She saw little of Guy, who came to take tea with them on only one occasion. He was busy searching for a suitable London house. But on Saturday, they were to attend Eustace's dinner party.

Chapter Fifteen

HETTY WORE ANOTHER of her new evening gowns to Eustace's dinner, a delicate white silk embroidered with silver thread.

Guy complimented her, spoke briefly to her aunt, then escorted her to the carriage.

"You seem distracted," she said. He'd merely smiled at her when she complimented him on the clever arrangement of his neckcloth.

He tucked her hand in his. "Not at all. My thoughts are always with you."

She doubted it, but was charmed by it, nevertheless.

The carriage pulled up at a townhouse in Curzon Street where an elegantly dressed couple climbed the stairs.

Eustace greeted Guy and Hetty at the door, seeming more animated than usual, and escorted them to the drawing room where the guests chatted and drank champagne.

Hetty's fears that she would face the critical judgement of the *Ton* again, faded when they were introduced to an interesting group of people: the Earl of Liverpool, England's prime minister and his countess, a famous actress, the editor from *The Times,* the reverend from St. George's in Hanover Square, and a foreign prince who clicked his heels and bowed over her hand.

In the dining room, mouthwatering aromas blended with the scent of hyacinths in a silver bowl. Fascinated, Hetty hung on every word as they conversed during the lavish and delicately flavored courses. Liverpool spoke emotionally about the state of the country, the depression, and political uncertainty, social discontent and unrest and the difficulty of reform, while the dishes were brought and covers removed.

While a footman poured gravy over her veal olives, a rousing discussion began on the veracity of the social movement called the Luddites, who opposed progress and the loss of jobs. Its members were known to have destroyed or damaged machinery in the industrial northwest of England. The unsuccessful march of the Blanketeers was mentioned.

"Blanketeers. That is a curious name, Mr. Randall," Hetty said to the man beside her.

The publisher from Fleet Street, nodded. He explained how four hundred spinners and weavers marched from Manchester to London to hand the government a petition. They were named thus because they carried their blankets with them. Most were turned back or arrested by the magistrates and yeomanry before they reached Derbyshire.

Hetty was incensed for them. "And not one made it to London?"

"Rumor has it one protestor did arrive and handed over his petition."

"I'm glad," Hetty said. She found it terribly sad.

The mention of Bonaparte's name produced murmuring around the table. While the prime minister declined to comment, Mr. Randall expressed the view that the French general would never escape Saint Helena where he had been sent last October.

Further down the table, Guy remained silent. She thought he looked unhappy. He was yet to reveal his true feelings about Napoleon Bonaparte. The discussion of politics came to a halt when the famous tragedian, Sarah Siddons, a forthright older lady, declared they'd all become too serious. An amusing discussion followed concerning *Bertram,* the current play on in Drury Lane, which continued through the dessert course. Then the ladies rose from the table and left the men to their port.

After an hour, Eustace's guests began to depart. He saw them to the door. Rain had begun to fall, and footmen scurried about with umbrellas. Hetty looked for Guy, who had not emerged from the dining room. Finally, she went in search of him. She found him in the library seated behind a satinwood desk, scanning a sheath of papers.

"What on earth are you doing?" she asked shocked.

He dropped the papers into a drawer and rose, crossing the room to her. "Now don't frown at me. We don't have time for this. Come, we must say our goodbyes to your godfather."

She stepped in front to him. "Don't be so insufferable. You were spying on him."

Voices sounded in the corridor outside. Eustace said in a loud voice, "I can't think where they've gone."

Guy pulled Hetty into an embrace and pressed his mouth to hers.

"Well, here they are," Eustace said, smiling, the reverend at his side.

Guy bowed. "I apologize for my poor manners."

"Young people. So passionate. Best you marry without delay," Reverend Dewhurst said. "The banns can be read this Sunday. I believe the first of April is free for a wedding."

"But my parish is in Digswell, Reverend," Hetty said, embarrassment making her cheeks burn.

"That won't be a problem if notice is sent," the reverend answered. "Would you not prefer to be married at St. George's?"

"We should be honored. Thank you, Reverend," Guy said. "But I have matters to settle before I can set the day."

"Very well. Please advise me as soon as you can."

With the rain loud on the coach roof, Hetty tried to read Guy's expression, aware they would reach her aunt's home in a matter of minutes. "Have you altered your opinion of Eustace?"

"I'm beginning to understand how things stand," Guy answered. The cool tone of his voice made her anxious. "Are you cold?" He moved across to sit beside her and placed an arm around her shoulders.

Hetty laid her head against his shoulder. "Have you learned anything more?"

"Who is behind the attacks? No."

His voiced sounded strange, tight, unlike himself. "But you don't think it is Eustace, do you?"

"I don't know yet, Hetty." He sounded impatient. Was there something he wasn't telling her?

"You would tell me if there was another attempt?"

He sighed. "There hasn't been. Eustace approves of our marriage. Perhaps there won't be another."

"Then shall we end this engagement? Everything is becoming too complicated." She sagged as bitter disappointment took hold. It had cost her a lot to say it.

His arm tightened around her. "I'm aware of how difficult this is. Can you be patient for a little while?"

Hetty nodded. She'd never been so far out of her depth before. She appealed to him with her eyes, wanting to know how he felt.

As if in answer to her unspoken question, Guy tapped on the roof with his cane. The panel in the roof slid back. "Yes, my lord?"

"Drive through the park."

Guy closed the blinds as the carriage turned into Tyburn Lane and rolled on toward Hyde Park Corner. He pulled Hetty onto his lap. Cradled in his arms, she leaned against his hard, heated body.

He took her chin in his hand. "Hetty," he murmured against her lips. When his mouth sought hers, demanding a response, she could only obey as her thoughts fled. He drew away and untied her cloak, sliding it off her shoulders, and bent to kiss the hollow at the base of her throat. "You smell so sweet, my love," he said, "like a flower garden." His voice was muffled against her skin. She was filled with an odd kind of yearning. She stroked his thick hair, finding it silky to the touch.

Guy undid the hooks on her bodice. When he pulled it down to reveal her chemise and stays, she grabbed his hand as confusion filled her. She wanted to encourage him and stop him both at once.

He paused, his intense gaze searching hers. "If you want me to take you straight home, just say so, Hetty."

He looked different, dangerous, potent, which both thrilled and disturbed her. Her breath quickened, lifting her bosom as he slid the straps of her chemise further down her shoulders. She stilled, as he bent to kiss the rise of her breast. He traced a line down her throat, his fingers lightly calloused, not the pampered hands of a lord. A cautionary voice entered her mind. She knew so little about him. "Where were you before you came to England?"

He straightened and sighed.

"I WILL TELL you, but not now, Hetty." Hetty's hair was a halo of rich color in the dim light from the carriage lamps. Heat pooled in his groin, and his determination not to give in to desire, wavered. He could stop. He would. But not yet. Not until he'd tasted her, he would have that at least if his life was to end soon by the hand of an assassin or at the end of a rope. He took a curl and raised it to breathe in the floral fragrance while longing to loosen her tresses from their pins, to slide over her naked shoulders. He trailed a finger down the smooth column of her neck to a brown areola peeping from the top of her corset. He freed her breast and bent to kiss it. This time Hetty didn't stop him. She pulled him to her.

"Oh, that's lovely," she whispered.

HETTY BREATHED IN his clean musky scent and ran her tongue over her lips. Ripples of sensation rushed over her skin as he took a nipple in his mouth. "Guy..." She went limp as threads of fire traced their way to throb low in her stomach. He turned his attention to the other taut, sensitive nipple. She inhaled sharply when he eased her skirt up, his fingers stroking her bare skin above her stocking.

"So soft," he murmured, a low sound deep in his throat.

"Are we going to..." she asked between great gasps.

He angled his mouth to kiss her. To silence her.

He drew away. In the dim light, his eyes were serious and passionate with intent.

"Guy..." Tantalized and aroused, Hetty couldn't finish the sentence for the life of her. She loved to lie in his arms, her body eager for his touch. She wanted... she wasn't sure what it was she yearned for. But, perhaps not yet. Not here. Powerless to stop him, she grew afraid it would spoil something they shared. Something fine.

Suddenly, Hetty found herself deposited back on the seat. Guy cursed. "I'm not taking you here in the carriage. Not your first time, Hetty."

Hetty gave a sob, feeling part relief and part disappointment.

"I'm sorry, Hetty." He leaned back with a grimace and adjusted his pantaloons. "I should not have treated you in that manner."

"I want you, too, Guy." While it thrilled her that she moved him so, she hated the distance that had sprung up between them.

He eased a lock of her hair from her cheek. "I haven't forgotten your wish to remain unmarried."

She stiffened. She now hated the very thought of being a spinster. To condemn herself to a life without love? It seemed unthinkable. She could no longer defend her earlier pronouncement although she feared the life of a lonely poetess would be her future.

"Such a dry and passionless life. And you are far from passionless, Hetty."

She huffed out a breath, determined to gather together at least some shred of dignity. "I will meet famous poets here. Aunt Emily expects Wordsworth to call again, Byron, too, when he's in England." She was aware of how halfhearted she sounded.

"Neither of those gentlemen will keep you warm at night," Guy muttered through tight lips. He tapped on the roof with his cane. "King Street please, Jason."

"Right you are, my lord."

Hetty's need to argue the point over something that no longer appealed to her, evaporated. He looked so serious in the dim carriage light. Was she enough for him? Why had he changed his mind? Had he not desired her enough? She placed a tentative hand on his arm. "Did you intend to make love to me tonight?"

"No! That was not my intention." He shifted uncomfortably in his seat. "Oh, but I do, Hetty. I definitely do."

Thrilled, she said, "Then why can't we…"

His eyes locked with hers. "I don't want you as my mistress."

"Oh." It was a stark declaration. Did he mean it? Even that would be better than being alone.

He took her hands in his. "I have several things I must sort out before we can continue this conversation."

"Will you tell me what they are?" she asked gently. He had not told her he loved her, so she supposed he didn't.

"No, Hetty. I won't." He tipped up her chin and placed a light kiss on her mouth. "You will keep at me I know," he said with a smile. "I only ask you to be patient."

"Oh, Guy. I care for you." It was an admission that a woman wasn't supposed to make until the man declared himself. But she couldn't play games. Not when danger seemed to lurk in every corner.

His mouth curved with tenderness. "I care for you, Hetty, very much indeed."

"Oh, Guy." She touched his cheek.

His eyes beseeched her. "Hetty… tomorrow evening, I am engaged to escort Lady Georgina to a ball."

She frowned. He looked guilty. Bitter disappointment flooded through her. "Alone?"

"With Strathairn. I am indebted to these people who have taken me in."

"Will you dance with Lady Georgina?" Hetty wrestled with her emotions, she knew the request was unfair, she had no real claim on him.

"I don't expect to." He framed her face with his hands. "Know this, Hetty. I do not desire Lady Georgina. If I was able to marry tomorrow, it would be you. No other lady is in danger of capturing my heart."

If it wasn't a declaration of love, it was very close to it. A luminous glow of happiness threaded through her as the carriage pulled up in King Street.

As he placed his hand on the door latch, she stopped him. She didn't want him to leave her, to go off to face danger without her. "What are you planning to do?"

"Strathairn is making inquiries."

She remembered John's hard gaze. "Lord Strathairn would be a good man to have on your side, I should think."

"He has made some useful connections during his years away at war," Guy said. "You're right, a better man at my back I couldn't find." Guy opened the door. "I have accepted an invitation for you and your aunt to Lady Bloxham's rout on Saturday. You met her at Lady Eleanor's soiree, remember?"

"I look forward to it." Hetty remembered the lady only too well. She'd looked through Hetty as if she hadn't been there.

"I'll call for you both on Saturday evening, *ma cherie*."

Hetty hurried inside, aware that her lips were swollen from his kisses. Her aunt appeared on the stairs in her dressing gown and nightcap. "Your gown is rumpled, and your hair is coming down. I trust that you behaved with decorum."

Her aunt's voice lacked conviction, Hetty thought. "Guy has invited us both to a rout on Saturday at Lady Bloxham's."

Her aunt followed Hetty up the stairs. "Oh well, that is nice indeed. I've met Lady Bloxham. She is a devotee of the romantic poets. I shall be pleased to spend time in her company."

Hetty shut her door. It had been such an extraordinary evening, she wasn't sure what to make of it. What had Guy found in Eustace's library? What did he keep from her? But most pressing was the need to know he loved her. She had witnessed his desire, but men were made that way, were they not? While his words were designed to put her at ease, she still didn't know his true feelings or intentions.

Chapter Sixteen

A T BREAKFAST AUNT Emily raised her eyebrows when Hetty told her Guy was escorting Lady Georgina to a ball.

Aunt Emily buttered her toast. "I shouldn't worry about Guy's feelings for you," she said. "Judging by the state you were in last evening." She made a clucking sound with her tongue and shook her head. "Perhaps I should be more diligent as chaperone."

Hetty frowned. "Lady Georgina is an earl's daughter, and she's pretty."

"Lady Georgina is young and caper-witted. She has been kept in cotton wool and is a trifle spoiled." Aunt Emily reached for the jam. "Guy speaks ardently of his plans to make improvements to his estate. I suspect he intends to get his hands dirty in the process. He would want a wife who wished to spend a good deal of the year in the country. He has too much sense to marry a young lady who would prefer a coxcomb for a husband."

"Sense doesn't always feature into one's decision to marry," Hetty said, stirring her tea.

Her appetite had deserted her after a restless night. An ominous feeling seemed to hang over her. It was what Guy hadn't said that worried her most. But she'd seen no evidence that Guy wished to become a fashionable leader of society. She'd begun to understand him, his faults as well as the finer points of his character. He would seek to protect her, something she valued but also annoyed her. He would be a stalwart friend to the last, but he was unequivocal in his demand for loyalty from others. She suspected Guy would never forgive Eustace for doubting him even if he was proved innocent of any crime. Guy had come into her life shattering her dull existence. Sometimes lying in bed at night, it all seemed like a dream, from the moment she first saw him lying on the road.

She loved his passion, his humor, his masculine pride and would trust him with her life. What would the future hold for her without him? It seemed a dreary prospect.

THE VALET PUT down his brush. "All done, my lord."

"Thank you, Hobson."

Guy had borrowed John's valet to ensure he was suitably attired. He was grateful for all Strathairn had done and continued to do for him. But Guy hated being watched. He was confident he could handle himself well in a crisis. It galled him that he was seen to be an enemy of England and that John acted on instructions from Sidmouth, the Home Secretary.

Guy left the bedchamber and made his way down the staircase to the salon. He was glad of his decision not to enlighten Hetty about the cloud which now hovered over his head. It would be impossible to reassure her, she'd want to know every detail, and he refused to have her involved.

He'd hoped the Bow Street runner would unravel the mystery; but as yet, he'd turned up nothing, and the mystery of the Frenchman who wanted him dead only deepened. Was this to do with Forney's letter?

John awaited him in the salon. "Care for a whiskey to fortify you? These affairs seldom offer spirits."

"Thank you." Guy took the proffered drink.

"There's a gentleman I hope will offer marriage to Georgina," John said. "It's my hope that she'll realize the great advantages that come with it."

"Isn't she a little young?"

"She turns eighteen soon. Many marry at that age."

Guy thought her too silly for marriage, but he wouldn't dream of saying so.

"I'm playing it down," John said. "If I endorse him, she may think I'm manipulating her and dig in her toes."

"Are you two talking about me?" Georgina hurried in, tucking a scrap of lace into her reticule.

"Yes, in endless fascination," John said, cocking a brow.

She giggled. Her maid hurried in with her evening cloak. "Shall we go?" She slipped an arm through Guy's and fluttered her lashes at him.

"You shall have all the male guests at your feet tonight," Guy said.

"And will that be you, too, Guy?"

He laughed. "What is this occasion?"

"Beatrice Taylor's eighteenth birthday ball, of course." She rolled her eyes at him as if he should have known.

"But of course. How did I come to overlook it?" Guy grinned at her.

More than half an hour later, they arrived at the mansion in Hampton, the gardens alight with lanterns.

As soon as they were announced and entered the ballroom, a crowd of hopeful young blades came to crowd around Georgina to beg a dance. It was not surprising, for she looked quite lovely in her silky white gauze gown, flowers and ribbons in her dark curls. "Promise me a dance, Guy," she whispered before a gentleman led her to the dance floor for the quadrille.

Out of respect for Hetty, Guy had decided not to dance. He planned to move amongst the guests to test society's mood. He steeled himself for variations of the cut direct. Any whiff of scandal and the ruthless *ton* would turn their backs on anyone of whom they disapproved.

Fortunately, no one gazed accusingly at him. A couple of the older gentlemen remembered his father and spoke of the tragedy that befell him with regret. No one even hinted at Guy being a dangerous spy. But then, he shouldn't be surprised. Spying was a secretive business.

John danced with Lady Sibella Winborne, an enchantingly beautiful dark-haired young woman, daughter of the Marquess of Brandreth.
How interesting that the few times he'd seen Strathairn enter a dance
floor it was with Lady Sibella on his arm. They were deep in conversation and smiling at each other. Friends of long standing? From what
Guy had come to understand, John sought ladies from lower down the
social scale. When they'd talked together in the evenings, nursing
brandies by the fireside, he'd insisted he had no intention of marrying
for years.

John laughed at something Lady Sibella said and lowered his head
to hers. Guy smiled to himself. A lady as lovely, and apparently as
amusing as Lady Sibella, might change his friend's mind.

Guy leaned against a pillar. A man should ask one of the ladies
without a partner to dance. But if he did, Georgina would put up a
good argument as to why he didn't dance with her. Hopefully, her
dance card was filled.

The dance ended. John was immediately drawn into conversation
with someone. Guy was tossing up whether to join them. He was yet
to find a comfortable balance in this company and feared he might be
de trop.

When a waltz was called, Georgina approached him. "I have kept
this dance free," she said.

Guy groaned inwardly. He should have made himself scarce. He
bowed. "May I have the pleasure of this waltz, Lady Georgina?"

"You may, Lord Fortescue." She smiled and rested her hand on his
arm.

As the first notes of a Handel waltz were struck, he swung her into
the dance, guiding her over the crowded dance floor.

"You might have danced with any number of eager young bucks,"
he said as he reversed her.

"I prefer to dance with you."

"I don't see why. My dancing is in no way superior to your last
partner. The Duke of Broadstairs, wasn't it?"

She gave Guy a fierce look. "You are the one of the few men who doesn't bore me. You are interesting. You have lived!"

"Are you flirting with me, Lady Georgina?"

She flushed and lowered her eyes.

"You do recall that I am betrothed to Miss Cavendish?"

"Of course. I quite like her. But I would make you a better wife."

"Let us enjoy the dance," Guy said, concerned they might be over-heard. "If I talk when I dance I get short of breath."

"Ho! You cannot fool me, Lord Fortescue. I am the right girl for you. If only you would admit it."

"Shouldn't you like to be a Duchess? The duke is one of your ad-mirers, is he not?"

"He's too young."

"Nonsense. He cannot be far off thirty."

"He's not...sophisticated."

"That is in his favor. You don't want to marry a rake. That way leads to heartache. Broadstairs could prove to be an excellent husband. You should consider it."

"You're not a rake."

"This is not about me." Guy raised an eyebrow. "You should talk to the duke. You might find you like him."

"I have. And I shall talk to him when we dance again."

"You may not get the chance. He seems charmed by the pretty young woman he's dancing with."

"Is he?" Georgina turned her head. She shrugged her slender shoulders. "Oh, that's just Amabel Gilliam."

"Amabel is amusing him. See how he laughs?"

Georgina raised her eyebrows. "So?"

He noticed her take another peek when they turned. "Could you make him laugh?"

"Of course, I can."

"Are you sure he will invite you to dance again?"

"As a matter of fact, he has requested the next waltz," she said airily.

"Then I shall watch and see if you make him laugh."

"I'll accept the bet. If I win it, what will you give me?"

"My compliments."

"Pooh!"

An hour later, Guy stood and watched Georgina dance with the Duke of Broadstairs. She flirted shamelessly. The poor man appeared to be lost. Guy hoped that if they married, Broadstairs would stand up to her. Georgina respected her brother for that reason.

The duke gave a loud guffaw, and Georgina's triumphant gaze sought Guy's. He nodded, then went to find John. Unable to locate him, he strolled out onto the terrace.

The Taylors' mansion was some miles from Mayfair. The estates were more generous, and this one had a large park bordered by a high brick wall. A fresh spring breeze ruffled the trees, and a full moon hung, a golden penny suspended in a cloudless sky. What a perfect night to share with Hetty. If he hadn't lost his papers, they might have been wed by now and living at Rosecroft Hall. He wandered down the steps and strolled beyond the flaming torches into the shadows. At the sound of rustling in the bushes behind him, he spun around expecting some night animal to emerge.

Something struck him hard on the side of the head. He saw flashes of bright light, heard a laugh, and sank into darkness.

"IT IS NOT like Guy to be late," Hetty said for the fifth time.

"No," her aunt repeated.

Hetty walked to the window and back, her skirts swirling around her legs.

"Do sit down, Hetty. I declare you have worn a path in my carpet."

Hetty sat but remained on the edge of her chair, listening for the sound of horses clattering over the cobbles.

An hour passed.

She rubbed her arms. "I'm afraid something has happened, Aunt."

"What can befall his lordship in a short carriage ride through Mayfair?"

"What if he's been hurt?"

"Someone would send word."

"What if Lady Georgina has beguiled him?"

"Beguiled by two different women within a few days? I doubt he's that susceptible," her aunt said.

Another hour passed with little said. Only the ticking of the longcase clock broke the silence.

It was after midnight when Hetty finally consented to retire. She lay stiffly in bed while jumbled thoughts crowded her mind. Guy might not tell her everything, but she'd never caught him in a lie. Nor was he a coward. If he'd decided he'd rather court Lady Georgina, he would tell her so. She thought about his passionate kisses and his declaration that she was the only one he would consider marrying. He could not have changed his mind within a few days, could he?

She punched her pillow and rolled onto her side as worry turned to anger. She'd asked him several times about his past, but he'd evaded her questions. Perhaps she'd been fooling herself and didn't know him at all. She turned over and tucked her hand under the pillow, staring blindly into the darkness. That wasn't true. She did know him, and the realization made her shudder with fear.

After hours of anguish, Hetty dropped into an exhausted sleep only to wake again before dawn.

Light filtered through a gap in the curtains and traffic rumbled through the streets. She heard the servants moving about.

Hetty sat up. Someone had knocked at the door.

Chapter Seventeen

A T THE LOUD rap of the knocker, Hetty, her heart racing, rushed
down the stairs, praying it was Guy. She reached the entry hall
as the maid admitted Lord Strathairn.

"I apologize for calling at cock's crow, Miss Cavendish," he said.
"But I wonder if you have any notion as to Lord Fortescue's whereabouts?"

His words produced a shudder of fear. She clutched her dressing
gown and shook her head, her plait swinging. "I don't. You'd best
come into the parlor, Lord Strathairn."

The big man followed her inside. Hetty sat before her knees gave
way. Still holding his hat, he perched on the edge of a chair as if ready
to leap up again.

"Lord Fortescue was to escort my aunt and me to a rout last evening, but he didn't arrive." She twisted her fingers. "Nor did he send
word."

As he took this in, he frowned. "Guy attended a ball with Lady
Georgina and me. He went missing during the evening." He looked
down at the hat he held in his hands. "I didn't worry at first. I have not
known him long but suspected, well, that a lady might be involved."
His lashes shuttered his eyes, making her wonder what he wasn't
telling her.

"A lady?"

"I expected it to be you, Miss Cavendish, for Guy seems single-
minded in that respect. When he did not return last night, I grew

alarmed." He shrugged. "Hence my unpardonable appearance on your doorstep before breakfast."

Hetty clutched the arm of the sofa. "He disappeared in the middle of a ball?"

"Yes. Held at the home of Lord and Lady Taylor at Hampstead. No one remembers seeing him again after he danced with my sister."

Guy danced with Georgina! Strathairn's words rang warning bells in her mind. She shook her head and tried to focus on what was important. "And your sister returned home with you?"

"Yes." His intelligent gray eyes studied her. "Georgina spent the rest of the evening dancing with a gentleman. They set the *ton* on its ear, I might add." He stood as if to leave. "Guy didn't mention returning to his estate?"

"If he was called back to Rosecroft Hall, he would have sent word. It is very unlike him to let my aunt and me down."

"I apologize for worrying you. I'll obtain the guest list from Lady Taylor. Someone might have learned of his direction."

Hetty rose, too. She swallowed to moisten her scratchy throat. "Would you advise me as soon as you have news, Lord Strathairn?"

"I promise." He took her hand. "Try not to worry, Miss Cavendish. He is a capable fellow."

After the door closed, Hetty rubbed her arms and paced the room. All the life seemed to have been sucked out of her. Through the window, Lord Stathairn climbed into his carriage. "Horse Guards in Whitehall," his booming voice instructed the jarvie.

Aunt Emily entered the room, adjusting her lace cap. "I listened at the door. I didn't want to greet him in my wrapper."

"Why would Lord Strathairn go to the Horse Guards?" Hetty asked.

"Likely he seeks help from his fellow officers."

"I wonder if he suspects Guy is not what he purports to be."

"You don't doubt him, do you?"

"No, I do not. But there's something Lord Strathairn didn't want to tell me." Hetty turned away from the window, massaging her aching temples. "Someone wants Guy dead, but it doesn't seem possible he was attacked at the ball. A guest would have witnessed it, and his body…" She swallowed. "… found." She moaned. "I must try to find out what happened." She covered her face with her hands. "But I don't know where to begin."

Aunt Emily patted her arm. "Hush, my dear. Be patient. I'm sure there is a quite logical explanation for his absence. We shall hear soon enough. I must say, when you first told me of these attacks on him, I put it down to coincidence. England can be a very dangerous place if you are wealthy and go about unprotected. But no one attempts to kill without a reason. And what reason might there be?"

"I wish I knew," Hetty whispered.

The hours passed in excruciating slowness which became almost unbearable. At times, Hetty feared she might lose her fragile hold on her emotions. She had hastily dressed, barely eaten, and jumped at every sound.

When the knocker rang through the house, it took Hetty a moment to realize she hadn't imagined it. She rushed into the hall to find Aunt Emily's maid, Sarah, at the door open-mouthed. A glamorous, dark-haired woman in a striped pelisse of Mexican steel blue stood in the porch.

"*Mademoiselle Cavendish? Je suis Duchesse la Châteaudunn, la sœur de Lord Fortescue.*" She put a gloved hand to her flushed cheek, her green eyes anxious. "Oh, pardon! English!"

Hetty sank into a curtsey. "How nice to meet you, Your Grace. Will you come into the parlor?"

Guy's sister reminded her of a tiny bird. The Frenchwoman barely reached Hetty's shoulder. But there was a family resemblance in the resolute look in her eye. She settled her skirts around her on the sofa.

"May I offer you coffee or tea, Your Grace?"

"*No, merci. Gee* wrote to me of your engagement. I wish we'd met under more pleasant circumstances. I am looking for him. I called at the address where *Gee* was staying but Lord Strathairn is away from home. The servants couldn't help me. A young lady said he had left without giving his direction. She gave me your address."

"I'm sorry, Your Grace. I've no idea where the baron is. I wish I did."

"You… you are worried, too. I can see."

"I must confess to becoming a little concerned."

"*Gee* has always been most reliable," the duchess said with a stricken look.

"Yes, that's what makes this so surprising," Hetty said. She resisted expressing the full force of her fears aloud, for the duchess looked close to tears as she fidgeted with her stylish reticule.

"He would never be…" She waved the reticule about as she frantically sought for a word. "So negligent."

Her concerns were compounding Hetty's. She wanted to rush right out to find him. "Could you furnish me with your address so that might I contact you, should I hear any news?"

"I've taken a house in Portland Place." She shook her head, causing the soft feathers on her bonnet to flutter. "But we must act, must we not? Where might we begin, Miss Cavendish?" She motioned to the street beyond the window where a luxurious carriage and four matched gray thoroughbreds stood restlessly, their heads held by a liveried groom.

Hetty stared at the lady opposite, who chewed her bottom lip awaiting her reply. She might be a duchess, but she was Guy's sister and shared Hetty's anguish. "We might go to Hampstead."

"That is in London, no?"

"That is where the ball was held at Lord and Lady Taylor's home. The last place where Guy was seen."

"Then we must drive there at once." The dainty woman rose on feet encased in blue suede half-boots the like of which Hetty had never seen, trimmed with silk rosettes.

"I must leave a message for my aunt. She is away from home."

"*Bon*," the duchess said.

"I'll fetch my pelisse and bonnet." Hetty's spirits rose as she hurried toward the door. Something to do at last, and a confidant in the tiny lady beside her.

GUY OPENED HIS eyes and stared into the dark. His first thought was a moonless night at midnight. But because the air was thick with dust and mold, he ascertained he was indoors. He moved his head gingerly. It ached, and every part of his body seemed bruised. Where was he? A memory flashed into his mind, a silvery moon, the sweet-smelling garden at Hampstead, and then... nothing.

He put his hand to the sore spot on the side of his head and discovered a lump with crusted dried blood coating his hair. He loosened his cravat, his mouth bone dry, his insides hollow with hunger. His last conscious thought came back to him, a demanding voice in the darkness. What did they ask him? Had he failed to supply the answer? His mind remained befogged. How long had he been unconscious? Once his eyes had adjusted to the darkness, he spied a faint light under a door. He staggered from what he recognized as a bed of coarse dusty onion sacks then, walked an unsteady path toward the light.

Once he located the door, he turned the knob, pushed the door open, and stood blinking in the glow of candlelight flickering in iron sconces along a low-ceilinged stone passage. Something came back, a memory of being dragged along a tunnel at some point, the rancid smell of earth and mold stifling him. His hands tied, he'd cried out and struggled and been hit again before the blackness claimed him. This must be a cellar. The weight of stone pressed down, disorienting him. The air rank with the smell of rat droppings and tallow made him swallow as nausea gripped him.

He fought to draw the stale air into his lungs, to strengthen him. To face whatever awaited him at the end of the passage. Bracing himself against the wall, he lurched toward the light, and stumbled into a wide cavern. A candle wheel hung from the ceiling, throwing the room into a chiaroscuro of light and shadow, the frigid air smoky. Without his coat, Guy shivered in his ruined evening clothes.

An arched door opened in the far wall, and he started toward it, coming to a halt as a tall man entered. He gestured with the pistol in his hand for Guy to leave the room.

Was he asleep or awake? "Who *are* you?" Guy wiped his eyes and took a step backward.

The man moved into the circle of light.

Stunned, Guy sucked in a breath and almost collapsed. He grasped the back of a wooden chair to right himself. It was like gazing into a mirror at his own visage. The face staring back at him was gaunt, the blue eyes harder. A long scar marred his cheek. But taken feature-by-feature, it was identical to his.

Guy passed a hand over his eyes. "It cannot be true! Vincent!"

"It's true all right. You'd best sit down before you fall."

Guy stared at him. He slumped onto the chair and put his hand to his throbbing head. "You speak better English than I."

"Papa taught us well, but one forgets, no? But I learn fast. You must when life isn't offered to you on a silver platter."

"I've longed to find you my whole life, Vincent. Although we all believed you to have perished in the attack on the chateau, Papa never stopped searching. He is dead now. Maman, too. Did you know?"

"He abandoned me to the fire. His own son. You were his favorite, Guy."

"That's not true. He was a fair man."

"He disapproved of everything I did."

"You were often damned difficult, but he loved you. We all did."

His hard face didn't soften, didn't acknowledge the possibility. "It matters not now."

"Why do this? What is it you want from me?"

"All in good time."

"You were not in our bedchamber when the fire started. Where were you?"

"Do you want food?"

"Yes, but first you must tell me what happened."

"First, I will fetch you the food."

He disappeared out the door again, shutting it behind him.

Guy sat with his head in his hands, it all seemed unreal.

His brother was soon back and pushed a plate of meat, a rind of cheese, and a heel of bread into his hands.

Guy was hungry, but he pushed it away. "I won't eat until you tell me."

"It is nothing to me whether you eat or not," Vincent said. "It will not matter in the end."

Guy felt the chill of those words. "What do you intend to do with me?"

"I'll explain later. While you eat, I'll tell you what happened the night of the fire."

Guy reluctantly picked up the plate. He broke off a bit of the bread and chewed. "Go on."

"I had crept downstairs to the kitchen to eat some leftover tart. When the crowd began to ransack the chateau, I was frightened. I tried to reach Papa and Maman's bedchamber, but the flames licked at the servants' stairs and blocked my way to the corridor leading to the family quarters. A servant rescued me as the house fell in flames around me. He carried me away half comatose for I had inhaled a lot of smoke. It was some days before I recovered. He cared for me and adopted me as his own. I was desolated when he told me my family had left France. You left me! Aristos were being rounded up and taken by tumbril to the guillotine. If I'd been found, that would have been my fate, too."

"We did not leave France for days, because Papa held out hope that you lived. Who was this servant?"

"Papa's chef. Remember Pierre Valois?"

Guy vaguely remembered a short, rotund man who gave him food when he was hungry. "Why did he not return you to us?"

"By the time it was safe to go back, you had abandoned me, and we knew not where you'd gone."

"We did not abandon you! The whole of our quartier was in flames. We believed you dead and still waited far too long. We barely escaped with our lives. Papa paid someone to continue to look for you, but he sent us word that he'd had no luck. Did Pierre take you away from Paris?"

Vincent nodded. "We lived in Calais. Pierre opened a restaurant there. That's where I grew up."

"You never tried to find us?"

"No. What was the point? You'd left the country. There was no way of returning to France during *The Terror*. And in the end, I didn't want to. I suppose my adopted parent's hatred of aristos rubbed off on me."

"Pierre was treated well. All Papa's servants were."

Vincent shrugged. "I do not remember. It's likely you don't either."

"Please understand. We would've died, too, had we stayed. There was Genevieve to consider and Maman was not well."

Vincent shook his head. He backed away, still pointing the gun at Guy. "Time to move."

Guy thrust the plate onto the table and lurched to his feet, his head still aching. "I am telling you the truth, Vincent. Why are you threatening me with that pistol? Put it away!"

Vincent gestured toward the door. "Back to the storeroom."

"And if I refuse?"

"I will shoot you. Don't doubt I mean it, Guy."

Guy searched his brother's fevered eyes. He did mean it. He had hired men to do precisely that. Vincent had lost his reason. But why was he still alive? He was glad to have time to appeal to his brother. Sure that Vincent could be talked around. Blood was thicker than water, wasn't it? Fear that he may not succeed, made his stomach roil as he stumbled back into the suffocating space. He would go mad, too, if he stayed there too long. "Why are you doing this?" he asked trying to delay. "Why did you send men to kill me?"

He was pushed through the doorway. The door slammed shut in his face, leaving him in the dark. "Tomorrow," came the muffled reply.

The next day, Vincent came for him again. "Will you at least tell me the reason for this?"

Guy's gesture encompassed the room, the table and chairs, and the pistol in Vincent's hand. He'd spent a sleepless night shivering in the freezing dark trying to understand it. To think of a way out of it, but he couldn't see past the fact that his brother was alive. It should have brought him joy, but for the fact that Vincent planned to kill him. Guy stiffened his resolve and decided to take his chances as they came, whatever the outcome.

"You owe me, Guy."

Guy shook his head, confused. "You do not need to do this, Vincent."

"But I do. I'm ready to become Baron Fortescue. I paid for that right."

"But I am the firstborn son."

Vincent shrugged. "A matter of a few minutes. Is that fair?"

"It is the way of the world. I am happy to share my life with you, although it won't make up for what you've suffered. Where are we?"

"The tunnels beneath Rosecroft Hall."

"How did you find a way inside?"

"Later! I need your identification papers. I've searched your chamber and the library here and turned up nothing. I tried to get you to tell me in Hampstead, but you were out to it. Tell me now."

"For God's sake, Vincent. This is madness. Sit down and we'll talk."

"*Non!* We shall just waste time. I need those papers!"

"I lost them when your men attacked me in the woods. I fell off my horse. But what good will they do you while I live?" Guy swallowed as the enormity of what Vincent planned became clear to him.

"I'll need them later. But first I must supply the British government with a body, so the authorities will stop searching for me. Once I convince them that this dangerous spy who has been masquerading as the baron is dead, I can become you," he waved his hand. "And take over your charmed life. We are identical, but for this. He touched the scar. And that I can fix."

Guy whistled through his teeth. "So, it's you in the documents Forney showed me!"

Vincent's mouth stretched in a wry grin. "*Oui.*" He looked down at the pistol in his hand. "Once you are dead, I will be accepted as the baron. But I must have the proof."

Vincent didn't have the papers. That meant his portmanteau was still out there somewhere.

"Let's go and search for them together?"

Vincent's eyes burned fanatically. "No, I think not. You are tricky, Guy, and might find a way to escape. You rode directly from London. I know where you were attacked. I shall find them after you are dead."

"You can't mean to kill me!" Guy searched for a sign that Vincent's determination might falter. His dry scratchy throat made his voice rasp. "Can I have some water?"

Vincent jerked his head toward a barrel in the corner.

"I rode away from the attackers before I fell. They could be miles away. I doubt you'll find them. I knew better where to look, and I failed."

A metal cup lay alongside the barrel. Guy scooped up water and swallowed thirstily. It was icy, and chilled him through to his very marrow, but the dryness in his throat eased. An ache thudded cruelly behind his eyes. "Even if you found them, your plan won't work, Vincent. You cannot carry off such a deception."

"After Pierre died, it was useful to take on your identity in France. To all intents and purposes, I am the baron. Vincent Valois died years ago."

"Weren't you afraid you'd come across me or someone who knew me?"

Vincent gave him a sly glance. "You were arrested with other hapless people and thrown in prison." He grinned. "I expected your head to roll at the guillotine like many others."

Guy frowned. "You didn't try to help me?"

Vincent shook his head. "You disappeared after they released you.

I was told you'd left France. Where did you go?"

"Spain." Guy wrestled with the fact that his brother had known where he was at some point and never approached him. "It won't work, Vincent," he said. "There are many who know me well here in England."

"You refer to Mademoiselle Cavendish."

At hearing Hetty's name on Vincent's lips, anger and fear tightened his gut. He curled his hands into fists. "Leave her out of this."

"I might, and I might not. That depends on the lady. I've come a long way and there's much at stake."

Guy welcomed the anger. It energized him. "If you hurt her, my friends will come after you."

"I want nothing from her. If she accepts the engagement is at an end, it won't be necessary to deal with her."

He had to stay alive. Even if Hetty did accept the engagement was at an end and returned home to Digswell, which he doubted, what would happen when Vincent took up residence in Rosecroft Hall? When she grew suspicious, it would place her in terrible danger. He wasn't prepared to let that happen.

"How did you find these tunnels?"

Vincent smiled with boyish enthusiasm. "Remember how often Papa told us stories about the tunnel that leads to the wood? And how it had been an escape route for priests during the reign of Queen Elizabeth. But I didn't know exactly where it was."

"You searched for it? How did you evade my servants?"

"I move about the house late at night."

"I made a thorough search for the tunnel under the solar and failed to find it. Where is the entrance?" Guy asked.

"I doubt I would've found it either had I started my search inside the house. I located the tunnel entrance in the wood. It lies close to the eastern wing."

"Near the fountain?"

"You can see the fountain through the trees; it's so close you can feel the spray from it when the wind blows. It's covered by a moss-covered stone tablet, which was quite heavy to lift. Steps lead down and the tunnel branches out into these storerooms. I daresay, priests lived here at one time. Maybe some even starved to death here, no?

Vincent's eyes gleamed. He acted as though they were young brothers again, sharing a secret. "I emerged in the far corner of the long storage room beneath the solar. The door fits into the wall so snug it would be impossible to find without some prior knowledge. You must locate the exact spot. Once pressed, it releases the catch."

"So, you can come and go undetected," Guy said. "Smart of you."

"I've learned to be, because life was hard."

Vincent nodded with a satisfied smile.

"I brought you here because it makes a perfect prison. I hefted you down through the tunnels. You are no lightweight! No one saw me. No one will ever discover you've been here." He raised a brow. "I shan't kill you here, though. If you behave, you may enjoy what there is left of your life."

Guy's heart thudded in his throat. "You would murder your own flesh and blood?"

"I don't blame you for the past, Guy. But don't try to change my mind. I've very little choice. There's nothing out there for me. If I fail, the British government will hang, draw, and quarter me. Not a good way to die. I burned my bridges in France. This or suicide is all I have left."

"You can't mean it," Guy said, chilled to the bone. Unthinkable, that Vincent should kill himself and be buried in unconsecrated ground.

"I do. Now Napoleon's finished."

"You were close to the general?"

"Napoleon relied on me. He called me *Le Renard*. There are those who plot to rescue him once more. They wish me to join them." Vincent shook his head. "I won't, because this time it will not work." He walked to the door. "I'll fetch more food from the next room. I want you fit enough for the trip to London."

"We return to London?"

Vincent cast him a pitying look. He went out, locking the arched wooden door behind him.

Guy recalled the disturbing words said in such a flat unemotional tone. He leaned his arms on his knees on the uncomfortable chair, his thoughts racing as he considered possible means of escape. Was it possible to wrestle the gun from Vincent? He looked to be every bit as strong as he, and right now in better shape, but Guy had to try.

As a boy, Vincent was often cruel. He ran wild and liked to torment animals and tease his little sister. But how did he become such a ruthless murderer? Guy was glad his father wasn't here to witness it.

Chapter Eighteen

I T TOOK TWO hours through roads clogged with London traffic before Hetty and Genevieve arrived in Hampstead Village. Lord and Lady Taylor's Portland stone mansion was surrounded by a high stone wall.

The duchess's name opened the door to them like magic. They were ushered into a drawing room papered in crimson, cream, and gold and seated on a sofa with cream velvet cushions and rosewood arms. Guy's sister wasted little time peppering them with questions in her thick French accent.

While Lady Taylor appeared captivated by the small duchess, Lord Taylor's thin face bore a haughty expression. "Lord Strathairn visited this morning," he said, as if one morning call at an inappropriate time was bad enough. He settled his boney frame on the chair and crossed his legs. "My wife and I had little to tell him. Lord Fortescue was last seen dancing with Lady Georgina Haldane. I have since sent letters to each of our guests. Many have replied with no knowledge of the baron's whereabouts."

"Lord Strathairn was in a fearful hurry." Lady Taylor twisted her mouth. "He has visited our other neighbors before luncheon. And I've no idea why he felt it necessary. It's nonsense to imagine Lord Fortescue was snatched from our home. He must have left of his own free will."

"Lord Fortescue would not be so ill-mannered to leave without seeking you out and thanking you," Hetty said.

"I'm sure he will return when it suits him." Lord Taylor's jaw stiffened. "The baron is new to London. He is entirely unknown to us. He was not invited but came with Lord Strathairn. We cannot say if this is his usual behavior."

Genevieve let out a little huff. "My brother has impeccable manners."

"But of course he has, Your Grace," Lady Taylor said hastily, with an annoyed look at her husband. "Perhaps some tea?" Her hand hovered over the bell.

"No, *merci*. We must continue our search," the duchess said, rising.

Lord and Lady Taylor rose with obvious relief. Lady Taylor patted the lace cap that covered most of her iron-gray hair. "It is to be hoped that the baron returns very soon to lay this mystery to rest. We wouldn't wish any scandal to attach itself to us, especially with our daughter's season upon us."

"There is little point inquiring of the neighbors, as Lord Strathairn has been before us," Hetty said, when they found themselves out in the street.

The duchess having agreed, they entered the coach. Hetty wrapped her arms around herself, feeling the tremor in her arms. Rational possibilities had deserted her.

The duchess told the coachman to stop at the farrier's in the village. The blast of the furnace greeted them when they entered the forge. The solidly built man pushed his cap back with a finger. "The night of the Taylor's ball? Mostly fancy carriages and their liveried grooms. There was two men in their cups. So many shady coves roam the heath. The Bow Street boys often bring bodies down from there."

Hetty shivered. "Tell us everything, even the smallest details could be important."

"I told 'is lordship who called earlier. When I was walking 'ome down Hampstead Road, I passed these two coves. One was lugging the other. Said 'e was drunk when I inquired. Toffs they were, probably been to the ball, so's I minded me own business. 'E bundled the drunker one into a curricle and drove off fast. But then they's always drive fast, don' they."

Hetty grasped the man's sleeve. "What did they look like?"

"No need to rush me, miss. I was gettin' to that." He shook off her hand and took a step back. "Didn't see their faces. Similar in size. Tall and dark-haired, both of 'em."

Hetty clutched her hands, finding cold sweat on her palms. "But which way did they go?"

"Took the north west road, but from there, who's to say?"

"Could it have been Guy? He might have been hurt." Hetty allowed the footman to assist her into the coach. "But who would the other man be?"

"Lord Strathairn's residence," Genevieve instructed the coachman.

WITH AN EYE on Vincent, Guy ate the bread, sausage, and cheese. The pistol had never wavered in his brother's hand. If Guy managed to escape, would he be able to find his way through the labyrinth of tunnels before Vincent found him? Guy was no longer under any delusion about what his brother was capable of. Vincent would shoot him down in cold blood.

"Do you remember your childhood, Vincent? The happy times when we swam in the lake and fought duels with wooden swords?"

"*Oui.* The apple fights in the orchard. And that time I set fire to Genevieve's doll's hair." He laughed and shook his head. "She cried and cried."

As the memories came, they shared them, lapsing into their native tongue. As Guy indulged his brother, the hope flickered to life that he could convince him to give up his awful plan.

"You can't do this, Vincent. Don't you see? We'll enjoy a good life, here. Together."

Vincent frowned. "This changes nothing. I've burned my bridges." When he reverted to English, his persona changed. He became more intent on his purpose. Guy didn't know this man and was forced to accept that Vincent was committed to his wicked plan. The pain and the hurt of it tore through him as if he'd already been shot.

His thoughts returned to a means of escape. If he was able to find his way to the room under the solar, he'd make for his chamber where he kept a brace of pistols. It was an enticing thought. Then they would be on equal terms, although he doubted he could shoot Vincent if it came to that.

"Do you have ale?"

Vincent nodded. He disappeared into the next room and soon returned with a tankard. As he put it down on the table, Guy jumped up. He threw the plate of food at Vincent's head.

Startled, Vincent put his hand to his head, dropping the pistol, and Guy rushed him. He punched his brother's solar plexus and met hard muscle. Vincent fell to his knees and groped for the pistol which had skidded under the table.

Guy kicked Vincent's rear end and knocked him flat to the floor.

"Bastard!" Vincent cried, scrabbling for the gun. He was between Guy and the weapon and would reach it first.

Guy turned and bolted through the door into another large store-room. Vincent had made a bed for himself there. Through another door, beyond it, he found himself in a dim rock-walled tunnel where only one candle flickered in a wall sconce. He fled down it. When the tunnel branched into two, he didn't hesitate, he took the right fork. Around a corner, he skidded to a halt at a dead end. This didn't make sense. It must lead somewhere. If this led into the room below the solar where was the door? Cursing at finding himself cornered, Guy ran his hands feverishly over the wall as he searched for any protrusion. There was no time to retrace his steps to the other passage which would surely lead him to the garden. Somewhere behind him came the rumble of his brother's untroubled laughter.

Vincent was confident he had him. "You can't escape, Guy," he called. "Surrender. Don't make me shoot you. I don't wish to carry a dead weight all the way to the curricle again. But I will if I have to."

Gasping, Guy's searching fingers alighted on a button-like protuberance. He hit it hard. A click sounded, and the door swung open. Vincent cursed. The passage brightened. Vincent had snatched up a candle and was coming fast.

With a grim smile, Guy leapt through and put his shoulder to the door, closing it behind him. He swung around in the pitch dark. Which way out? He trailed his hand along the wall, searching for a doorway. From the shape of the room, he gained confidence. It was the long chamber under the solar. He paused to orient himself, then stumbled forward to where he thought the steps leading up to the kitchens and solar were, and fell onto them, barking his shins. He scrambled to his feet and took the stairs two at a time. His heart hammered and his breath came in large gasps. He cursed that his strength was deserting him.

In the main house, he passed the solar, a tired dusty room where the family had once gathered but not used for a very long time. Nearby came the clatter of plates and the chatter of the servants in the kitchen. Not wishing to endanger them, he ran up the next flight of stairs. On reaching the upper corridor, he made his way to the east wing. The butler walked toward him along the passage.

Hammond stopped dead. His cool persona dropped away as his mouth dropped open and shut again.

"Come with me, Hammond!" Guy pushed the astonished man backward and ran toward his chamber.

Performing a swift about-turn, Hammond huffed behind him as they raced through the house. On reaching his chamber, Guy took out his pistols and loaded one, expecting Vincent to burst through the door at any moment.

"M-my lord," Hammond stammered, his cheeks crimson.

"My twin brother is here in the house. He is armed and extremely dangerous."

"Your brother, my lord?" Hammond's eyes widened with bewilderment. Guy didn't blame him, but he had no time to explain.

With both guns loaded, Guy placed them in his waistband, then opened the door and peered into the corridor, surprised to find no sign of Vincent. "Take care. He intends to kill me. Keep the servants out of the way and send a footman for the magistrate."

"Right, my lord." Hammond scurried away toward the servants' stairs.

With a firm grip on the pistol, Guy edged along the corridor, listening for any movement.

A servant girl emerged from a chamber. She squeaked at the sight of him in his dirty clothes and bloodied hair.

"Go and find Hammond." He jerked his head back, indicating the way he'd come. She rushed away.

When Guy reached the main staircase, he found Vincent in the hall below, and saw the reason he had not been right on Guy's tail. He looked up at Guy, his lips stretched in a manic grin, blood dripping from his chin. He had freshened the wound on his face with the knife he held in his left hand. "When I take your place, the baron will have a scar. Foolish of you, Guy. You should've run."

Vincent raised his pistol.

"Your plan to kill me has failed, Vincent. The servants know."

"I'll make them believe I've killed the imposter."

Guy leaned sideways against a pillar which offered him a little protection. "Shall we both die here?"

"You won't shoot me."

Guy was inclined to agree with him. He had no wish for his brother's blood on his hands.

An explosion echoed hollowly around the huge hall. Stone chips from the pillar peppered Guy as he leapt back.

Vincent climbed the stairs, slightly off balance as he reloaded his pistol.

"I have a loaded gun, Vincent."

"You won't shoot me," he repeated.

Guy took his chance and rushed him. He took six stairs at a leap and crashed into Vincent. They both tumbled down the stairs, landing hard at the bottom.

Bruised and winded, Guy retrieved his pistol and approached Vincent, where he lay crumpled and still.

Hammond and the rest of the staff appeared as Guy crouched to examine him. He took his brother by the shoulders and called his name. Vincent's head lolled, all the strength and fierce determination gone from his body. Guy lost his breath and his throat closed. "The fall broke his neck," he said, his voice an anguished growl.

"He looks so like you, my lord," Hammond said in a hushed tone.

Sadness engulfed Guy like a dark shroud. He sat on the step with his head in his hands.

Two of the maids began to wail and were ushered away by a footman.

"Did you send for the magistrate, Hammond?" Guy asked, lifting his head.

"I did, my lord, he should be here soon." Hammond opened the front door.

A horse galloped up the gravel drive.

The rider dismounted and ran up the steps.

Guy climbed to his feet. "John!"

"So, you are here." Strathairn walked into the room. "What has happened?"

Strathairn stared down at Vincent who lay on his back, his eyes staring blankly up at them. "Your twin."

"*Oui*. Vincent and I fought. We fell down the stairs. His neck is broken."

John nodded. "See to Vincent's body first. We'll discuss how to deal with the situation, later." He knelt beside Vincent and drew a tiepin from his cravat. It was of a bronze bird its wings outstretched.

"What are you doing?" Guy asked with a gasp.

"We might have need of this." John handed the tiepin to him. "An eagle. A Napoleonic symbol. Like those that sat atop regimental flag poles."

"To lose an eagle would bring shame to a fighting unit," Guy said. "Vincent told me he was close to Napoleon." Hating to hold the thing in his hands, he gave it back to John and turned to the butler. "Hammond, have two footmen move my brother into one of the bedchambers. Wait for me in the library, John."

Guy went to oversee the laying out of his brother. He gazed down at the face he'd longed to see again since he was twelve years old. He sat for a moment in the still room staring at nothing, his mind grappling with the horror. When he finally left the room and returned to John, he was barely aware that his body ached for the pain in his heart was so intense it almost brought him to his knees. He walked to the drinks table. "Whiskey, John?"

"Please."

Guy sloshed amber liquid into two tumblers and handed one to John. He sat and took a large swallow as warmth spread through his cold insides. It failed to remove the hollow pain and sense of loss. He doubted anything ever would.

"So, this is the spy Whitehall has been looking for," John said.

Guy nodded, his shoulders slumped.

"He was a murderer. I'm sure he would've killed you, Guy."

"I have no doubt of it."

"The government must be informed. Lord Parnham will handle it."

"I see."

"But Parnham will be disappointed."

Guy glanced up. "Disappointed? I should think he would be relieved."

"Vincent was to lead us to the spies' nest."

"You've learned nothing from following Forney?"

"He's being cautious. He approached you believing you to be Vincent and expected more from you. Your reaction would have surprised him."

Guy gingerly touched his head. "Perhaps."

A curricle rattled its way up the drive.

"See to that wound while I consult the magistrate. He will need to view the body. After that, we must return to London."

Guy searched his friend's sharp gray eyes. He was bone-tired and had no strength left to argue. "As you wish, but I won't leave until Vincent is interred in the family crypt."

"Yes, of course."

Guy sighed. "What must Hetty be thinking?"

"I visited Miss Cavendish. She is concerned, naturally."

"*Zut!*" Guy rested his head in his hands. It had taken quite a battering of late. "I must get word to her."

"Sorry, Guy. Parnham expects us at Whitehall," John said. "Send a note to put Miss Cavendish's mind at rest. But say no more."

Chapter Nineteen

ETTY PACED AROUND the parlor earning an appeal from her aunt. She had barely slept after the trip to Hampstead. When she and the duchess called at Berkley Square, they were told Lord Strathairn had not returned. They could do nothing but go home and wait. Hetty had never found waiting easy, but now it was a torment.

Fanny wrote to say she would call at two o'clock. Hetty groaned. "Oh, not now. I can't see Fanny while all this is happening!"

She and Fanny hadn't met since she'd come to London. She guessed that Fanny's season had been carefully orchestrated by her mother. Fanny had been presented in the Queen's drawing room and would have danced at Almack's. She would be bubbling over with news. Hetty only wished she was in a fit enough state to enjoy every detail.

As the clock struck two, Fanny swept in, dressed in a very smart half-dress of striped primrose yellow sarcenet, richly trimmed around the hem. Her face was rounder, and she'd developed quite a confident air. Pleased to find her looking so at home in her new surroundings, Hetty hugged her. Lady Kemble followed in a Turkey-red gown and puce turban.

"Almack's is de trop," Fanny said, ignoring her mother's frown as she selected another tart from the cake stand. "You require a voucher from one of the lady patronesses to attend." She giggled. "I danced with so many partners I can't remember their faces, let alone their names."

"No one was of particular interest to you?" Hetty asked, as her aunt poured more tea.

Lady Kemble took the flowery china cup and saucer with a nod in Aunt Emily's direction. "Viscount Rothwell is enamored of Fanny. As are several gentlemen."

Fanny wrinkled her nose. "Rothwell is too old."

"Nonsense," Lady Kemble said. "He's years off forty with a large estate in Sussex."

"He seems old." A mulish expression tugged Fanny's mouth down at the corners. "I don't care for him." She replaced her cup in its saucer. "Mr. Bonneville pleases me."

"Forget Bonneville. He is known to be in dun territory and is in the market for a rich wife. Your dowry would not be acceptable to him, Fanny. He merely flirts with you."

"I've met Mr. Bonneville," Hetty said. "He has big, sorrowful brown eyes like a puppy."

Fanny gave a trill of laughter. "That's Bonneville precisely! Such a dear face."

Lady Kemble turned her frown on Hetty. "You do look peaky, Miss Cavendish. You must make sure you get your sleep. A young lady in search of a husband needs a good complexion."

Hetty swallowed and looked away.

"Hetty is a little tired," Aunt Emily said quickly. "Her social life has been such a whirl."

There was an uncomfortable silence, during which Hetty strained her ears for any activity in the street outside.

"Do you know if Lord Fortescue is in London, Hetty?" Fanny asked.

"I'm not sure where he is at present," Hetty replied, careful to modulate her tone. She rubbed her bare finger. It distressed her, but she'd decided to remove her ring. News of her betrothal had not reached Fanny's ears, and it wasn't prudent to mention it now. She fought to maintain her composure, but her hand shook, and her cup rattled in its saucer.

"You're very fidgety, Miss Cavendish," Lady Kemble said with a sharp-eyed stare. "I was surprised to learn your father permitted you to come to London."

"Is it so very surprising?" Aunt Emily's eyes glittered. "My brother loves his daughter and wants the best for her."

"I'm sure he does." Lady Kemble put down her cup and saucer. She rose from her seat. "We must go. We have many calls to make, and then Fanny needs to rest before the ball this evening."

Fanny cast Hetty a sympathetic glance. "I do hope you are enjoying your time in London. We must get together for a coze soon."

Hetty returned the hug. "I'd like that, Fanny."

After they left, Aunt Emily breathed a sigh of relief. "Mrs. Kemble is a spiteful woman."

Hetty shrugged. "I fear she doesn't like me." It seemed unimportant now.

"That's because you're prettier and more intelligent than her daughter," Aunt Emily said with a fond smile.

"Prettier than Fanny? Come now, Aunt." Hetty kissed her cheek.

"You've had little chance to shine. When you become a baroness, you will come into your own, my dear. See if I'm not right."

Her aunt clung to the idea that Guy meant to marry her. If only he was safe, she'd accept whatever happened, even if it meant losing him.

In the afternoon, a footman delivered a letter. Hetty pounced on it. It was from Guy. Her hands shaking, she sank into a chair in the entry hall to read it.

Guy's note was appallingly brief. He was at Rosecroft Hall and would call on her when he returned to London. Exasperation fought with relief as she hurried upstairs to tell her aunt.

THE MORNING AFTER, Vincent was buried in the family crypt in the Digswell churchyard. Then Guy and John traveled to Whitechapel in Vincent's curricle, John's horse tied behind.

At Whitehall, Lord Parnham, a man in his fifties with thinning gray hair, put a plan to Guy. "You are in the enviable position of gaining these conspirators' trust. You can lead us to them."

"And just how might I do that?" Guy already had an inkling and dreaded to hear what Parnham would suggest. Bruised and saddened, he just wanted to be with Hetty. Lord Parnham's grave voice broke into his thoughts.

"Your twin brother adopted the title while working to free Napoleon. We would like you to become him. No one could possibly suspect you."

"But I don't believe Vincent had any intention of joining them. He wished only to take my place at Rosecroft Hall."

"They are not to know that," Parnham said. "But it confirms the view that he has not been in contact with them."

"But I neither know any of these conspirators nor what they plot." Guy held out his hands, palms up. "This is madness! Vincent had a scar on his cheek. That would give me away immediately. Why do you need me?"

"Because we've lost our agent. One of Lord Castlereagh's fellows got close enough to learn the secret code they go by. Unfortunately, he became too confident, and they grew suspicious. They slit his throat and threw his body in the river."

Guy scrubbed his hands through his hair. *"Nom de Dieu!"*

Lord Parnham leaned forward in his chair. "This will work. Forney has seen you without a scar. It's unlikely the rest of them have ever met Vincent. You are identical. They will not doubt you even if they have met him. It will give us the time we need to act. And it will draw out the rest of them. If you call one wolf, you invite the pack. Once you have entered their midst, we will pounce."

"But they must suspect you're on to them."

Parnham shook his head. "No one has been arrested. They will be confident they're safe."

Guy eyed him. "I'm not trained in espionage."

"We'll help you with that."

Guy's eyebrows arched. "I cannot imagine how."

"Lord Strathairn will assist you with the finer details."

He'd had enough of the violence men do to one another. Guy huffed out a breath. He was spent. "I intend to visit my fiancée, Miss Cavendish. She will be concerned about me."

Lord Parnham shook his head. "I'm afraid that's impossible until this is over."

Guy pushed back his chair and stood. "Then I won't do it."

"Sit down, please, Fortescue." Lord Parnham motioned him down again. "You can send word that you are ill."

Guy shook his head as visions of Hetty banging on Strathairn's door swam into his head. "That wouldn't keep Miss Cavendish away."

"I'm afraid my orders come from Viscount Sidmouth, the Home Secretary. I must insist," Parnham said. "The future of England far outweighs the demands of one young lady."

"This is preposterous. You cannot insist." Guy swung around to look at John. But he shifted in his seat and wouldn't meet Guy's eyes.

"These saboteurs plan to strike here in London. Would you prefer to allow them to continue to work against England? To assassinate the prime minister or the Prince of Wales? To stir the masses to riot and work against the Crown?"

"I would not," Guy said with heat. His love of England was deeply ingrained. "What do these Frenchmen hope to gain by this?"

"They are not all French, some are Englishmen. But the delusional souls are united in their quest to free Napoleon," Parnham said with a tight-lipped smile. "Their reasoning being that as he escaped from Elba, he can do so again. Destabilizing this country's government and stirring up the mood of the people will aid them in their cause. The present unrest plays into their hands. There's revolution in the air and some of these Englishmen prefer England to revolt instead of–in their opinion–remaining enslaved. They hate Liverpool's Tory government. They hate the Regent and his reckless spending and intend to ferment trouble wherever they can. There are organized societies with the same aim.

"What concerns us most is a new threat to the regent's life. We have prevented one attempt recently. He's unpopular, but to lose him would prove disastrous for England."

Parnham held out his hands, palms up. "Your life has been badly affected by revolution, has it not? You do understand why England needs you to do your duty, Lord Fortescue?"

Guy released a long breath. "I'm quite prepared to do as you wish. But only if I can visit Hetty. She must be told the truth. I know she can be trusted."

Parnham's clever brown eyes assessed him. "On reflection, it might seem odd if you stopped courting Miss Cavendish. You may tell her about your brother if you wish. Continue as you were, but she must not learn of your mission. It would be too dangerous. Do I have your word?"

Guy had to agree. The last thing he wanted was Hetty involving herself in this, and he was sure she would. "You have it."

Parnham rose, came around the desk, and shook Guy's hand. "Then it is done. You are to infiltrate the group to discover their plans. Best you don't come here again. I expect to learn something from you in the coming days. We'll keep in touch through Strathairn."

"And the scar?" Guy traced a line down his cheek.

"We might give you a fake one, but the count has already seen you so that won't serve." Parnham tapped the desk with a quill. "We shall have to trust no one has met Vincent."

Guy crossed Whitehall with John to the carriage. "Hetty and I will marry as soon as my sister arrives in London to identify me," he said. "Should I die, I want Hetty to inherit all my unentailed property."

John eyed him as he settled back on the squabs. "You French are a pessimistic lot, aren't you?"

Guy shrugged. "It would be foolish to be anything else, would it not?"

"I have your back, Guy. Remember that."

"I'm not likely to forget it," Guy said with a rueful smile.

Chapter Twenty

HETTY BEAT THE maid to the door. She threw it open, and all but fell into Guy's arms. He looked so weary and sad that she stilled. His cheek was bruised and there was a cut on his chin. Her questions fell away as shock dried her mouth.

He greeted her aunt in a sober voice, then sank onto the sofa.

Hetty sat beside him, her concern and curiosity getting the better of her. "What happened?"

Guy held up a hand. "I shall tell you."

She swallowed, not knowing what to expect and fearful of what he might say. She was sure it wasn't good.

Guy's voice was strained as he related the happenings of the last week.

When his voice fell away, Hetty, horrified and confused, rubbed her arms, and tried to sort through what he just told her. His twin brother whom he had thought dead in France was a veritable monster. He'd tried to kill Guy and take his place at Rosecroft Hall.

"Vincent accused Papa of deserting him when the fire engulfed our chateau. But he did not. I couldn't make him believe it. He hated us." He sounded so bitter it made her yearn to try to soothe him. "Life is cruel. Fate has cheated me of a brother."

When Guy lapsed into silence, her aunt offered her heartfelt sympathy and excused herself.

Hetty moved closer to Guy on the sofa. "My poor love."

Guy placed an arm around her shoulders and drew her close. The muscles on his arms were hard with tension. Tears blinded her.

"It's over, Hetty." He cradled her face in his hands and wiped the tears from her cheeks with his thumb. "I've missed you," he said quietly, and kissed her. "Will you be my wife?"

"Oh, Guy, yes. I love you." her heart throbbed with love for him. She coiled her arms around his neck and kissed him. As he held her, Hetty stroked his hair and discovered a lump. She pulled away. "You've been hurt."

Guy shrugged. "I'm lucky to have a hard head. Hopefully, I still have my wits."

She leant her head against his shoulder. "It's all over now." She sighed with relief.

His arm tightened around her.

Hetty sat up. "Guy!"

His eyes widened. "What is it?"

"Your sister, Genevieve has arrived in London. We traveled to-gether to Hampstead where you were last seen. She has taken a house in Portland Place."

Guy grinned. "Genevieve is here?"

"As soon as I received your letter, I sent a servant to let her know you were safe."

"*Merci.*" He sobered. "You and she went to Hampstead?"

Hetty wished he didn't look so defeated and unlike himself. "We traveled in your sister's opulent turquoise carriage," she said with a smile. "The coach is lined with fine parquetry, paisley silk curtains, velvet upholstery, and gold carriage lamps. I've never seen the like!"

A smile tugged at his lips. "Genevieve is never without her com-forts."

"She was determined to find you."

He drew away and stood. "I must go to her."

"Of course, you must. I like her very much, so please tell her I hope we meet again very soon."

"Tomorrow, I'd like to show you the Mayfair house which I found the day before Vincent..." Guy shook his head. "There might be a delay, Hetty." He rubbed his hand over his nape. "I must consult with my solicitor and I must ask your father. After that, the banns must read. Reverend Dewhurst at St. Georges will advise us of a suitable date."

"Oh, Guy." Hetty gazed at him with longing. "I do so want to be with you."

He pulled her into his arms and took her mouth in a kiss. "Tomorrow," he promised, drawing away.

She touched his cheek still unsure, still unable to fully trust in their future and wondering why. "But is everything all right now?"

His eyes looked shadowed. He took her hand in his big one and kissed it. "*Oui, mon cheri amour.*"

After Guy left, Hetty told her aunt about the house.

Aunt Emily hesitated. "But I cannot go with you. I have an engagement with the poetry society."

"That's all right, Aunt. It's no longer a false engagement. We are to marry." Hetty paused, something still wasn't right. His eyes were troubled. Was it because he mourned his brother?

"Well, of course you are to marry," her aunt said with a laugh.

Hetty, about to leave the room swung around. "You knew?"

"I did. That first day. When I saw how he looked at you."

"You don't find it surprising that a baron should wish to marry a poor man's daughter?"

"Poor? Your father is very careful with his money, but he is far plumper in the pocket than he makes out, Hetty."

Startled, Hetty remembered the dowry. "I had no idea. We live comfortably but simply in Digswell."

"That is your father's preference. But he might be called a nabob. He made a good deal of money with the East India Company while in India."

"Father a nabob? I can't believe it!"

"Nevertheless, it is true. The Cavendish family is a very old and important family even if we do not hail from its upper echelons. You are quite sure your baron is wealthy?"

"His father lost properties during the Revolution and Guy's estate, Rosecroft Hall, is sorely in need of renovation. But he appears to have the money to repair it."

Aunt Emily scooped up the gray cat at her feet and followed Hetty up the stairs. "It doesn't matter, my dear. I'm quite sure he loves you."

Hetty didn't care if Guy was as poor as a church mouse. "I am looking forward to seeing the house tomorrow."

Her aunt paused, a hand on the banister. "It's regrettable that I cannot see it, too. We plan to discuss Coleridge's poem *Kubla Khan*. He wrote it in '97, but he reserved it for private readings until this year when Lord Byron persuaded him to publish it. Such a pity you'll miss it." She paused for breath at the top of the stairs. "I trust you to act with decorum tomorrow, Hetty. I expect there will be someone there to show you around the house."

"I daresay, Aunt." Hetty hoped there wasn't. She needed time alone with Guy. Almost losing him had frightened her, and she sensed there was something else he wasn't telling her.

DESPITE THE JOY of an emotional reunion with his sister, Guy felt drained when he walked through the door of his temporary home in Berkley Square. He and Genevieve had reminisced about their childhood memories. Genevieve was appalled at what Vincent had done but was still sad that she'd been unable to attend his burial. She expressed her approval of Guy's choice of bride. "You could not do better than Hetty, *Gee*," she said.

Guy agreed. He hoped he would live to enjoy what promised to be a wonderful life.

Strathairn's butler approached him at the door. "My lord, a parcel arrived for you today."

Mystified, Guy tore off the paper. Inside were his evening coat, hat, and cane. A letter written in Lord Taylor's bold strokes explained that Guy's coat and hat had been left in a cupboard and overlooked by the maids until recently. He and Lady Taylor hoped all was well with him and that next time he visited them he would come to say goodbye before departing into the night and worrying all those who cared for him.

Guy shook his head and went to join John in the library.

His friend spun the bronze tiepin in his fingers. "It would be smart for you to wear this eagle pin when you meet with Count Forney."

Guy looked at it with distaste.

"We have reason to believe the secret code they use might be Longwood," John said. "The house on Saint Helena where Napoleon has been incarcerated."

Guy raised his brows. "So, I'm to visit him and use that word?"

"Yes and declare yourself to be one of them. Once you are drawn into his group, we will make our move."

"I may not be admitted a second time."

"I doubt you'll be turned away. But if he refuses, send the tie pin to him."

Something tugged at Guy's memory.

The door opened, and Georgina entered. "You wished to see me, John?"

Guy stood, ready to excuse himself.

"No, stay, Guy," John said. "We shall need to speak further." He beckoned Georgina into the room. She came to stand in front of him, unusually meek with her hands clasped together. She glanced at Guy. "What became of you at the ball, Guy?"

"Never mind quizzing Lord Fortescue, Georgina. His activities do not concern you. As you are no doubt aware, I have received a morning visit from Julian, His Grace, the Duke of Broadstairs, who has requested your hand in marriage."

Georgina gave a confident smile. "And what did you tell him?"

"That at seventeen, you are too young."

Her face fell. "No! You didn't," she cried. "You wouldn't! I am eighteen in three months' time."

John grinned. "Everything you wish for falls into your lap, does it not? I'm sure it is not good for your character."

Georgina rolled her eyes. "Pooh! See how he teases me, Guy?"

John smiled. "I told him the marriage can take place when you turn eighteen."

"Then I am betrothed?"

"It would seem so. He will call tomorrow, no doubt, with a handsome betrothal ring."

Georgina squealed in delight. She kissed her brother on both cheeks. "You are a beast. I shall be glad to leave home."

She turned to Guy. "I shall kiss you, too, Guy. I am so happy!"

Before her brother could protest, she had kissed Guy's cheek and flounced toward the door.

When it closed, John shook his head. "I'm fond of my sister. But I'll be relieved to hand her to Broadstairs."

"Does she love the duke?"

"I imagine so. She's been busy making him jealous for some months."

Guy laughed.

"Now…" John turned serious. "Any questions?"

"You've jogged my memory," Guy said. "Something Forney mentioned that I thought odd at the time. He said he enjoyed England when the shadows in the wood grow long."

"Longwood!" John's eyes gleamed. "That confirms the password! We have the wolf by the ears! We'll get him and the whole pack along with him."

"Preferably before they get me," Guy said with a grimace.

Chapter Twenty-One

"**I** HAVE THE key."

Guy led Hetty up to the front door of an impressive house in South Audley Street. Doric columns flanked the doors with a pretty fan-shaped window above.

Hetty took a deep breath as she looked at the handsome man beside her. An hour spent alone with him was enticing.

Guy unlocked the door and led her into the marble hall where elegant stairs curved away to the upper floors.

"It's very grand." Hetty's hushed voice echoed around the lofty space.

Guy took her hand and led her through the empty rooms. Then they mounted the stairs to the upper stories.

"This is the drawing room." He threw open a door.

Crimson silk walls rose above the dark polished wood of the wainscoting, rising to a high plaster ceiling. The Adam fireplace was of white marble. Tall French windows opened onto the garden. She crossed the bare boards to inspect the magnificent carved fireplace. "I can imagine it furnished."

"That will be your domain." Guy gazed down at her. "How pretty you look today. The lilac suits your hair."

She smiled. "I'm glad you didn't say red hair."

"I have learnt my lesson."

She reached up and touched the cleft in his chin. "The first of many."

He pulled her against him. "That sounds threatening."

She laughed. "It's only fair to warn you."

He tilted up her chin. "Ah, but you are not fair."

"Why am I not?"

"The way you look at me when I want you so."

Her hand at his nape, she pulled him down for a kiss.

"Hetty," he murmured when they parted. "Don't torture me. Let's examine the rest of the house."

She smiled and took his arm. "Yes, I'd love to."

Guy threw open another white and gold paneled door. "This will be our bedchamber."

Hetty found it difficult to breathe. The room was empty of furniture but was carpeted in the pinks and blues of a rosy dawn. Another handsome fireplace where she could visualize flames crackling cozily in the grate as they lay in bed together. The thought thrilled her.

She pressed her hands together and gazed up at her handsome fiancé.

Hetty was determined to have Guy make love to her today. Her breath quickened as she walked to the window. "We overlook the garden." She pulled off her lilac pelisse and kid gloves and began to untie her bonnet strings.

Guy came to stand behind her, resting his hands on her shoulders. "What are you doing, Hetty?"

"I'm a trifle warm."

Aunt Emily wished her to act with decorum, but her aunt wished she'd experienced love with the man she adored. It seemed to Hetty that Aunt Emily compensated for a life not lived by immersing herself in poetry.

Hetty turned into his arms. She reached up to slide a black lock back from his forehead as his eyes roamed her face.

So much had happened. It seemed irrational, but Hetty feared he'd be snatched away from her. He was tense, she could sense it when she touched him, and she wondered why. He was withholding something from her. Perhaps if they became lovers, he might tell her, although she doubted he would listen to her and stay safe.

"Shall we view more of the house?" When he drew her away toward the door, she silently took his hand and tried to pull him down with her onto the dense carpet.

"What mischief are you up to, Hetty?" Guy said, removing his hand as if he'd been burned.

She sank down. "Lie with me."

He shook his head, doubt in his eyes. "We should wait."

Afraid he might not desire her after all, she tucked her legs beneath her, suddenly foolish.

Guy laughed and sat beside her. "I swear I'm never sure of what you'll do next."

Hetty hesitated. She wasn't entirely sure how to proceed but determined they would not leave there today without making love. She trusted Guy to keep her safe from scandal. Now that she'd made up her mind, her senses were on fire. A twist of desire curled deep inside her.

Guy eyed her cautiously but kept some distance between them. She reached out to him. "Kiss me."

He leant over and gave her a gentle kiss, pulled away, then with a soft moan, moved closer, and kissed her again. One kiss turned into many, and his tongue thrust against hers, teasing, taking. Desire built to a heavy throb low in her belly. Her nipples tingled.

He drew away. "You are playing a dangerous game, *ma cherie.*"

Something odd had happened to her breath, she was gasping, her heart pounding. "I know, but it's worth it, isn't it?" She ran a finger along his bottom lip.

Guy kissed her throat and untied the strings at the back of her gown to lower it, kissing the swell of her breast. A delicious ache spread over her breasts, and her nipples tightened into rigid buds.

She shivered with expectation at his deliberate movements. He seemed a different person as her shift was pulled down to expose her breasts. Suddenly shy, she put an arm across her breasts.

"Don't hide from me," he murmured huskily, removing her hand.

He lowered his head and took a nipple in his mouth.

As exquisite sensations flooded through her, Hetty gasped and raked her fingers through his dark hair.

GUY COULDN'T RESIST kissing her full creamy-skinned breasts. Lust slammed into his body as he cupped a firm globe and teased the taut nipple with his tongue. It tasted deliciously of woman with a delicate floral scent. But he could not let it go far. Not when he feared he may not live long enough to marry her. He'd already gone further than he intended. Her long slender legs enticed him, and a wicked voice in his head urged him to settle between them and make her his own. Her soft words of encouragement made him want her so much he had to fight not to take her right there on the carpet.

"*Mon dieu!*" he groaned. "We must stop this, Hetty."

"What? No." Her beautiful eyes were unfocused, which made his blood run hot.

As his last shreds of resistance slipped away, Guy pushed her back, his mouth sliding over hers. He nipped at her full under lip, evidence of her passionate nature.

When Hetty gazed deeply into his eyes, revealing the trust and respect she held for him, he pulled away, making a valiant effort at restraint.

"This is not going to happen," he said, his voice hoarse while aware the evidence of his body made a mockery of his words.

"You're trembling," she whispered. "I don't think you mean it." She pressed herself ruthlessly against him, hip-to-hip, her hands sweeping over his back. He gave a strained laugh.

"Hetty, have mercy!"

He struggled to resist as hot blood surged through his body. His hand stroked up the soft skin of her inner thigh under her petticoats and located the soft feminine folds at the apex. Hetty's body tensed, she flushed, and with a small sigh of pleasure, gave herself up to him.

With a moan, Guy stroked her hot damp flesh while she wriggled, uttering mews of pleasure. His free hand went to his breeches as desire drove him to mount her. They were panting with need, and his brain, turned to mush, ignored the danger.

There was a time when he would have taken her and worried about the consequences later. But not now. Surprised at how much he'd changed, and knowing his love for Hetty had changed him, he pulled his hand away from his breeches and focused on her enjoyment.

Hetty clutched at Guy's shirt and emitted small shrieks as he continued his rhythmic stroking. "Guy, oh that's so..."

She moaned, sank back, and opened her eyes.

Guy smiled at her. "It was agreeable, my love?"

Hetty's eyes had a dreamy look, and her pink tongue toyed with her bottom lip. Guy struggled to inhale as he moved to ease the discomfort of his swollen shaft straining against his breeches. He wanted her so much he fought for air. Somehow, the bitter reminder had found its way through the fog of lust enveloping his mind. What he faced tomorrow. He could die and leave her unmarried and pregnant. Withdrawal was never a guarantee. He moved to put distance between them.

GUY'S DEEP GROAN vibrated through her. She bit her lip, contrite. When he jumped to his feet, she saw with a small measure of satisfaction how she had affected him before he turned away to adjust his clothing. "Get dressed, Hetty," he said, his voice tight. "I shall be back in a moment. And then I think we should leave."

Filled with an odd languor, Hetty struggled with the ties of her gown. Her muscles seemed to have gone to water. Tears gathered, and a sob formed in her throat. He had proved remarkably un-rake like. Was he disappointed in her?

She climbed to her feet and straightened her clothes. She was struggling with the ties on her gown when he returned.

"Let me assist you."

She studied his face as he helped her into her pelisse. He was so handsome, so wonderful, and her behavior had been appalling. "Thank you." Despite her best efforts her chest heaved, and her voice trembled.

Guy sighed and placed his finger beneath her chin to raise her gaze to his.

Hetty gave a sigh of relief at the amusement she found there. He touched his lips lightly to hers. "What motivated this attempt at seduction?"

"I'm afraid I'll lose you, Guy," she murmured. "That you're not telling me everything."

"You aren't going to lose me," he said and pulled her against him, his hand cupped her head as he took her lips in a long passionate kiss. "Sweetheart. I would like nothing better than to make love to you. But I know more about life than you do, so please, just once, will you let me take care of you?"

"But I wanted to give you pleasure," she whispered.

"You think you didn't?" He laughed and tucked a lock behind her ear and bent to give her another brief kiss. "I plan to make love to you in the proper manner. In our marriage bed."

At those words, any vestige of remorse fled. "I remember the stories you told me–when you believed me to be a man–of making love in hay lofts, carriages, fields, and wasn't there one incidence involving a table?"

Guy laughed. "You have changed me." He shook his head. "I am not that man anymore."

Guy was an honorable man, one of the things she respected and loved about him, but she didn't want him to change from the passionate and thrilling lover described to her in the woodland hut. She was determined they would do all those things together because she wanted to eradicate the memories of his past lovers. Lords were known to take mistresses, but he would never wish for anyone but her.

She tied her bonnet ribbons firmly beneath her chin. "I've yet to see the dining room. I fancy a long table, with enough room for all our friends and family."

Chapter Twenty-Two

WHEN GUY LEFT Hetty at her aunt's home, he considered how his attitude to so many things had changed. He'd come to England with the somewhat arrogant intention of finding a bride to fit his station. He was even prepared to set up a mistress if he had no real affection for his wife. He'd suffered so much loss and heartbreak, he believed himself incapable of deep feeling for anyone and impervious to further hurt. Now his happiness depended upon an amber-eyed, willowy young woman who was far too spirited for her own good.

Hetty filled his mind, heart, and soul. It had been a great struggle not to take her as she lay there on the carpet inviting him to do so, her lush mouth made for kissing and her lovely body bared to his gaze. He didn't fully understand why he hadn't. Perhaps, because he sensed what lay behind her determination.

Hetty was troubled. Guy had been unable to fool her when he attempted to reassure her that that all was well. He was worldlier and far more conversant with the tragedy their making love might cause, and he would not take advantage of her vulnerability. As a young man, these thoughts would not have troubled him, but, now they did.

After dinner, Guy joined John in the library, where they discussed John's time spent with Wellington during the Peninsular Wars, or at least what John would reveal. Much of what John was required to do during those years he'd probably never repeat to anyone. War left men scarred. Although John was a stalwart friend, Guy could only get so close until he came up against the wall John had built around himself.

There was much in Guy's past, too, that he'd rather forget. After downing his third whiskey, Guy relaxed enough to talk of his years spent on the Continent before coming to London.

"In Paris in '08, I had the misfortune to be in the wrong place at the wrong time. I was arrested and thrown into the Conciergerie." He threw down the last of his drink to obliterate the bitter taste in his mouth. "Most don't emerge from that prison alive, but for some reason, I was released. I didn't wait to find out why. Over a million men, women, and children died in France during that time. Many in that prison. I left France, sick to my very soul."

"And you took up arms against Bonaparte." John raised his glass to him.

"Another million souls perished under Napoleon. Spain was in an even worse state than France. The land was scattered with the corpses of dead soldiers and horses. Villages ransacked and burned. The women raped and murdered. Stock and grain destroyed leaving those left to starve to death." He took a deep breath. "I ended up at Girona, with such anger I wanted to kill, but instead, I acted as aide and secretary to Colonel Anthony O'Kelly from Roscommon, preparing dispatches, and translating documents into English, and working with the women. I refused to kill my countrymen. My hatred for Napoleon didn't extend to the men who served him, although I was ashamed of their atrocities in that country." He sighed.

"But in Girona, I witnessed so much foolish bravery, against enormous odds. Some six thousand French troops of Napoleon's army laid siege to the fortress of Monjiuch, demanding the surrender of the Ultonia Regiment. Colonel O'Kelly refused. The blockade went on for eight months."

To speak of it tightened Guy's throat. The words took him back to that grim time in his life when, as a despised aristocrat, he'd tried to help desperate people, but there were so many and so little he could do. Before the Revolution, his father had helped all those on his estates. Guy had helplessly witnessed these people being overrun and dying where they stood. And he reached a point where he didn't know or care what would become of him.

"Those were troubled times, my friend." John broke into his thoughts as he refilled Guy's glass from the crystal decanter.

"I grew fond of those whose lives I shared. Mrs. Lucy MacCarthy, wife of Colonel Patricio Fitzgerald MacCarthy, sought permission from the Spanish Army High Command to organize a women's unit. The Company of St. Barbara, they came to be called. They carried ammunition to the troops and risked their lives to care for the wounded."

"Yes, they were indeed admirable." John lit a cheroot and puffed a cloud of smoke into the air.

"Heroines to the last." Guy looked down at his glass, as his thoughts took him back there, amid the thunderous barrage and the confusion, the groans of the men, their blood running over the stony ground. He aided the women. "They ran the gauntlet of shells raining down, bombs and grenades, carrying the wounded in their arms to the hospital." His voice broke, and he took another deep sip from his glass. The whiskey rolled over his tongue, thick and smoky with a hint of peat, warming the chilled knot in his chest. "When thirty-three thousand more French troops arrived and demanded O'Kelly surrender, he allowed the citizens a democratic vote." He gave a hopeless shrug. "They voted no."

"Brave, but foolish."

A long, heartfelt sigh escaped Guy's lips. "Over six hundred soldiers, along with Colonel O'Kelly, perished."

"How did you get out alive?"

"After Lucy died by her husband, Fitzgerald's side, I organized an escape with those civilians left. We slipped away at night amid the chaos."

Guy had walked for miles despite the wound in his thigh where a bullet had grazed him. After parting company with the others who wished to make their way farther west, he found a tiny hamlet untouched by Napoleon's forces. A peasant family took him in and cared for him until he was well, generously sharing their few provisions.

"As soon as I was able," Guy told John, "I returned to offer them aid. The house was a smoldering ruin. Soldiers had taken their livestock and destroyed the crops, they had murdered the farmer, stripped, and violated the wife. She'd been taken in by relatives and was like a ghost."

Guy left what money he had. "I ended up in Barcelona, where for a time, I lost myself."

There was a long silence as they stared into the flames remembering lost comrades.

John stretched. "Tomorrow, we need to make a plan."

Guy raised his brows. "*Oui*, tomorrow." He hoped those days in Spain had helped him hone his instincts for danger, and to trust his gut feeling. He would need those skills now.

"It might be wise if I move into a hotel, John."

John nodded.

WHEN SHE WOKE in the morning, Hetty gasped and curled her toes, remembering. Sarah entered with her hot chocolate, as the bells rang out over the city, calling people to church. "It's a beautiful day, Miss Hetty. Listen, you can hear the booming bells of St. Paul's Cathedral." She drew back the damask curtains to reveal puffed white clouds in a patch of delph blue sky.

Hetty stretched her arms over her head, more aware of her body, her breasts, her nipples, and that vulnerable spot between her thighs. It was as if Guy's lovemaking had changed her and left her yearning. She finished her chocolate and sprang out of bed.

"What a lovely day! I fancy a walk in the park after church." With a sad pull of disappointment, she remembered Guy was not to visit her today. He had urgent business to attend to. How adroitly he'd evaded her questions as to what that business might be.

After church, Hetty strolled back to the house with Sarah beneath the trees as she recalled the time Guy had taken her to the park. The memory tugged at her heart. She wanted to see him. Wanted to be sure he was safe, though why she couldn't convince herself of it, puzzled her.

She sat down to a hearty luncheon of soup, bread rolls, and a large helping of custard tart. After a careful look, her aunt requested a description of the house. Hetty concentrated on the food and tried to avoid her aunt's penetrating gaze as she described in detail the impressive size and layout of the rooms. "It's situated in a nice street in Mayfair where new houses are being erected," she concluded.

She was relieved when her aunt made no comment, but instead discussed wedding gowns. Princess Charlotte was to be married in May. "Her wedding gown is said to have cost over ten thousand pounds," Aunt Emily said. "I read that it is to be of silver lama on net over a silver tissue slip with flowers and shells embroidered in silver at the hem."

"That sounds very lovely," Hetty said. "I shall want something simpler."

Her aunt nodded enthusiastically. "No time like the present to search for the fabric."

Hetty wished she could give it her full attention, but the unease she felt still clouded her mind.

The next morning, the duchess was admitted, dressed in another exquisite costume of cornsilk yellow, which made her eyes appear very green.

"How divine you look, Your Grace," Hetty said, much struck.

"*Merci*, mademoiselle. I must speak to you!"

"Of course." Surprised by her urgency, Hetty showed her through to the parlor. "Please sit, Your Grace. May I offer you coffee?"

"*Non, merci.*" A tiny frown marred Genevieve's normally smooth brow. She patted her breast. "I am not how you say... quiet, in here."

Hetty's pulse throbbed as she met the duchess anxious gaze. "I'm sorry. What worries you?"

"*Gee*. He called last evening but stayed only a minute before he left again. He is not himself."

"Oh?" Guy had been less than forthcoming about his plans, leaving her wondering herself what worry consumed him. "What makes you think it?" she asked uneasily.

"You sense it, too," Genevieve said. "*Gee* said he was unable to visit me for several days." She pushed out her bottom lip. "He said he'd be delighted to see me if I came to London, and now, *poof!*" She waved a hand in the air. "He says he has calls to make today and then disappears again! His behavior is most odd."

"I did wonder," Hetty confessed.

"I followed him this morning."

Shocked. Hetty widened her eyes. "You followed your brother?"

The duchess nodded. "*Gee* visited a gun shop, Manton's Gallery in Davies Street. He was inside for over an hour. I saw him go upstairs and heard him practicing." She wrinkled her nose. "I could smell the gunpowder."

"Well, I find that entirely—"

"When he came out, he carried a box under his arm."

"For hunting?"

"*Non.*" The duchess shook her head. "It was not a hunting rifle. Smaller. A pistol."

Hetty stared at her thunderstruck, her head filled with wild thoughts. Why would Guy need a pistol? Did he think himself in danger? Or did he just want to arm himself after all that had happened?

The duchess edged forward on her chair, looking ready to rise. "He has an appointment at two. If we start out now, we can follow him this afternoon."

Hetty blinked. "But Your Grace! I cannot follow him. Guy trusts me."

Genevieve's fine brows lowered a frown. "What of that? If *Gee* is in trouble, we must help him."

"But what trouble would he be in?" Hetty considered she'd done enough to unnerve him yesterday. "Surely with Vincent dead, it is at an end. What if he sees us? He will be *so* angry."

"Leave that to me." Genevieve nodded sagely. "I will handle *Gee.*"

"Are you sure?" Hetty found herself unable to resist another woman who preferred action to talk.

"I am. Send the maid for your things. My carriage waits outside."

Hetty informed her aunt she was riding in the park with the duchess.

When they were assisted inside the coach, Genevieve gave instructions for Berkley Square, and they moved off down the street at a fast clip. They arrived within minutes, for it was but a pleasant walk from her aunt's house. Hetty swallowed, her throat dry. She could visualize Guy's scowl when he caught sight of them.

They left the groom to walk the horses in Berkley Street and followed the graceful curve of the footpath to where the row of mansions faced onto the park. Unsure quite what to do next, she and Genevieve huddled down behind a tree. Minutes passed.

"He has a two o'clock engagement, so he must leave soon," Hetty said, half wishing to give the idea up.

Another five minutes passed. They were discussing whether to leave when the door to number eight opened. Genevieve pulled Hetty down the servants' steps of the house opposite. Through the railings, they watched Guy, dressed in a brown coat and fawn trousers, walk along the pavement swinging his cane.

"It is as I suspected. He calls on someone," Genevieve hissed. Guy reached the corner and disappeared behind a stone wall.

"Is that a bad thing?" Hetty began to question the duchess' sanity as the women hurried back to the carriage.

"Drive around the corner and follow the man in the brown coat," the duchess instructed the startled coachman. "Don't lose him whatever you do, but don't make us conspicuous. I shall reward you if you succeed," she added.

With eager agility, the footman jumped onto the box, and the coachman moved the horses on.

They caught sight of Guy in Berkley Street. He turned left into

New Bond Street. They followed and arrived to find him hailing a hackney.

The coach trailed behind at a discreet pace as the hackney wove through the London streets. It pulled up in Cavendish Square, and Guy alighted. He looked neither left nor right but climbed the steps of an impressive residence to knock at the door. Minutes later, a butler admitted him.

"This square bears your name, mademoiselle. Surely it's a family connection?"

"A distant one," Hetty said.

"I wonder who my brother might visit here," Genevieve said. "Do you know?"

"No." Hetty studied the four-storied townhouse. "It might be best if we get out and let the coachman walk the horses."

"Make enquiries as to who lives here, Jacque," Genevieve said to the groom.

"*Oui, ma dame.*"

He hurried to knock at the servants' entrance of the neighboring house.

Moments later, he returned. "A Corsican gentleman, *ma dame.* Count Forney."

Genevieve shrugged. "I do not know him."

A lady entered the pretty park at the square's center and with a smile, left the gate open for them. Hetty and Genevieve chose a seat facing the house and opened their parasols. Hetty hoped it would afford them some disguise if Guy should walk past them.

Chapter Twenty-Three

G UY WAS RELIEVED when Count Forney's butler admitted him. At least he wouldn't fall at the first fence. And with time to consider, he was eager to succeed in his mission.

He was shown into the grand salon where the count greeted him in surprise. "I did not expect to see you again, Lord Fortescue."

"It is my practice to be careful, Count."

Guy pulled back his coat to better display the bronze eagle pin nestled in the folds of his cravat. "The days grow long, and I find I miss the countryside, the charm of the wood."

Forney's eyes widened when he caught sight of the pin. He gave an oily smile and shook Guy's hand. "Then I wasn't wrong. You are one of us."

"I had to be sure about you, Count. You understand?"

"*Oui,* indeed I do. We cannot be too careful."

"The stakes are too high to be careless."

"*Bon.* I shall take you this evening to meet the others. They have long since wished to meet you. Your exploits are legendary."

Guy bowed. "You are too gracious."

"We require your expertise in our quest to rescue Bonaparte. We must act with great speed before the English have him killed."

"I should be happy to offer all the assistance I can. Where do we go to meet them?"

"My carriage will call for you. Where do you stay?"

"At Grillon's Hotel in Albemarle Street," Guy said.

"At ten of the clock, then."

Guy emerged into the square. He glanced at the two women in the park who chatted beneath their parasols and continued. He must report to John. Tonight would put an end to the whole infernal scheme. He had no real faith in these so-called spies, for they appeared more like mischief makers. A plan to free Napoleon was bizarre. Their idolatry of Vincent seemed amateurish to him. Had the Home Secretary been ill informed? Yet, he surmised, amateurs they might be, but obsessed and determined they were, nonetheless.

He crossed the juncture of Henrietta and Margaret Streets and began to walk down Holles Street, making his way to Oxford Street, where he had a better chance of finding another hackney. The streets were busy with horsemen, and vehicles of all kinds. Many people walked the pavements visiting the shops. Guy cursed and stopped suddenly causing a peddler selling pies to give him a hopeful glance as he wandered past. A grand aqua carriage waited on the next corner, the four matched gray horses held by a liveried groom. Not only did this fit Hetty's description of his sister's carriage perfectly, it was surely the purple and blue of the duke's livery. He was sure of it. He walked up to it. "Where is the Duchesse la Châteaudunn?"

Learning of her direction, Guy swiveled abruptly. The two women in the park, hidden behind parasols… Could it be? "Zut!" he muttered and strode back to the square. Had he not been so angry, he would have laughed at their stricken expressions. It was one thing for him to be in danger, but he would not have two of his favorite people in all the world drawn into the arena.

"And what might you be doing here?" he asked in glacial tones.

"I took the duchess to meet a friend of mine, but she is not at home." Hetty's face flushed crimson, and she refused to meet his gaze.

"You are a very bad liar, Hetty," Guy said. He raised his brows at his sister. "Who is behind this absurd notion?"

"I am," Hetty blurted.

"Non. 'Twas I." Genevieve revealed a sisterly lack of fear at his wrath. "You are in trouble. We wish to help."

He ground his teeth. "You can help enormously."

Two sets of pretty eyes looked at him in fascination. "How?" Hetty asked in a breathless voice.

"By going home and staying there."

"Oh." She looked at Genevieve, who made a moue with her lips.

"Then you don't deny you are in trouble?" Genevieve asked.

"I do deny it. You are being absurd. Allow me to escort you both to your carriage."

"But where do you go? Why don't you come with us now?"

"Because I have a prior engagement. You are both outrageous. Must I tell you every detail of my life?"

When his sister began to object in a flood of voluble French, Guy held up his hand. "*Assez!*"

The unmanageable pair climbed into the carriage. "Can we give you a lift somewhere?" Hetty asked with a sweet smile.

"No!" He slammed the door. "I shall call on you both tomorrow."

"Why not call this evening, *Gee?*"

Guy ignored Genevieve's question. He instructed the coachman to take them directly home.

Hetty stared back at him from the window with a worried expression as the carriage trundled away down the street.

HETTY WATCHED GUY stride away. "He's very angry," she said. "Will he ever forgive us?"

"*Pooh!* He was bluffing. I know my brother."

"But you believe him to be in danger?"

"*Oui.* His eyes are evasive. When he was a boy and up to no good, he looked just like that. And what other reason would he have for not coming to visit one of us this evening?"

Hetty studied Genevieve. She had no way of knowing if the duchess's opinion could be relied upon. Guy had been very angry. She shivered, his eyes had pinned her in place. But… He was worried and tense, otherwise he would have recovered his good humor, laughed, and joined them. She recognized the way he'd clenched his jaw, and he had avoided her eyes when questioned. "There is nothing we can do."

"We shall follow him again this evening."

"He may not be going out this evening," Hetty reasoned.

"He must be, otherwise he would call on us," Genevieve said with French practicality.

"But, he'll be on the alert for us now."

"We'll dress in costume," the duchess said promptly.

"What kind of costume?"

"Men's attire, and we'll hire a hackney."

"Where will we get... Oh!" Hetty bit her lip. "I do wish I'd brought them to London."

Her Grace stared at her. "*Quoi?*"

Distracted by the sudden likeness to her brother, Hetty muttered, "It is nothing. I'll explain later."

"I can borrow some clothes from my staff. The footmen are huge, but the younger servants aren't so big. No one visits before nine in London. I'll come to you at eight of the clock."

An alarming thought struck Hetty. "W-what if Guy is visiting a woman?"

"A mistress?" Genevieve asked, in a matter-of-fact tone.

"Yes." Hetty swallowed a lump in her throat. Had she driven Guy into the arms of a Cyprian?

His sister shook her head. "She would not keep him from me for days at a time. And he is in love. A man in love does not visit a courtesan. Not *Gee*. I may not have seen much of him for years, but I remember him as a loving son and a kind brother. He rescued our Maman and me when our chateau was burning, and my papa had gone to find Vincent. Gee fought a man much bigger than he, who tried to attack us. I don't know where he found the strength, but he punched him to the ground and he led us to safety."

That was the man Hetty knew.

"Gee wrote to me when he could," Genevieve continued. "As a child he was honorable. Vincent never was. The twins were opposites. The light and the dark. This does not change."

The coach drew to a stop in King Street. Hetty alighted as another problem faced her. What on earth was she to tell her aunt?

Hetty walked in and found the house in upheaval. A maid scurried past with her arms full of linen. "What has happened, Sarah?"

"Your father has arrived," Sarah said. "Your aunt has put him in the guest bedchamber next to yours."

"Papa?" Hetty's voice quavered.

Aunt Emily bustled out of the parlor. "He has news." She gave a conspiratorial smile. "I shall let him tell you himself."

As she trudged up the stairs, Hetty searched her mind for an appropriate reason to be absent this evening. She knocked on her father's door with the hope that a suitable excuse would spring from somewhere when the need arose.

Her father stood before the mirror adjusting his neckcloth. He turned as she entered, and she was struck by how lively he appeared. His beaming face looked years younger.

"My dear." He kissed her cheek. "I had to come and tell you the news. I have asked Marina Illingworth to be my wife, and she has accepted."

Pleasure for him threaded through her. His future with Mrs. Illingworth was sure to be a happy and fulfilling one. "Papa, that's wonderful news. I'm so pleased for you."

"Are you really, my dear? I hoped you would be."

"I like Mrs. Illingworth very much."

"She is a sensible woman."

"Indeed, she is."

"I thought we might have a small celebration this evening. If you are not otherwise engaged?"

"I'm afraid I do have an engagement tonight," Hetty said cautiously. "I received an invitation from the Duchess Châteaudunn, Guy's sister."

Her father's face fell. He considered her words and recovered a little. "The Duchess Châteaudunn, you say?"

"Yes, she has come from France for a visit. Will tomorrow night serve? We can invite her and Guy."

"Well, yes, I should like that. I should have written, but I wanted to tell you the news myself."

She hugged him with a fresh flush of guilt. "I'm glad you did. I'm pleased to see you're in excellent health. When is the wedding?"

"Come and sit down." He took her hand and steered her to the sofa. "I thought it safe to proceed and have the Banns read." He frowned. "Has the date for your wedding been set? I've been expecting a letter from you."

"Not as yet. Guy has other matters to attend to. He plans to obtain a special license and arrange for the wedding to take place at St. Georges in Hanover Square."

His eyes widened. "St. Georges? The vicar and I had expected... Well of course, that is fitting for a baron."

Hetty clasped her shaking hands together. Marrying before the eyes of the *haute ton* terrified her. She could hear the talk now. Cavendish? A branch of the family live in Digswell?

"I'll learn more about it when Fortescue calls for you tonight."

"I'm afraid not. Guy has another engagement."

"An engagement that does not include his betrothed?" He studied her. "You are happy, Horatia? I judged him to be a good man."

"Guy's the very best of men, Papa." The words almost stuck in Hetty's throat, her guilt overlaid with uneasiness. Was Genevieve right to follow Guy when this matter was surely none of their concern? It was most unlike Hetty not to act on a premonition, but the duchess depended on her, so she would not let her down.

"Good." Her father rubbed his hands together. "Let's go downstairs. I have yet to enjoy a good chat with your aunt."

After dinner, Genevieve called for Hetty in her carriage at the appointed time. She was introduced to Hetty's father, who was immediately charmed by her.

When she climbed into the coach, Genevieve thrust some clothes into Hetty's hands. "Put these on."

"Here?"

"*Oui.*" She lowered the blinds.

As the carriage rocked along the street, they removed their gowns. Hetty struggled into the ill-fitting clothes that reeked of horse.

"I'm sorry. They belong to the stable boy," Genevieve said. "They were the only ones that would fit you." She gave an apologetic shrug. "You are so tall and slim." She held out a pair of scuffed shoes. "These will be too large for you. You'll need to stuff the toes with paper."

Hetty admired Genevieve's nimble fingers as she tied a credible cravat without a mirror. Her clothes were more suited to the gentry. She wondered whom the duchess had coerced into giving them up and had a ridiculous vision of her ordering a local clerk to remove his clothes. She stifled a nervous giggle, tugging on her black tricorn as Genevieve tucked her dark hair beneath the hat.

A watchman called, to whoever would listen, that the weather remained fine. The coach halted for them to alight at the stand in New Bond Street beside the water trough. A night coach passed them, and link boys lit the way for a chair carrying some important personage.

The bare wisp of smoky cloud hiding the crescent moon slowly drifted away. A cool breeze stirred the trees and fanned the stench of fresh horse manure, stinging Hetty's nostrils. She shivered in the thin clothing, more from apprehension than cold.

No available hackneys were waiting at the stand. A peddler strolled up to them with a box of clocks strapped around his neck. Hetty waved him away as her frustration grew. She and Genevieve walked up and down. The minutes turned into half an hour.

"It's growing late. We will have missed him." Hetty rubbed her arms.

"I see one!" Genevieve darted out to wave it down. Hetty followed, unable to move very fast as the shoes slid off her heels.

"Don't have smallpox or the plague, do you?" the jarvie asked before they climbed in.

"Certainly not," Hetty growled. "Berkley Square, if you please."

"Toffy kind o' place for the likes of you, ain't it?"

Hetty squared her shoulders. "Mind your manners, my man, or you won't get a tip."

"No offense meant." The jarvie pushed his hat back and drew his whip.

They rattled past elegant stone and brick houses as they approached Berkley Square.

"There he is!" Guy walked up Brutton Street, a tall hat on his head, his long dark coat flowing about his ankles. "Follow that man!" she called to the jarvie.

"What kind o' smoky business is this?" he asked.

"Nothing for you to worry about," Hetty said. "Just think about the extra money you'll earn."

The jarvie turned the hackney and drove after Guy, who had disappeared into New Bond Street. An empty hackney passed him and slowed. Guy waved it on, content to go on foot to his destination. They caught sight of him again as he turned from Grafton Street into Albemarle Street. He walked past the grand façade of the Royal Institution and disappeared into the Grillion Hotel.

"What do we do now?" Hetty asked as the jarvie pulled up outside the hotel. "He'll be here to meet a friend and may be there for hours."

Suddenly, the hackney doors were flung open, and a man thrust a pistol into their faces. "Out."

Chapter Twenty-Four

A TALL MAN stood there, another beside him. Both men's faces were obscured by shadows.

Hetty stilled the clink of coins in her pocket as she climbed down, having heard of some people being robbed, sometimes just for their handkerchiefs. Genevieve followed her to the pavement, unusually silent. Hetty couldn't be sure that a scolding tirade wouldn't erupt from Genevieve's lips and get them both shot.

She hurriedly spoke before the duchess could. "We has nothin' of value 'ere," she croaked, her voice lowered to a bark by the fear that tightened her throat.

The tall man grabbed her by the arm while the other attempted to drag the struggling Genevieve into the light cast by a street lamp. "What business do you have here?" the tall man demanded.

"They look like pigs, they do, miss," the jarvie offered from his seat. "From Bow Street I'll be bound."

The light fell on the tall man's face. Hetty gasped. "Is it you, Lord Strathairn?"

"What the devil?" He whipped off her hat. "Miss Cavendish. Why are you dressed like that and talking that way? Those clothes reek of the stable. And why are you following Lord Fortescue?"

"We are most worried about *Gee*," Genevieve said, finding her voice.

"I'm sorry, Lord Strathairn." Hetty finally remembered her manners. "I'd like you to meet Duchess Châteaudunn. Lord Fortescue's sister."

Lord Strathairn's accomplice whistled. "I'll be damned!"

"I appreciate your concern, Your Grace." Lord Strathairn spoke through clenched teeth. "But you'll make matters worse for the baron if you remain here. Please go home."

"I demand you tell us what this is about," Genevieve said, having regained her poise. Her voice rang with imperiousness, and the other man hesitated then made an awkward bow.

"It's secret government business that does not concern you, Your Grace," Lord Strathairn said in a cool tone. "Have no fear. We shall keep your brother safe. Please leave now or you'll both spend the night in a Bow Street cell."

"Guy's on secret government business?" Hetty gasped. That would certainly account for his odd behavior. "If you're sure…"

"We'll guard him like a baby." The Runner–if indeed he was one–gave a guffaw which was cut short by Genevieve's icy glare.

"I do hope so, *monsieur*," the duchess said. "There will be trouble should you fail."

Once back in the hackney, Hetty instructed the jarvie where to take them. He moved the horse on without further comment, apparently struck dumb by what he'd witnessed.

"What on earth is Guy involved in?" Hetty asked. She'd experienced cold fear before but was now chilled to the bone.

The hackney turned the corner into Grafton Street and passed a lane behind the hotel. Hetty caught sight of two men exiting from the rear of the building.

"Look, there's Guy!" Hetty clutched Genevieve's sleeve. She hung out the window. "Stop the carriage!"

The jarvie cursed as he pulled the horse up.

Genevieve craned her neck. "They are entering a carriage."

"I can't run in these shoes! You go! Tell Lord Strathairn," Hetty said. "I'll keep their carriage in sight."

"*Oui*." Genevieve climbed down onto the pavement. She paused. "But what if we lose you?"

"Hurry! Tell Lord Strathairn. He will follow us."

As the duchess ran back to Albemarle Street, Guy's carriage passed Hetty's. She watched it go and shouted to the jarvie. "Don't lose sight of that carriage!"

"You meet all kinds in this 'ere job," the jarvie said with a crack of his whip.

The hackney moved at a clip to the next corner in time for Hetty to see the carriage that bore Guy trundle down Dover Street toward Piccadilly.

Hetty looked back. Lord Strathairn was half a block behind driving a curricle, the other man beside him. Had they forced Genevieve to go home? Hetty bit her lip. Genevieve would be furious.

At Piccadilly, the hackney was slowed by a stream of evening traffic. Ahead, a slow wagon loaded with wares rattled along at a snail's pace. With mounting horror, Hetty watched Guy's carriage disappear into the gloom. "Have we lost them?" she yelled, trying to make herself heard above the noise of clattering wheels and pedestrian chatter.

"Not bloody likely," the jarvie yelled back. "When Pete sets his mind to it, he doesn't fail."

"There they are," Hetty called. "They're heading toward the Strand." She had no idea if Lord Strathairn still followed or was held up in the traffic.

They traveled under the stone gateway of Temple Bar and the nearby Inns of Court where judges, barristers, and silks wandered the courts and chambers in their robes. Then the printing shops, churches, inns, and coffee houses in Fleet Street. Ahead, Guy's carriage turned into Bridge Street, where a motley crowd overflowed the pavements. "Could they be heading for the river?" she yelled.

"Looks like it," Pete yelled back.

A group of sailors gathered in a pool of lamplight to eye a pair of well-dressed gentlemen intent on some evening's entertainment.

As Guy's carriage turned into Earl Street toward Puddle Dock, they barely avoided a cat streaking across the road. They stopped outside a warehouse, only feet from the moss-covered steps leading down to where a sea of masts swayed on the Thames. Boatmen rowed passengers over the river during the day, but it was now deserted but for one lantern lit wherry winking out on the river.

"Smokey business," Pete muttered. "Best we stop 'ere." He pulled up the horse at the top of the lane, beside a pen filled with ducks and fowl settling for the night.

Hetty covered her nose at the stench of manure mingling with sea-coal smoke. Fingers of mist rose from the water and curled around them while clouds shrouded the moon in a ghostly haze. Muffled by the mist, it was deathly quiet but for the creak of boats rocking on the swell.

In the poor light, Hetty jumped down onto the sandy gravel in time to see two vague shapes enter the building. She whirled around with the hope of finding Lord Strathairn coming behind them, but the lane was empty.

She shuddered as a rat scuttled across the ground intent on its own pursuits. "You can leave me here, Pete."

"You shouldna go after 'em, miss," Pete said. He removed his hat to scratch his head. "Don't like the looks of this 'ere place at all. They might be ark pirates, being so close to the river as they are."

"What are ark pirates?"

"Those who rob an' plunder on the river, miss. Anyways, there's something smoky goin' on behind that door."

"Go, if you'd rather." She reached into her pocket and drew out some coins for him, dismayed at how much her hand shook.

"Hold on a bit," Pete said, deep furrows forming in his brow in the light from the lantern he held. "I didna say I'd leave, did I? You might be a bit dicked in the nob, but you ain't short of pluck, and I ain't about to cast you to the birds of a feather in that there place. I'll stay 'til your friends show up, that I will."

Relieved, she smiled gratefully at him. "Thank you, Pete. I'll go and see if I can hear what's being said."

"Not sure you should, but you be careful, miss."

"I will."

She picked her way down the lane toward the warehouse, edging around a stinking and rotting animal corpse on the ground. The mist thickened, extinguishing all light. She faltered, unable to see the way. Distant sounds reached her, echoing through the fog. Was it a carriage? She stood still, unsure whether to return to the hackney. Had Pete decided to leave after all? Moving closer, light flickered around an ill-fitting door at the side of the warehouse. She crept forward and placed an eye to the crack. She could make out only blurred movement in the flickering candlelight and the indistinct hum of voices. Frustrated, she hesitated. Should she go and find Lord Strathairn?

An arm around her waist pulled her backward off her feet. A smothering hand covered her mouth and nose, clamping down on her scream.

GUY WAS CONVINCED they'd lost Strathairn when he and Forney left by the rear of the hotel. He looked around the bare candlelit warehouse at the dozen men who stood to greet him. They had been sitting at a table drinking brandy. Heavy curved wooden ribs marched across the ceiling like the inside of a whale's belly. An anchor propped against a wall alongside a pile of fishing nets. The strong smell of rotten fish lingered in the air.

"Please take off your coat, baron," Forney said, hanging his on a peg near the door.

Guy did the same, ruing the fact that his new gun was in the pocket. He fought to appear calm as he greeted each man around the table. So far, none had questioned his authenticity. Whenever a man eyed him, however, saliva dried in his mouth and his heart banged against his ribs. Despite John's instruction, he was poorly prepared for this dangerous gamble. One question could strip him bare.

The last man in the room to be introduced was a Monsieur Delany, a short, dark-haired man with shifty brown eyes.

Delany leaned forward and shook Guy's hand. "Baron, it's good to see you again. We met that memorable night before Napoleon escaped from Elba."

Every muscle in his body tense, Guy forced himself to smile and speak warmly. "*Oui*. It is good to see you again, Delany."

"Your contribution to Napoleon's escape was the result of great cunning," Delany said.

Away from the halo of light cast by the candles on the table the rest of the room lay in shadow. Guy stepped back and turned his head to hide the absence of a scar. When had Vincent been wounded? Did these men know of it?

"We are eager for you to lend your astute advice to this new plan, Baron."

"I am eager to do so."

Forney handed him a glass of French brandy. "Raise your glasses, gentlemen. We toast our future success."

Guy tossed back the liquor and welcomed the burn sliding down his tight throat.

"I've thought long and hard about where we strike, and when," Forney said. "We must learn from mistakes of the past. If Fawkes had been better prepared, King James, his family, and the aristos would be no more."

"That was because the schemer Francis Tresham gave them away!" Delany said, his gaze around the room ferocious.

Forney rubbed at the deep grooves on his forehead. "Today, it is even more difficult, for the palace is searched by the yeomen of the guard before every state opening of parliament. We need the element of surprise like the successful assassination of Spencer Perceval in the lobby of the House of Commons."

"I vote we assassinate the cabinet when they're all together and establish a Committee of Public Safety to oversee a radical revolution," said the Frenchman, Robillard.

"I should think many would thank us if we shot Liverpool," offered Diprose, a fair-haired Englishman.

A ripple of amusement passed through the room.

"Which is why we won't," Forney said. He took Guy's arm and pulled him into the light. "Baron, I want you to take charge of this mission. I place our future success in your hands."

"I would be honored," Guy said. With growing dread, he stepped up to the table where detailed diagrams of a possible assassination plot were spread out over the surface. These men were not so amateurish after all. Details of the route taken by a carriage down Pall Mall, with times and access routes marked. Who would be where and what role they would take, was carefully detailed. Was it to be the Regent? And might it be a credible plan? He rose from studying them and caught sight of Delany staring at him with a puzzled expression. "Who is our target then, Forney?"

"Princess Charlotte," the count said.

"The princess?" Guy suppressed a shudder. They were fanatical, and very dangerous because they did not care what risks they took.

"As she recently announced she is with child, we need to act now. Her death removes the only heir to the throne before she gives birth. The public see her as a sign of hope, a contrast to her unpopular father and her mad grandfather. Her death will further destabilize the Regent. The princess is popular. Her death will throw England into deep mourning. The best time to strike is when she goes to church."

Guy struggled to keep his horror from registering on his face. He leaned over the detailed plan, then shook his head. "I don't like it."

Forney's eyebrows shot up. "Why not, Baron?"

"Because Napoleon wouldn't. You must know that he counts on Princess Charlotte to help secure his release. She is sympathetic about his exile because of her distress for her mother, so badly treated by the English. Such an act would put the authorities on the alert, which won't help our cause to free the general. We can do better than this. Let's not rush in where angels fear to tread. Give me twenty-four hours and I'll come up with a better plan."

"But that is the genius of it," Forney said. "Bonaparte is mistaken to look to the princess for help. He won't get it. If we act on this, the English aren't so likely to suspect Napoleonic sympathizers when searching for the culprit."

Guy's fingers itched to pummel the man to the ground. "You would condemn Napoleon to exile by removing his last shred of hope. He would be very angry indeed. I'd hate to be the one to tell him."

"Yes, there's that to consider," said Jackman, a tall thin Englishman. The rest murmured their agreement. "There's no saying the princess will survive childbirth. A better choice would be the Regent."

"That was recently attempted. The Regent's carriage windows were broken." The other Englishman called Simmons, pushed himself forward. "It could have been a gunshot, although no further evidence was found. But now Lord Liverpool's government has reacted with force. The Habeas Corpus Act has been suspended, and anybody under the merest suspicion of conspiracy can be thrown into Newgate and kept there."

The majority in the room voted against the murder of the princess or the regent. Relieved, Guy released a breath, only to stiffen when Forney spoke again. "I have also considered Lord Bathurst, Secretary for War, and the Colonies. He would be a cruel loss to the government."

"Mm. An excellent idea. Give me those twenty-four hours. I'll come up with a fail-proof plan," Guy repeated.

"Every hour we delay makes it more dangerous," Diprose said, stalking up and down. "Whitehall will get wind of it."

"Still, we can't go off half-cocked." Forney folded his arms. "Baron, you have your twenty-four hours. Once the new plan is formulated, we will act."

As they moved toward the door, it opened. A burly man entered with a young lad struggling in his arms. "See what I found lurking outside."

Forney glared. "A stable boy, Smith?"

Smith eyed the boy's chest. "This boy has a fine pair of cat's heads!" He whipped the lad's hat off, and red locks fell to cover her shoulders.

Forney's mouth dropped open. "*Qui est-elle?*"

Guy groaned inwardly as he met Hetty's frightened gaze.

Chapter Twenty-Five

S MITH'S HANDS CUT painfully into Hetty's arms. She opened her
mouth to speak but snapped it shut when Guy's warning gaze
locked with hers. An overdressed Frenchman stalked before her, his
arms behind his back. "Dressed as a stable boy? What game are you
playing, mademoiselle?"

Hetty raised her chin, praying it didn't wobble and struggled to
shake herself loose from Smith's grip. "I followed my betrothed here. I
believe he planned to betray me with another woman."

"Your betrothed?" The Frenchman's heavy brow cleared. "You are
the baron's *fiancée*?"

"I am. Even if he does not wish to admit it." She cast Guy an in-
dignant glance.

Guy stepped forward. "The lady is correct, Forney. I am rendered
almost silent with rage, Miss Cavendish. To follow me! *Mon dieu!* And
dressed like that. Go home immediately!"

Whatever was occurring here, Hetty's presence would not help
Guy. Strathairn was the man to assist him. She was quite happy to
leave if only Smith's ham-like hands would release her. She gazed
down at her filthy stockinged feet, numb with damp and cold. Where
were her shoes? That ruffian had pulled her right out of them. From
the first she hadn't wanted to take part in this escapade. And now, if
she and Guy escaped with their lives, she doubted he would ever speak
to her again.

But first, they must find some way out of this dire situation.

"Please fetch my shoes, my good man," she said, determined they didn't see how afraid she was. "As Lord Fortescue merely attends to a matter of business, and not a lady, I'll be on my way."

The men laughed.

"Will you, mademoiselle?" Forney asked, his gaze unsettling her.

"Miss Cavendish is a little foolish, gentlemen," Guy said. "You know how women are. They lack sense." He laughed. "She won't be of any bother to us."

Hetty stamped her foot then grimaced. "Well, really, Lord Fortescue! What a bore you've become, to be sure." She twisted around causing Smith to drop his hands. "My *shoes*, if you please."

"*Oui*, get the lady's shoes, Smith," Forney said. "We don't want to leave anything to chance."

Smith nodded and left the room.

"It might be prudent to detain Miss Cavendish until our work is done," Delany said. "Don't you agree, Baron?"

"I must insist on a private word with my fiancée. This is a delicate matter; her father is a wealthy man with powerful friends. I should prefer not to annoy him. I'm sure you understand."

Delany took a step closer to Guy. "While I understand your reason behind this betrothal, Baron, in the circumstances, I cannot keep your secret. You must understand."

Guy turned to stare at him. "*Pardon?*"

"Your marriage. Your French bride, the baroness."

"You have a... wife?" Hetty's knees went from under her. The burly fellow reappeared with her smelly shoes in his beefy hands. He grabbed her by the elbow and pushed her onto a chair. Was this Vincent's wife they spoke of? But he was not Baron Fortescue. Surely Guy hadn't married and failed to tell her? What was he doing here with these bad men? Was he working for Strathairn, or was the earl after him? No! Genevieve would have told her, and she could never believe such a thing of Guy. She just wished she understood. Sagging with exhaustion, she blinked away the tears threatening to blind her. She attempted to put the shoes on, but the stuffing in the toes had gone, and they fell off again.

"Damn you, Delany." Guy glared at him. "I planned to make a haven for myself in England, where I can operate without fear of discovery."

"I'm sorry, Baron," Delany drawled. "You should take better care of your women. Eugène, Baroness Fortescue, would be outraged." He gave an exaggerated shiver. "You should fear a knife in your back if you ever return to France."

Guy shrugged. *"Encore Je suis embarrassé."*

When Guy refused to look at her, Hetty leapt up from the chair. "I embarrass you? I demand you take me home." She swallowed a sob. "I wish never to set eyes on you again."

"If you intend to retain your cover, Baron, I suggest we deal with Miss Cavendish," Forney said coolly. "We are conveniently placed close to the river. Let the fishes remove the thorn in your side."

Horrified, Hetty gasped.

"That would be madness, Forney." Guy stepped closer to her. "You'll have Bow Street down upon us in a minute. Her father is a friend of the Prince of Wales. The search would be directed at me."

"Close to the Regent, eh?" Forney studied Hetty and nodded.

"But this girl has come here alone, dressed as the lowest of servants. Her father would have no notion of her direction," Delany argued.

"If you take such action, you can count me out of any further plans," Guy said.

"I believe you are fond of the girl," Delany said, with an unsympathetic grin.

Guy cocked an eyebrow. "Is that a crime, Delany?"

"It is if it weakens you, as I see it has."

Guy's hands curled into fists. He took a step toward the man he'd called Delaney. "I should like a chance to show you how weak I am."

Delany stared. He snatched up a candle from the table and thrust it close to Guy's face. "Where is your scar, Baron?"

"What scar?" Forney and the other men crowded around.

"The baron had a scar on his cheek. It went from below the eye almost to the chin," Delany said. "This man is an imposter."

"*Sacré bleu!*" Forney cried. "Could this be true?"

"Delany lies. I never had such a scar," Guy said. "I believe he is the charlatan here."

"The baron I met had a scar." Delany appealed to the men in the room. "He suffered the wound fighting alongside Napoleon. I swear it!"

Forney stood, his gaze fixed on Guy.

"Kill the carroty-patted harridan. Kill them both I say," the tall thin Englishman said, his clipped voice chillingly unemotional, his eyes like pale blue ice.

"My hair isn't red," Hetty whispered. What had she done? Oh, what had she done!

"Ridiculous! Who else might he be if not the baron we have urgent need of?" Forney said. "He has already uncovered a serious fault in our plan."

"I am the man Napoleon called *La Renard!*" Guy strode around the room looking every inch a dangerous spy. "Why do you doubt it?"

The tall Englishman nodded. "The Fox! The baron must be he. How would he know this otherwise?"

Delany scowled. "I tell you he had a scar."

"I need time to think," Forney said. "To be sure."

Delany pointed at Hetty. "Let him prove his loyalty. The woman must die tonight."

"I need to prove nothing," Guy said coldly. "But I can withdraw my support to your plans. See how well you do without me."

"Shall we put it to the vote?" Delany asked.

"*Oui.*" Forney handed the big man a pistol. "Watch them both, Smith."

The men retired to the end of the room and spoke in low voices.

Guy's arm stole around her. She straightened her back, desperate not to give in to the urge to collapse against him. "When I tell you, run for the door," he whispered in her ear.

"Get away from her." Smith shoved the pistol into Guy's side.

Hetty tried to quell her shaking. She did not want to leave him, French wife or no. But knew she must. Her presence here only complicated it for Guy.

The men began to argue in loud voices, their ranks split by indecision. Forney asked for time to prove Delany's theory. "If truth be told, the baron is more important than you, Delany," the other, shorter Englishman said in a threatening tone.

Delany cursed and leapt at him.

"Stop this at once," Forney cried as the men struggled to keep the two apart. "We must keep cool heads."

Smith became distracted by the fight at the end of the room, and his pistol wavered.

"Run, Hetty," Guy hissed. He leaped forward and administered a lightning kick to the gun in Smith's hand. It clattered away over the floor.

Hetty stumbled to the door, leaving her shoes behind. She hauled it open. It banged behind her as she ran blindly into the dark, straight into the solid body of another ruffian.

A pistol shot echoed behind her. "Guy!" she cried with a sob. Strong hands picked her up and shoved her aside as several men rushed past her, kicking down the door.

"Get right away from here Miss Cavendish!" There was a lethal note in Strathairn's quiet voice.

Hetty ran, stubbing her toe, her hand against the rough wall as she felt her way toward the glow of carriage lanterns at the top of the lane.

The hackney was empty, the horse eating from a nose bag.

"Pete?" she rasped, staring around her.

Pete emerged from behind the vehicle, adjusting his breeches. "I'm mighty glad to see you, miss." He paused and eyed her askance. "Although I don't much want those feet of yours on me floor, that I don't."

She looked down. Something revolting had attached itself to her stocking. "I'm frightened. I think my fiancé has been shot." She yanked the wretched stockings off.

"Best you climb inside, miss." Pete exhibited admirable calm as he took her arm and gently coaxed her toward the step. "You look done in, you do."

She climbed into the carriage and sagged against the squabs, her gaze fixed on the halo of light radiating from the open warehouse door.

"After you'd gone, I planned to go in search of the runners, miss," Pete explained. "But I needn't have. There was a dozen of 'em right here."

"Thank you, Pete. You're a good man," Hetty said with a gulp. "The Prince of Wales should give you a medal."

Pete grinned. "Zounds!"

Like a ghost, a stranger emerged from the darkness. "Take the lady home, jarvie."

"Right you are, sir."

"But I need to wait." Hetty pleaded. "Guy—"

"Someone will send word." The darkness swallowed him up again.

"Walk on." Pete slapped the reins and moved the horse on as she searched the dark for a glimpse of Guy. Shadows danced in the candlelight spilling over the road from the open warehouse door, the shapes impossible to discern.

"You'd best tell me where you live, miss," Pete called.

Hetty shuddered and sucked in air. "King Street, Mayfair, thank you, Pete." As they entered Fleet Street, the clocks chimed one. Would her father wait up for her? Her chest grew so tight she found it difficult to breathe.

"Glad to see you 'ome safe, miss," Pete said after he'd pulled up his horse in King Street.

Hetty piled coins into his hand. "I wish I had more money to give you, Pete. I am so grateful to you for your help tonight."

"Can't says I know what all that was about," Pete said, removing his cap and rubbing his head. "But all's well that ends that way."

But was it? Was Guy safe and well?

Candlelight shone out from the downstairs windows as she entered the gate. The door was unlocked, so she slipped inside, hoping to scurry upstairs unseen.

Her father stalked into the hall. His mouth dropped open, and his ears reddened. "Horatia!" he bellowed. "What is the meaning of this? Why are you dressed this way?"

A hysterical giggle rose to block her throat. "Might we talk in the parlor, Papa?" She wished she could shed the smelly clothes but knew he would not be inclined to wait for her to do so.

He clamped his lips into a thin line. "The servants have retired, and you shall not walk on the parlor carpet. Come to my bedchamber."

Her father tossed her a towel to wipe her feet before she entered. She stood on the mat before the fire, conscious of the stink rising from her breeches and her filthy feet, her hands tightly clasped in front of her. She longed to sit, but hadn't been invited to, and she didn't want to add spoiling her aunt's chair covered in a maroon printed fabric to her lengthy list of wrongdoings. "Even though there's much I don't know, I'm afraid what I can tell you will take some time."

Her father removed his handkerchief from his pocket and laid it on a chair. "For heaven's sake, sit, child. Then please explain yourself. I can think of no earthly reason for your behavior."

He had not called her "child" for many a year. Would he ever trust her again?

She took a deep breath. "It all began when I took The General for a ride—"

"You rode The General?" he roared.

She perched on the edge of the chair. "Papa," she rasped, as her throat ached for water, "if you interrupt me after every sentence, we shall be here until morning."

He gave her a look that would have made many a soldier quiver from head to toe, which produced its desired effect on her. "As I was saying, while riding The General, I came across Guy unconscious on the road—"

Her father made a choking sound and waved at her to continue.

By the time she'd covered most of what occurred during this evening's debacle, her father's face had gone through several color changes varying from white to puce.

There was a long pause while he struggled to control his temper, and when he spoke, his voice didn't sound like his own. "I must say I doubted my sister's ability from the first. She is far too wrapped up in her own pursuits to be the right chaperone for a spirited girl like you. But I did trust Fortescue to take good care of you in my absence. I can see I asked too much of him. It seems it was too much for any man. But I never expected you to be so rash in your judgment, or to lie to me."

"I'm sorry, Papa," she said in a small voice.

"And I must say, I am disappointed in the baron for encouraging such behavior."

"But he didn't. Guy is a brave man. He endangered his life working for the government." Might he have a wife? Tears filled her eyes. "I hope he's not hurt. I'm not sure what happened. I heard a shot."

Her father jerked forward on his chair. "There were shots fired? *Dear God.* I quake at the idea of you in such danger."

She sniffed and wiped her nose with the back of her grimy hand. "We'll learn more tomorrow."

His nostrils quivered. "Go to bed, Horatia. I shall tell you what I've decided in the morning, when I've had time to think on it."

"I'm sorry, Papa," Hetty said again. There was nothing more she could say. She rose and picked up the handkerchief, offering it to him. He shook his head with distaste. Blinded by tears, she hurried to her bedchamber. She had never been so alone. It seemed her life in London had come crashing down around her ears. Digswell, with its church fetes and afternoon teas, lurked dismally in her future.

GUY WATCHED WITH relief as John and his cronies rounded up the conspirators. Delaney spat at Guy and cursed him as the men were dragged outside. Guy kept his pistol aimed on the hunched figure of Smith, who groaned and clutched his wounded shoulder as he joined the rest of the conspirators in the wagon on their way to the cells in Bow Street.

John appeared at Guy's side. "Forney's gone missing–out through a back door. My men are searching for him, but it appears he had a boat waiting. I'll get the Thames River police onto it."

Guy grabbed John's arm. "Did Hetty get away safely?"

"Yes, you need not worry on that score."

"Damn it! How did she come to be here?" Guy would never forget the shock of seeing Hetty dangling from the thug's brawny arms.

"She and the duchess were shadowing you," John said.

"My sister, too! *Mon dieu!* Where is she now?"

"We had a difficult time convincing Her Grace to go home. In the end, one of my men took her to Portland Square in a hackney." A reluctant grin stretched John's mouth. "She was dressed like a solicitor's clerk from Lincoln's Inn."

"Couldn't you have stopped Hetty from getting mixed up in this? They almost threw her in the river," Guy said angrily. "You lot cut it as fine as the hairs on a gnat's bollock."

"I'm very sorry, my friend." John shook his head. "Some of these men have influence. We needed enough proof against them to put them away permanently, and things got out of control very fast. Don't blame Miss Cavendish or your sister too much. They acted without delay, to alert us to your exit by the back lane."

"Did they indeed?"

John nodded. "And Miss Cavendish kept on your tail. She'd make a damn good spy."

Guy scowled as he climbed into the carriage beside Strathairn. "So, you and your cronies lost sight of me, John?"

"There'd be the devil to pay if we did, Guy. We had no intention of it. Several of our men followed you. You could not have escaped us."

Guy huffed out a tired laugh. "No sense in telling Hetty that."

"Might be wise not to reveal all of it. I fear it might encourage her, should you wish to continue to work for us?"

"No chance of that." Guy grimaced. "Hetty will be in a terrible fix though when she arrives home in that state. Her aunt will be livid."

"You'll have to put things right."

Guy frowned. "Can you drop me off in King Street?"

"I'll be pleased to. We'll discuss this evening's events later."

When they arrived outside her aunt's townhouse, it was in darkness apart from one lighted window upstairs. "She may have been able to sneak in unobserved. I won't be thanked for knocking on the door. I'll go first thing in the morning. I'm for a bath, a Cognac, and a few hours' rest."

John stretched out his legs and sighed. "An excellent idea."

Knowing Hetty was safe, Guy enjoyed being back in the luxurious surroundings of John's home. He lay back in the bath in his chamber and let the warm water soothe his tight muscles. Might this business be at an end? They must capture the French count, but even if they failed, he was now alone, his web of spies in prison awaiting trial. While Hobson fussed around him, Guy's thoughts returned to Hetty. He admired her spirit and her quick thinking, but her rashness worried him. Once married, it seemed his life would continue its unpredictable course. He was more than ready for a quiet life. She had only leapt to his defense. And though he loved her, he worried that he might not be able to give her the life she craved. He didn't want to crush her spirit. She had been unhappy in Digswell. Water mixed with blood as he stepped from the bath into the towel his valet held for him.

Hobson peered at him. "Why, my lord, you have a fresh wound in your side."

"It's just a scratch, Hobson. But you may dress it for me."

When he and Smith had grappled for the pistol, it fired. The bullet struck Smith in the shoulder. Guy had attempted to staunch the flow of blood gushing from Smith's wound with his handkerchief. Unfortunately, the big bounder had pulled a knife and slashed clean through Guy's waistcoat and shirt, the blade finding his ribs.

Hobson shook his head. "Might need a couple of stitches, my lord."

"I doubt it, Hobson. It's not deep. Please wrap a bandage around it. Then I'm for bed."

Chapter Twenty-Six

THE NEXT MORNING, she dressed carefully in a white muslin morning gown and entered the breakfast room, heavy-eyed from little sleep. She resisted rubbing her eyes and seated herself at the table. Her father put down the newspaper. "I intend to return home after luncheon."

She straightened and eyed him cautiously. "Oh, will you? I'm sorry your visit has been so brief and so—"

His chest swelled with indignation. "You are to return to Digswell with me, Horatia. I have no intention of leaving you here. London is a den of iniquity. It is a miracle you were not hurt or worse. I shall not trust to luck that you'll remain so."

His tone softened when he saw tears gather at the corners of her eyes. "My concern is for your safety, my dear. I could not endure it if you died before me."

"Guy and I planned to wed soon. If he's..." She fought a fervent desire to dissolve into hysterics.

"I also need to think about your wedding, Horatia. I was pleased when the baron offered for you. But now I see there was some ulterior motive. That you have been supporting him in some dangerous endeavor."

"Yes, but all that has changed. We love each another, Papa." She wished she was able to inject some enthusiasm into her voice, but she wasn't entirely sure that Guy still felt the same way, and the mention of a wife still hovered in her mind. She needed him to come and reassure her that it wasn't true, and nothing had changed.

"I've sent a note off to Eustace. I wish to discuss this matter with him."

Her hands clenched in her lap. "Yes, Papa."

It appeared that, at this moment, Eustace was the only ally she had, and she hoped he might persuade her father to allow her to remain here. She would not leave until she'd heard from Guy. Was he hurt? Was there already a baroness in France? So many unanswered questions filled her mind, she feared it was in danger of exploding.

"And there's this matter of a Truesdale being buried in a rather rushed manner in the Fortescue crypt. I wasn't aware that the baron had any relatives living in England."

"It was Guy's twin brother, Vincent. He'd just arrived from France when he had an accident. He fell down the stairs at Rosecroft Hall."

"How tragic! Everyone was speaking of it in the village."

It was fortunate that Lady Kemble was away from Digswell, for she would have made it her business to uncover the truth.

"So, Guy is now in mourning, poor fellow, and may not wish to marry so soon." He pushed back his chair. "You need to eat a good breakfast, Hetty. Everything will seem brighter on a full stomach."

Left alone at the table, Hetty pushed buttered eggs around her plate. She couldn't eat it if her life depended on it.

"Perhaps some toast, Miss Hetty?" Sarah asked as she poured Hetty another cup of tea.

"Yes, thank you Sarah. And thank you for doing my hair so nicely."

"It's my pleasure. Such lovely hair you have."

Hetty nodded with a vague smile. That awful villain called her a carroty-patted harridan, last night, when she feared for her life. The milkman's son had once told her that witches had red hair. "If a witch puts a spell on you," he went on to explain, "the only way to remove it is to take an item of clothing which is worn close to the witch's skin and burn it in the place where she was born." He annoyed her so much Hetty threatened to put a spell on him.

The color of her hair would never concern her again. She sniffed.

As long as Guy liked it. Guy! A tremor passed through her. She would not relax until she saw his dear face again and knew that he was all right.

GUY WOKE AND groaned. He felt as if he'd been trampled underfoot by a herd of cattle. Then the night's disastrous dealings came back to him, along with the pain in his side. The wound appeared to be deeper than he'd first thought and bled in the night.

After breakfast, he visited a physician who put in several stitches and bandaged the wound again, warning him to rest. "You were lucky, sir, an inch deeper..." He shook his head.

Guy shrugged painfully into his coat. A knife wound didn't bother him overmuch, but he shuddered when he recalled how close Hetty came to being thrown into the Thames. And his sister, too, who behaved with such bravery he wasn't sure whether to scold her or embrace her. He would call on her later this afternoon. With all that had been going on since she'd arrived in London, he'd had very little time to enjoy having her with him again. She was his one connection to that happy time in France before everything came to such a brutal end.

On the way to King Street, he reflected soberly on the whirlwind months since he'd come to England. Vincent's reappearance and subsequent death left him bitter with disappointment and sadness. Eustace's distrust of him rankled, and he'd been bailed up by footpads, shot at by highwaymen, and thrown into a den of mad conspirators, escaping by the skin of his teeth. Any desire for excitement had vanished, and at this moment, it seemed entirely possible it would never return.

His nerves stretched thin, he longed for a quiet life at Rosecroft Hall. There was so much there he looked forward to getting started with, and he didn't wish to spend another season in London anytime soon. The grouse shoot and some hunting would provide ample excitement.

He wasn't sure how much Hetty's father and Aunt Emily knew. If they'd been told, they would be justifiably angry having put their trust in him. It would require great diplomacy to put things to rights.

Chapter Twenty-Seven

HETTY WAS SLUMPED in the chair toying with a piece of toast and strawberry jam when her aunt entered the breakfast room. "Try to eat a little more, Hetty. Cook says you sent back the buttered eggs untouched."

Hetty shook her head. "I won't, thank you, Aunt. I seem to have lost my appetite. Are you angry with me, too?"

"I'm dismayed, my dear. I have not been vigilant enough. And I believe your ardent nature has led you astray."

"I hope Guy is all right," Hetty whispered. "It was dreadful, Aunt."

"Your father told me very little about what happened last night. I'm not sure I wish to learn the whole."

Hetty firmed her lips. It wasn't fair to draw her aunt into this when all she wanted was a quiet life. It occurred to Hetty that Aunt Emily would never have fought for her lover. Her aunt had a gentle nature evident in her contemplative poems, which lacked the spontaneity of Burns or the passion of Byron. Nor did she suffer Hetty's impatience, which right now made her want to hire a hackney and go to Guy.

Eustace arrived before luncheon. He hurried in with a worried expression and gave Hetty a reassuring hug before her father ushered him, along with her aunt, into the small room she called her bookroom. The three of them had been closeted there for half an hour when Genevieve appeared at the door, her eyes wide with distress. "Those men sent me home. What happened?"

"Have you heard from Guy?" Hetty asked.

"*Non!*"

With an eye on the bookroom door, Hetty drew the duchess into the parlor. She gave Genevieve a potted version of the evening's events, leaving out any mention of the pistol shot she'd heard.

Perhaps her voice had given her away, for Genevieve pursed her lips and frowned. "But *Gee*... Is he all right?"

"I hope so." Hetty cast her eyes down. "Father is taking me back to the country in a few hours. I doubt I'll be allowed to visit London again for years."

"You are betrothed to *Gee,* are you not?" A look of horror tightened the duchess's features. "Your father blames him for this?"

"No. Father is furious with me."

"*Pourquoi?*"

"He saw how I was dressed. I had to tell him."

"Oh. Then I am sorry."

"It cannot be helped." Hetty eyed her carefully. "Those men spoke of a Baroness Fortescue who lives in Paris."

She looked puzzled. "Maman died many years ago."

"No, Guy's wife."

Genevieve's eyebrows rose. "But *Gee* has no wife."

Hope took root in Hetty's breast. "Might he have married and not told you?"

Genevieve glowered. "*Non!*"

"Then perhaps she is Vincent's wife."

"Then she is *not* the baroness," Genevieve said with a fierce shake of her head. "Vincent lied to her."

Hetty had always known in her heart it couldn't be true. "She should be informed that her husband is dead."

"Gee will write to her. And I will visit the poor woman when I return to France."

At the rap on the door, the frazzled maid rushed along the passage to open it again. Hetty jumped up as her aunt emerged from the bookroom to greet the next visitor.

"Lord Fortescue!" her aunt exclaimed. Her heart racing, Hetty grinned at Genevieve, whose eyes danced with relief and anticipation. They both rushed to find Guy divesting himself of his hat and coat. He looked entirely whole, and his usual unflappable self.

Her first thought was to throw herself into his arms, but she held back. On closer inspection, he seemed reserved and rather distant. Had he not forgiven her for her interference? She wanted him to, desperately, even if they failed to marry.

Genevieve didn't suffer any such hesitation. With a flood of incomprehensible French, she gripped her brother's waistcoat and peered up at him. "I talked Hetty into following you last night, *Gee*. It was me. I brought the clothes."

Guy winced and eased her away. "That was rash of you, Genevieve."

Hetty saw the pain in his eyes. "Guy! You're hurt," she cried.

Before Guy could respond, Hetty's father and Eustace entered the parlor.

"Might I have a word, my lord?" her father asked.

Hetty's rush toward the bookroom was abruptly halted when her father held up his hand. "Alone!"

Hetty wished she could place her ear against the library door, but with Genevieve and Eustace beside her, she was forced to remain in her seat.

She suspected that when Genevieve put her mind to it, she could charm any male living. She sat beside Eustace and patted his hand while sympathizing with him about his gout in her Gallic manner. Eustace, who was on close speaking terms with the Regent no less, was flushed with a foolish smile.

At least the problem of Guy's claim to the title had been put to rest with Genevieve's arrival, Hetty thought, turning back to the library door. Her aunt had gone to consult the cook, expressing the notion that when everyone had said their piece, they would be hungry.

DISAPPOINTMENT WAS WRIT large on Colonel Cavendish's face. Closeted in a room piled high with tomes, he was at pains to express his displeasure without offending Guy.

"I must apologize for what occurred, Colonel," Guy said. "It was not my intention to involve your daughter."

"I depended on my sister to take care of Horatia in my absence." Cavendish shook his head. "I would never have allowed her to come to London had I known she would be placed in such danger."

"I quite agree with you," Guy said wearily. "But Horatia is quite spirited."

The colonel grimaced. "Too true, my lord. I can hardly blame my sister, or indeed you, can I, when Horatia rode my stallion around the countryside without my knowledge? And goodness knows what else."

Guy moved painfully on the seat as the gash over his ribs throbbed. A good thing that Hetty's father didn't know the whole of it.

The colonel's fingers formed a steeple. "I wish to offer my condolences on the death of your brother. A tragic affair."

Guy nodded. "I would like to discuss it further with you, Colonel. But not now, you understand."

"But of course. Horatia mentioned some special mission for the government. I trust that is at an end?"

"My involvement certainly."

"Good. Mr. Fennimore had expressed some doubt as to your claim to the title. I'm pleased that business is also now settled, as I'm sure you must be."

"I'm eager to put my estates in order," Guy said.

"Excellent. Quite right. Horatia is returning to Digswell with me today as Mrs. Illingworth and I are to marry in a week."

"Congratulations to you both, sir," Guy said.

Colonel Cavendish climbed to his feet. "Horatia is anxious to speak with you. I admit to being very angry when she came home dressed in that manner last night, without even shoes on her feet. I led her to believe I opposed your marriage. I do not." He frowned. "She is impulsive, but a good girl, of whom I remain very proud. You must begin the way you wish to go forward, Baron. Lay down some rules."

"I couldn't have put it better myself, Colonel," Guy said, shaking the Colonel's hand. He suddenly felt lighter. He didn't want a marriage governed by rules, but he and Hetty did need to talk.

Chapter Twenty-Eight

THE BOOKROOM DOOR opened, and her father emerged, followed by Guy. He looked serious and very pale. Hetty leapt to her feet. Guy took her by the hand. "I must speak with you." With a nod to the others in the room, he drew her into the empty bookroom and shut the door.

His dark eyebrows beetled. "Do you realize how dangerous it was for you to become involved in this affair? And after I asked you never to do it again."

"I do." Hetty blinked as his angry gaze sliced into her. "I don't think you're about to thank me for it," she said, attempting a little humor.

It didn't work.

"Promise me that you will *never* to do anything like that again."

"To be honest, I've had quite enough excitement of late—"

"Promise me." He tipped up her chin and searched her eyes.

"I promise," Hetty said, and her lashes swept down, to hide her absolute relief to find him alive and relatively unscathed.

"Good. Come and sit down."

Seated beside him on the small sofa, she inspected him. His features looked finely drawn, making him appear even more elegant and devastating. He moved awkwardly as if in pain. She had a strong urge to hug him, mother him, make love to him. The force of her feelings turned her breath to a deep sigh. "Did that brigand, Smith, shoot you?"

"No, he did not."

"But you are hurt."

"A mere graze."

"I can see the pain in your eyes, and your jaw is working. You do that when you're distressed."

"Of course, I'm distressed, Hetty. I don't want a wife who goes off half-cocked at every little thing."

She huffed at the unfairness of it, but she would not cast the blame at Genevieve. Except for the smelly disguise, she had been eager to join her. "I didn't go off half-cocked, as you put it. But I have no desire to take such risks again."

"You will accuse me of being overly protective. But I am not about to apologize for it."

"You have no need to worry," she said, tracing a finger over his tense jaw. If Guy was ever in trouble again, how could she keep such a promise? But there was no sense in telling him now. She prayed there would never be a need for her to break it.

One heavy brow slanted in disapproval. "Don't make the mistake you can fool me, Hetty." He framed her face with his hands and planted a hard kiss on her mouth.

"I'm glad that's settled," she said with a sigh, and leaned her head against his shoulder.

"There's another thing. And this is most important. I want you to understand what marriage to me will be like. In the future, I'll need to travel to inspect my other properties and take my place in the House of Lords. And then, we will attend the London season. But for now, I wish to remain in Digswell."

Guy was too honorable ever to cry off, but did he still want to marry her? Or had she driven him away by going off half-cocked as he put it? Distress tightened her rib cage. "Papa insists on me going home with him today."

He nodded. "To attend his wedding."

"And afterward?" she asked, needing him to say the words.

"We shall marry as soon as possible." A smile lingered on his lips. "I find myself becoming very impatient, Hetty."

Her breath quickened as she looked into his hot blue eyes. "Oh, yes, Guy."

Guy eyed her carefully. "I shall purchase a special license from Doctor's Commons and visit St. Georges to set the date."

Hetty grew hot. A poker seemed to have lodged in her spine. Her fear that she would become the subject of drawing rooms and be snubbed was bad enough, but not at her wedding. "Very well."

His dark eyebrows rose. "You're happy to be married in London?"

A baron should marry at St. Georges, Hetty knew. "I am, it's just that, it will be such a big affair and will take much organizing, then be weeks away." She glanced at the black armband he wore, feeling he might prefer a quieter ceremony in the little Digswell church. "Of course, I want it, if you do, Guy."

"Perhaps in the circumstances we should marry in Digswell," Guy said, a smile tugging at his lips.

Relief threaded through her. "Oh yes. Perhaps we should."

Guy laughed and slipped an arm around her waist, pulling her against him. "As we both reside in Digswell, the banns can be read next Sunday. As soon as your father returns from his honeymoon, we shall marry."

Her aunt knocked on the door. "Luncheon will be served directly."

Hetty sighed. Now that her aunt had decided to be an assiduous chaperone, Hetty felt like a rabbit being watched by a hawk. "We are to marry in Digswell, Aunt."

"That is good news. I shall have to consult my fashion magazines. I wonder what brides are wearing this season?" Aunt Emily disappeared again.

Hetty met Guy's gaze and laughed.

EUSTACE TOOK GUY aside. "I'm sorry we got off to such a bad start."

"You were right to be cautious," Guy said, not wishing to stir the waters, although the man's ungenerous attitude toward him still rankled.

"And I'm aware of your disappointment concerning the condition of the hall."

"I've become more aware of the problems here in England," Guy said, striving for diplomacy.

Eustace shuffled his feet and refused to meet Guy's eyes. There was not going to be an explanation or a sincere apology. He obviously struggled to come to face his culpability. "I will leave Rosecroft after I attend your wedding."

Guy had a grudging sympathy for him. It couldn't be easy to leave the home he'd lived in for the last thirty-odd years. "You are family and will always be welcome under my roof, Eustace, as I've been at pains to tell you."

Eustace's lips firmed in a determined line. He shook his head. "Now that my health requires the constant attention of a doctor, I shall remain in London." He smiled. "You are to bring your new bride home to Rosecroft Hall, Guy. You don't need Horatia's old godfather lurking in corners."

Guy returned the smile. "But you will visit us. I know she would wish it."

"Once in a while perhaps, to visit friends. There's another thing I should mention. When a thief began stealing from the big houses in the county, I sent paintings and statuary to London for safekeeping. Some *Meissen* and *Sèvres* china, too. I will have it returned."

"*Merci.*" Guy bowed, marveling at his ability to hold his tongue. Relieved that some had survived being sold to finance Eustace's gambling debts, proved by the wagers and *iou's* he'd found in Eustace's library drawer, he decided never to utter a word of reproof. Hetty loved her godfather, and who was he to try to change it?

"Ah. I see luncheon is served," Eustace said with obvious relief as the maid opened the dining room door. "Emily tells me we're to have mulligatawny soup, a collection of breads, and salad. I confess to being rather peckish."

"I don't believe I've encountered mulligatawny soup," Guy said.

The food the English ate still had the power to surprise him.

"A recipe the colonel brought back from India and quite hearty."

Still beset by low spirits, Guy returned to find Hetty chatting with Genevieve. He narrowed his eyes at Genevieve and was given a lift of her eyebrows in response. Although he was enormously fond of her, he admitted he'd feel a little relieved when she returned to France. One recalcitrant lady in his care was enough.

Hetty rose with her sweet smile, took his arm, and they walked into the dining room together.

Chapter Twenty-Nine

ETTY'S FATHER AND Marina had left to spend their honeymoon in Bath. At Malforth Manor, the wedding guests still lingered after a splendid wedding breakfast.

Fanny promised to be Hetty's bridesmaid. Exhibiting great determination, she'd thwarted her overbearing mother's attempts to manipulate her into a marriage with a man of her choosing. Fanny was soon to wed to Mr. James Bonneville. Hetty was pleased for her. It seemed she'd begun to reveal more of her mother's forceful personality.

"Mama is furious, but once Uncle Jasper took my side, she had lost the fight," Fanny said with a laugh. "He is the head of the family and quite wealthy. With no children of his own he dotes on me."

Lady Kemble detached herself from a group of ladies and came to her daughter's side. "How very discreet, Miss Cavendish, to have kept your courtship a secret from us."

"It was a wonderful surprise to get your letter," Fanny said. "But I did notice how the baron couldn't take his eyes off you at Mother's dinner party. Even while he danced with me."

Lady Kemble frowned. "Miss Cavendish has been much in his lordship's company over the past months. She is Mr. Fennimore's goddaughter, after all." Her frown faded when Genevieve came to join them. "I confess to being quite envious of your gown, Your Grace. The splendid cut of the sleeves and the richness of three rows of embroidery around the hem are perfection."

"You are too kind, Lady Kemble," Genevieve said.

"I assume your modiste resides in Paris?"

As Genevieve and Lady Kemble discussed fashion, Fanny took Hetty's arm and drew her away. "You must forgive Mama. It is her disappointment that makes her waspish."

"Think no more of it, Fanny." Hetty watched Guy over her friend's shoulder as he talked to the vicar, at least a head taller than all the men present and by far the most handsome. Nothing could hurt her today, not even Lady Kemble's ungenerous comments. "No doubt when your mother comes to know Mr. Bonneville, she will warm to him. Where do you plan to live after you marry?"

"With Mama in Digswell for a time. James is to inherit from an elderly aunt, but at this moment, he is rather squeezed for funds."

"That means we shall see more of each other."

"Yes, won't it be wonderful?"

"Fanny? We are leaving," called Lady Kemble.

As Hetty stood at the door to say farewell to her friend, Guy came and slipped an arm around her waist. "I am returning to the hall." He kissed her cheek. "I'll see you there tomorrow."

Mortified by her laxity in London, Aunt Emily seemed determined to rectify it now. She'd become as diligent as a Spanish duenna. She insisted on accompanying Hetty to Rosecroft Hall the next day which upset Hetty's plans.

She had hoped to have a quiet talk with Guy. Everything was in readiness—the license had been obtained, the church booked, and the settlement signed. Her pin money was most generous. There was nothing to worry her specifically, and yet she did worry. Guy had been quiet since London, and she sought his reassurance.

Rosecroft Hall bustled with a horde of newly acquired servants as furnishings were replaced, others taken down to be laundered, windows polished, and carpets removed to be cleaned. Men on ladders worked in the grand hall. Gardeners toiled about the grounds weeding and pruning shrubs. Summer was drawing to a close.

Guy seemed quiet. The brilliant blue of his eyes had dimmed. She searched in vain for that devastating look he used to give her, the one that made her weak at the knees without him having to say a word. She could find no spark of humor when she gently teased him. He had not come to terms with his brother's death, and she wondered if marrying so soon was wise.

She yearned to hold him and draw him out. If he could talk about it, surely it would be better than bottling it up inside.

Hetty seized the moment when they all sat in the drawing room after luncheon. Her aunt and Genevieve engaged in conversation while Eustace nodded by the fire. "I haven't seen the rest of the house. Could you show me our bedchamber?"

He raised a dark brow at her request but climbed to his feet.

"Where are you going?" Aunt Emily called.

"Guy is showing me more of the house," Hetty said, giving her a warning look.

"I will enjoy a tour also," her aunt said in a firm tone, rising to her feet.

Genevieve followed along as the four of them toured the house.

Guy threw open a door. "Eustace has kindly vacated the blue suite. The servants have made it ready for us."

The beautiful suite was dressed in royal blue velvet, featured a huge four-poster bed. The prospect of lying in bed with Guy made her face warm. Drawing a deep breath and trying to rid herself of the scandalous image, she walked through a door to her dressing room, a generous-sized boudoir with a huge wardrobe, bureau, and a Cheval glass. An escritoire, chair, and bookcase, was placed by the window. "I shall enjoy sitting here, looking over the park." Hetty examined the dainty desk and opened each small drawer. She found an inkpot, sand container, blotter, and quills and ornate metal pens awaiting her use. "How thoughtful." She smiled up at him.

"For your writing, letters, and so forth," he said.

"Not to mention penning poems," Aunt Emily said. "Thoughtful indeed."

As her aunt and Genevieve descended the stairs, Hetty slipped her arm though Guy's. "We've missed the spring and most of the summer."

"We shall enjoy them all the more, next year," he said with a tender glance.

The love and the promise in his eyes was all she needed.

Guy would find Vincent's death hard because they were twins, Hetty decided. Genevieve didn't suffer the same sense of loss. She confessed to missing her children but remained her exuberant self, contributing much to the preparations.

Hetty was grateful for her enthusiasm and her flair. She happily granted Genevieve full rein over the decorations for the church and the great hall at Rosecroft. The wedding dress had arrived from the modiste in London to be admired by those allowed to see it.

Aunt Emily claimed the wedding breakfast as her domain and spent time discussing it with Guy's new chef. Still concerned about her troubled bridegroom, Hetty was happy to leave it to them.

Her father and Marina arrived home two days before the wedding. How fond they were of each other. Hetty was delighted that he'd married a kind and capable woman and wouldn't be alone.

The day before the wedding, her father called her into the library. "I hope you'll be as happily married as I have been, first to your mother and now to Marina."

"I know I will, Papa," Hetty said. "I love Guy very much."

"Good, my dear." The tips of his ear tinged red as he tapped out his pipe. "I can't prepare you for marriage as a mother might. Perhaps your aunt?" The flush spread to his neck. "But then, my sister is herself unmarried."

Hetty hurried to spare him. "There is no need. I am marrying a patient loving man. I'm sure I shall manage."

"Yes, yes. Of course, you will." He rose, easing his shoulders with relief. "Shall we join the others for tea?"

GUY LED HIS horse over a gate and into the fields of Rosecroft Hall as the setting sun cast shadows over the ground. After an earlier deluge, the air was redolent with earthy smells. A cold breeze touched his face. The nights had turned chilly as summer tipped into autumn. He'd arrived in England in winter full of confidence and ready to take up the mantle of a country gentleman.

So much had happened that his dreams had lost relevance in his fight to stay alive. Now he must take up those dreams once again. He would not let Vincent's memory destroy the present. Even though his brother had chosen to disregard it, a special bond existed between them. Through the years, Guy had sensed Vincent still lived. And now he knew his presence was gone from the earth.

The prospect of his life with Hetty filled him with hope. He loved her optimistic nature. Once they'd married, the world would right itself. He urged his horse into a canter and rode back to the stables. His best man, John, would arrive this evening, and he looked forward to his company. Guy valued their friendship. John had trusted him and stood by him when he had little reason to do so.

Guy's spirits lifted as he approached the house. Tomorrow was his wedding day.

Chapter Thirty

T HANKFULLY, AFTER DAYS of intermittent rain, the day dawned fine, the sky the soft blue of a duck's egg. Hetty, her stomach fluttering with nerves, stood while her aunt, Genevieve, and Molly fussed around her. Aunt Emily smoothed the boat-necked, white Indian muslin gown decorated with a band of seed pearls high under the bosom. Genevieve arranged the dainty silver and pearl tiara she had lent Hetty over her soft curls. Hetty wore her mother's pearl drop earrings and the matching pearl necklace.

They stood back to admire their creation. Genevieve clasped her hands. "*Tres magnifique!*"

Aunt Emily kissed her cheek. "You make a beautiful bride, Hetty."

Hetty stared at her reflection and smiled. "You have been wonderful, thank you." The woman in the glass, who surely wasn't her, smiled back. She dabbed on a delicate floral scent, which Genevieve had given her, and picked up the ivory fan, a gift from her aunt. She performed one last slow revolution in front of the mirror. Could this eradicate Guy's memories of her shoeless in that horrid warehouse, smelling of something indescribably awful?

The villagers and tenants who couldn't fit into the church hovered around the entrance as Hetty, on her father's arm, walked down the aisle. Fanny followed in white muslin with blue ribbons decorating her bonnet. The Digswell ladies, seated on the pews, craned their necks to take note of the gowns in the first stare of fashion. Genevieve had festooned the church with every available white, hothouse bloom, filling the air with sweet scents. The pews were decorated with silver ribbons and bunches of flowers; the like of which Digswell had never seen.

Guy, handsome in an indigo tailcoat, a jabot peeping from his waistcoat embroidered in silver thread, stood at the altar with John Strathairn in gray beside him. He turned to watch her.

Hetty joined him at the altar and her father slipped away. She thrilled to see deep appreciation in his eyes. *"Belle,"* he murmured.

"You look very handsome." She smiled up at him.

The vicar cleared his throat.

GUY GAZED AT his bride standing beside him at the altar. Her lovely mouth trembled, and her slim fingers shook slightly in his as he slipped on the ring. Their eyes met, and his heart swelled. How blessed he was. He would protect and love her for all the days the good lord allotted him.

He repeated the words that joined them in wedlock, and she responded, her love for him shining in her warm brown eyes.

After signing the register, they left the church. Guy put his arm around his bride and assisted her into the landau decorated with silver ribbons and bells. Hetty smiled at him. His gaze on her mouth, he wanted to kiss his beautiful, spirited bride.

"I'd like a kiss," she said, guessing his thoughts.

Guy obliged with a long and passionate kiss as a cry went up from the small gathering waving goodbye, and they departed for their new life at Rosecroft Hall.

"Are you all right, darling?" Hetty asked as the landau lurched and jiggled its way over the rough road.

He held her tight against him and his lips found the soft perfumed skin below her ear. "I am now."

HETTY BARELY HAD time to speak to Guy as the wedding breakfast was served. The table in the dining room was laden with silver bowls of walnuts, hazelnuts, and hothouse grapes. A rich fruit wedding cake took pride of place in the center of the table. Their marriage was toasted with champagne. When everyone had eaten their fill of hot rolls, buttered toast, cold meats, ham, and eggs, and washed it down with steaming hot chocolate, an orchestra from London struck up in the minstrel's gallery and the country dancing began.

Hetty spied Marina sitting alone while her father chatted to Eustace and sat down beside her.

Marina smiled. "You have chosen well, my dear," she said. "Guy will prove a worthy mate for you."

"I only hope I will prove worthy of him."

Marina placed a hand on Hetty's arm. "You may not have understood my meaning. You are an adventurous young woman, by all accounts. Passionate and brave from what your father has told me. I am greatly in awe of such qualities because I know I lack them."

"But you are so calm and practical," Hetty said, surprised. "Why would you wish to be different?"

"I am not unhappy. I understand the value I bring to my marriage. But you'll achieve far more in your life. My one hope is to make my husband comfortable and happy."

"Then we are one in that aim."

Marina smiled. "But you shall prove an exciting companion, Hetty. Guy is the right man to appreciate a wife such as you."

Hetty kissed her cheek. "I am so glad my father chose you." She turned to watch her new husband across the room. He had joined Eustace and her father. Was Marina, right? Would Guy wish for those qualities in her? Could she become more acquiescent? For the first time, she was unsure. With a sudden need to be close, she crossed the room to him. The next dance was a waltz, and she wanted his arms around her.

Chapter Thirty-One

JOHN WAS ONE of the first to depart, his presence required in London on official business. The sun was sinking in the west as Guy walked with him to his carriage. "No news of Forney?"

"Unfortunately, no. It appears he has left the country."

Guy nodded. "I doubt we'll see him in England again. It would be foolish in the extreme for him to return. What of Countess Forney?"

"Her travel documents reveal she has returned to France."

"A tidy end to it, then."

"It is never tidy, my friend." John grinned. "Enjoy rusticating here with your bride. I will give you two months before we see you in London again."

Guy laughed. "You believe so?"

"You displayed talent in your handling of Forney and his cronies. We may have need of you."

"*Merci*, but I think not. To live at Rosecroft with Hetty is all I wish for."

John grinned. "We shall see. Farewell." He tapped the roof with his cane, and the carriage trundled away down the drive.

Guy and Hetty saw off the rest of their guests. As they walked back over the gravel drive to the house, he turned to his bewitching bride. "Your father has given us a wedding present."

Hetty's brows rose. "He said nothing to me. What might that be?"

"The General."

With a perplexed frown, she searched Guy's eyes. "Father gave you The General? He did not include me in this gift?"

"Au contraire, The General is yours. But, it is conditional on you being careful and not jumping over high gates which is dangerous with a sidesaddle."

Hetty raised an eyebrow. "Then I promise not to use a sidesaddle."

Guy chuckled. "It would be foolish of me to expect otherwise. You'll always surprise me, my darling."

"And that bothers you?"

"No, I expect it will be very good for me."

She giggled. "Do you think Father always knew I rode him?"

"I don't know." He traced a finger over her cheek. "He admires your spirit. As I do."

"I can't believe The General is mine." She smiled. "I'll ride him every day."

"May I ride with you?"

She pouted. "To rein me in?"

Guy leaned against the doorframe and pulled her against him, enjoying her warm curves. "Never. Because I don't want to be apart from you." He sighed. "I will try not to be too protective of you, *mon amour.*"

"And I'll try never to cause you to worry." She turned in his arms to laugh up at him.

He raised his brows. "You'll try?"

She laughed. "As long as you are not unreasonable in your demands."

He patted her derrière. *"Coquine!"*

Behind them, Hammond coughed discreetly. "One of the gardeners has brought something for you, my lord."

Guy expected it to be a wedding offering of some kind, from one of the tenants or the servants, but when the butler placed the object in his hands Guy was speechless.

"He found it under a hedge he pruned on the western boundary, my lord. It must have been dislodged when the horse jumped over it."

Guy looked at Hetty. "My portmanteau!"

"How wonderful!" Hetty put her hands to her cheeks. "Is everything still there?"

Guy unlatched it and searched inside. He removed the papers bearing the Fortescue coat of arms and the certificate of his birth, travel documents, and others pertaining to his ownership of several English properties. More importantly, his fingers closed over the box containing the seal matrix, a heavily ornate ring, which he disliked wearing. It was all there.

He took a deep shuddering breath. "Thank you, Hammond. And please thank..."

"Hislop, my lord."

"Convey my sincere thanks to Hislop. Tell him I shall speak to him directly."

Guy and Hetty walked along the passage. "Dare I hope this discovery means the fates are now in our favor?" Hetty said.

"You may, *mon amour*," Guy said. "But we will handle anything that comes our way, together."

They found Eustace in the library. "What a surprise." Eustace held out his hand. "May I see them?" He searched the documents. "Yes, this is the Fortescue coat of arms, the same as the one above the fireplace in the great hall." He nodded his approval and handed them back.

Hetty studied the azure chevron with its three golden birds. "What do these birds signify?"

"Nobility acquired through bravery, prowess or intelligence," Guy said.

"The martlet, or heraldic swallow, is seen to be swift and elegant," Eustace added.

"The birds don't appear to have feet," Hetty said.

"In a medieval myth, the swallow had no feet. It signifies that one has to subsist on the wings of his virtue and merit alone."

"Which perfectly describes my brother's life up till now," Genevieve said as she entered the room.

Guy smiled at his sister, aware of how much he would miss her.

"I'm for a ride. Who will join me?" Genevieve asked. "I want to see more of the estate. *C'est très beau.*" A mischievous smile lit her eyes. "I shall be gone from here in two days."

When Guy glanced at Hetty, she trembled at the hot impatience in his blue gaze. "We will miss you dreadfully, Genevieve," she said with honesty. "I shall be delighted to ride with you. Let's change into our habits."

The crisp air was scented with pine as they rode over the fields. Guy reined his horse alongside Hetty's while Genevieve rode on ahead. "I want to make love to you, but if we begin, we won't reappear until tomorrow."

She giggled. "It's courteous to remain with our guests until bed-time."

"*Oui*, bedtime," he said with ill-disguised impatience, and trotted after his sister who had disappeared into the trees. Hetty followed, suffering a good deal of impatience herself.

The sun was disappearing behind the mansion's roof when the three returned to the house. As they climbed the stairs with the intention of changing out of their riding clothes before embarking on a game of whist, Hetty turned to Guy. "You promised to show me the secret tunnel."

"Not me." Genevieve gave a shudder and laughed. She continued to her bedchamber while Guy took Hetty's hand and led her off toward the solar.

With a lit candle, they walked down past the kitchen into the depths of the hall. Hetty paused on the stairs.

"Are you afraid?" Guy asked.

She bit back tears. "When I think of what you endured here, I want to cry."

He pulled her close. "I have put that behind me, Hetty." He took her arm, and they descended to the floor below.

"I did wonder if you might prefer a calm and sensible wife like Marina."

He laughed. "I do not." He stopped her at the bottom with a hand on her arm, the candle dipping dangerously. "If you change into a milksop of a wife, I'll lock you up in the tunnel and get myself a mistress."

"I shall escape and pull out her hair!"

"That's more like the woman I love," Guy said with a rueful smile. His smile slipped away. "Vincent's death has been difficult to bear, Hetty."

She gasped and slid her arms around his waist. "Oh, my darling, of course it is."

He groaned as he held her within his free arm. "I don't want you to change. Just be that spirited young woman I fell in love with. I consider myself a very lucky fellow to have you."

Relieved, Hetty kissed him. "Come and show me this tunnel."

The long storeroom was shadowy and dim. Guy held the candle high and took a moment to gain his bearings. He walked to the far corner. With prior knowledge, he had little trouble locating the secret door. It sprung open, revealing a pitch-black passage. Unpleasant smells of damp and rat droppings flooded out.

"It's horrible." Hetty edged closer to him. "I've no intention of venturing inside."

"There's nothing to see as the servants have cleaned it out." He chuckled. "Unless you wish to follow the tunnel to its end?"

She shuddered. "I'll view it from the wood."

Guy dropped the candle. It rolled around, and before he could reach it, went out. "Are you, all right?" she asked.

"I am now." His arms found her in the dark and his mouth claimed hers. She held on to him as all her other senses came into play, his arousing male scent, the rasp of rough fabric beneath her fingers as his big, hard body pressed against her, his breath sweetened with the wine he had drunk earlier, the slide of his lips over hers, teasing her lower lip with his teeth, and the taste of him when he entered her mouth.

Guy moved to put space between them, still holding her upright. If he hadn't, dazed and breathless, she might have fallen. "Dash it all, not here, Hetty," he said heavily. "There are many ways to make love, and I mean for us to try them all. But not here, not now."

He picked her up and climbed the steps with her in his arms. In the upper passage, they met a maid who covered her mouth with a hand and dropped into a curtsy.

Guy carried her toward the main staircase.

"You can put me down now."

"If I put you down, someone will whisk you away," he muttered. "And I am going to make love to you. In our bed."

Hetty should have been embarrassed. They were expected in the salon for a game of cards. She clutched the velvet collar of his riding coat and gave herself up to the wonderful sensation of being crushed against his chest, listening to the steady metronome of his heartbeat. What she had yearned for was finally to happen. She wondered if he would do all those things to her, that he spoke of in the hut while the snowstorm whirled around them, which seemed like years ago now.

Guy entered their bedchamber, kicked the door shut, and slowly lowered her to the floor.

"We are finally alone, I can scarcely believe it," Hetty said as he turned the key in the lock.

They began to undress. It seemed a lifetime ago that she'd had helped him in the hunting lodge. She struggled to equate that man with the one before her; he seemed so changed. She had thought him an arrogant rake back then.

He methodically stripped her down to her chemise, and finding herself naked, she scurried to the bed.

Guy laughed. When the last stitch of his clothing was added to the pile on the chair, he walked over to her completely unconcerned about his nakedness. She clutched the coverlet to her chest and gasped at his beauty. Satiny olive skin stretched over long elegant bones and well-defined muscles. The wound in his side, now a purplish scar, testament to how close he'd come to death. Hetty was stunned into silence.

Guy came to where she sat on the bed. Wordlessly, he removed the coverlet from her fingers. She slid her arms around his waist and pressed her lips to the scar, then cupped his buttocks, strong and smooth beneath her hands.

He pressed her back on the bed. His arms resting on each side of her, erotic excitement sparked in his eyes as he lowered his head. His mouth demanded a response, and as she moaned against his lips, their kisses caught fire. She danced her fingers over the defined planes and soft dark hair of his chest and down, his galloping heart beneath her hand. Then tracing the line of dark hair over the ribbed muscles of his hard stomach to his taut member. Curious, she took it in her hand, testing the length, sensing the strength beneath the soft skin.

Guy lavished attention on her breasts, drawing each nipple to a peak with his tongue as he stroked her feminine folds and the pearl beneath. His teasing fingers drew ripples, then waves, and shudders from her body. Hetty arched against him, moving restlessly, unsure of what she craved, except more.

"Please, Guy, please...," she murmured, overcome with an urgent desire to be one with him.

"LET'S TAKE IT slow, *mon amour.*"

Guy seized control before Hetty's ministrations to his cock upset both their plans.

She coiled her arms around his neck and pressed her breasts against his chest. Their rapid breaths mingled as their passionate kisses robbed them of breath.

Hetty's eager responses matched his. He wanted her desperately but intended it to be memorable. The first time for a woman was not always good, he'd been told. Guy scooped her up in his arms and eased her back onto the bed. He planned to take his time, and continued to stroke, finding her moist and ready for him. She moaned and clung to him, pushing her hips up to meet his gently probing fingers. As she gripped his hair none too gently, he trailed kisses across the soft swell of her belly. His fingers tangled in the soft nest of fiery curls and he breathed in the musky smell of her arousal, following his fingers with his tongue.

"Oh, what are you doing?" Hetty gave him a wild look, her face flushed.

"Shush."

Hetty bucked her hips and moaned. She shook her head, pushed him away, and then pulled him back against her. "Yes, my love," he urged as she tensed and her thighs shuddered. She came with a long cry which turned into a deep sigh.

Hetty fell back and gazed up at him, her eyes half-closed as she flicked her swollen bottom lip with a pink tongue, looking utterly abandoned.

Guy groaned. It was time. This was too delicious, too exciting, and he'd wanted it too long.

He slipped between her thighs and pressed himself against her entrance, she stilled. Her body was ready for him, rosy and wet. He searched her eyes which gazed at him with love and apprehension. "This may hurt a little."

She shook her head as if incapable of replying.

With a thrust of his hips, he nudged inside her, met with a re-sistance, and pushed through. She drew her breath in sharply.

"Shall I go on?"

"Yes," she said cautiously.

"Am I hurting you?"

She bit her lip. "A little."

He paused.

"No, don't stop, please."

Guy began to move, slowly, as her body accepted him.

Hetty released a breath and drew him close.

He withdrew and pushed in again, then settled into a rhythm. As her body rose to join his, she threw back her head with a mew of pleasure. Her fingers dug into his shoulders as if she could pull him closer. Her body closed around him like a hot velvet glove, the pleasure so intense, he fought to retain control.

HETTY LAY SPRAWLED beside Guy, his hand resting on her breast, rising and falling with her rapid breaths.

"*Je t'aime ma chéri,*" he said huskily. "You are my life."

"Oh, my darling. I love you." She could barely speak, her body weighed down with a pleasurable fatigue. She settled beside him and closed her eyes.

She woke as the soft patina of moonlight slid across the room through the open curtains. It must have been close to midnight. While she'd slept, Guy had put a taper to the fire and pulled the covers over them. He stirred beside her, woke, and gathered her into his arms. She snuggled against the warm length of his body, settled her head on his shoulder, and slept again.

They woke to birdsong. Drowsy and exhausted, Hetty sat back against the pillows as they fortified themselves with the hot chocolate the maid had brought.

She put down the cup and pushed back the covers.

"Where are you going?" His eyes were heavy-lidded with sleep and awakening desire.

"I was just going to ring for the maid to draw my bath."

"Not yet." He drew her back into bed.

Hetty leaned into his hard body as the familiar sensations of warmth and need flooded through her. How she loved this man. Her need for him robbed her of breath as she pressed her mouth to his.

Hunger drove them downstairs at luncheon to find Genevieve and Eustace had tactfully gone to visit her father and Marina.

Ravenous, they devoured a late breakfast. Then, holding hands, they walked over the grounds enjoying order restored to the gardens, the hedges trimmed, the parterre garden free of weeds, the roses pruned, and the lawns scythed. Gardeners were raking up the first of the autumn leaves to fall and burning them, the smoke coiling into the sky. Rosecliff Hall had been restored. But to Hetty, it was more than a restoration. Rosecroft Hall had been lifted from the mortmain past, which had held it in thrall ever since Guy's father had deserted it. "I can't wait for you to see how glorious the estate is in the spring."

"We may not be here in the spring," Guy said.

She looked up at him. "Why? Where shall we be?"

"Genevieve wants us to visit her in Paris," he said with a grin.

"Oh, Guy. I'd love to!"

He lifted a curl to press a kiss on her neck and warmth spiraled down her spine. "I knew you would. But Genevieve may have to wait. It may not be advisable for you to travel."

She leaned into him and smiled. "Might I be with child?"

"Perhaps." He leveled a glowing look at her.

"I expect the others will return soon." She wanted to be alone with him and found a similar need in his eyes. He began to turn back to the house.

She tugged at his arm. "Let's walk to the summerhouse by the lake."

Guy's brows rose. For a moment, she thought he might refuse, but then his eyes smoldered with desire and he grabbed her hand.

Epilogue

Rosecliff Hall, Spring 1817

H ETTY WANDERED THE glorious gardens, breathing in the floral
scents carried on the breeze. Footfall behind her made her turn.
Guy walked down the path. "Are you ready to leave, *mon amour?* The
carriage is being brought around."

She smiled and took his hand. "I'm saying goodbye to the garden."

"It's only for a few months. We'll come home when it gets too
hot." He raised her chin with a finger, his blue eyes questioning.
"Looking forward to London?"

"But of course. The Mayfair house has been made ready for us,
and I can't wait to see it." Hetty turned for one last glance of the
sunlight brightening the new spring green in the trees. She didn't want
her perceptive husband to see the dread in her eyes.

"You will be a great success, Hetty."

She took an anxious breath and shook her head. "You are biased."

"Not at all." He grinned and shook his head. "We shall see."

After they'd journeyed to France to visit Genevieve in her chateau
and met her charming husband and children, they'd returned here and
spent the following months closeted in Digswell, through Christmas,
and the fierce winter that kept them snowbound for one whole
delicious month. Now the moment had finally arrived. She must face
the *haute ton* as the Baroness Fortescue.

She took Guy's hand, and they walked up the path to where the
coach waited, while footmen loaded the trunks. As Hetty's maid and

Guy's valet traveled with them, she wouldn't have a chance to talk to him privately about her concerns. She squared her shoulders, she must deal with this herself. She wanted him to be proud of her.

"Our house party proved to be a great success, was it not?" he reminded her.

"Because they are our friends."

"You shall make many more friends this season."

"I hope so."

Their house party held at Rosecliff Hall last October had been great fun. John came with his sisters and their husbands. Georgina, now Her Grace, Lady Broadstairs was still lively, but she'd gained considerable poise. Her husband, His Grace, proved to be an amiable fellow and not at all haughty. Eleanor's husband, Lord Gordon Fitzherbert, had rallied enough to make the journey, but looked thin and pale. Hetty found him to be bookish, calm, and patient, as many with serious infirmities could be. He'd been unable to join the men on their shoot and spent his time in the library where she and Eleanor had joined him for a cozy afternoon discussing poetry. Hetty liked his sense of humor and the twinkle in his eye, but she feared that he would not live overlong.

They settled in the carriage, and the horses trotted down the drive and soon left Rosecroft Hall behind. Digswell was not a great distance from London, but Hetty felt as if she was about to make a very long journey.

Hetty's first real experience of the *ton* came a week after settling in London. Lady Montague's was the first ball of the season. She wore her new peach silk gown lavishly trimmed with old lace, which she thought suited her.

They stood with other guests waiting to be announced at the door of the elegant ballroom. The orchestra played Mozart, and beneath crystal chandeliers, guests drank pink champagne seated on sofas and chairs around the walls where a variable garden of flowers in vases perched on occasional tables.

"Baron and Baroness Fortescue," a footman proclaimed loudly. A hush fell. To Hetty, it seemed as if time had stopped, before chatter began again. Their host and hostess warmly greeted them, then Hetty, her hand resting on Guy's arm, continued into the room.

In a moment, they were surrounded by friends and others begging to be introduced.

"We have been so eager to meet you." Mrs. Drummond, a large bosomed lady in gray, sank into a curtsy. "Your prolonged stay in the country after your marriage has had everyone talking."

"Oh, I didn't realize." Hetty employed her fan, imagining the talk would be unfavorable.

"Yes, indeed, my lady. The beau monde could do with an injection of new blood, and to find such a glamorous couple in our midst." Mrs. Drummond flicked a glance at Guy. "If you'll forgive me for saying so, well…we are all delighted."

The following hours became a blur as they chatted, ate supper, and danced. It was close to dawn when the carriage took them home. Hetty slipped off her dancing slippers and snuggled within Guy's arm. "Well?" He ran a hand gently up her arm. "Was it so awful?"

"Not at all. Really quite pleasant. I met many interesting people." She yawned. "I am fatigued though. They keep such appalling hours in London."

His deep chuckle made her lift her head to observe him. "With my preference for the country and your fear that society would shun you, we may never have come."

She ran a finger along his jaw. "But we will continue to come every year, will we not?"

Guy groaned. "If that is your wish, *mon amour.*"

THE END

Made in the USA
Columbia, SC
12 August 2018